an Agreement with the Soldier

SADIE BOSQUE

First edition

Editing by Tracy Liebchen
Cover art by The Brazen Wallflower Designs

This book was professionally typeset on Reedsy.
Find out more at reedsy.com

To my best friend Daria. If an infatuation with the same guy didn't draw us apart, neither can the distance. Love you forever.

Contents

Acknowledgement

To my fabulous Beta readers:
  Nicole Yost
  Michelle Lokeigh

Special thanks to my editor and an amazing author, Diana Bold

The story would not be the same without you. Thank you for making my experience in publishing a novel unforgettable.

Author's Note

This work of fiction contains adult content, strong language, violence, off-page death, bullying, nightmares, and pregnancy.

Reader discretion is advised.

Prologue

September 4, 1801
  Dear Brother,
  I know it has only been a week since you went away. But I miss you a lot, and I wish you would come back already.
  Your favorite sister,
  Sam—seven years old.

November 7th, 1801
  My Dear Sam,
  I've missed you a lot too. I promise, I shall come home on leave as soon as I can. However, I do enjoy it here in the army. It suits me well. I've found a few friends already.
  Please, keep writing to me every day. I want to know all the minutiae of your life. I want to see you grow up. Or at least read about your life in vivid details.
  Your favorite brother,
  Ben

March 6, 1804

Dear Brother,

The winter is very cold and dull in Hampshire. Tell me, what are the West Indies like? Is it cold there, or is it sunny and extremely hot? Is the grass there similar to ours? Are there exotic butterflies? What is the sky like?

P.S. Attached is a sketch of our house during the gloomy weather.

Your favorite sister,

Sam

November 14, 1804

My Dear Sam,

I've just received a bulk of letters from you. I am certain you're fretting over me, wondering why I am not writing back. Let me assure you I am well. The mail here is less than reliable, but at least I've received most of your correspondence.

Nature here is indeed different from ours. The leaves are bigger, the colors are richer and brighter. The sky, however, is the same. On a cloudless night, I can see the stars. When I look at them, I can imagine I am back home.

P.S. The likeness of the manor is uncanny. Please continue sending me your sketches. I would love to see your progress.

Your favorite brother,

Ben

December 29th, 1805

Dear Brother,

Adam found your last letter to me and took exception to your calling yourself my favorite brother. He refused to take me out on rides until I had to agree that he was my favorite. Let's hope he doesn't say this to Alan and Richard, or I shall not get any exercise at all.

Since the only thing we have in common is the sky, I started learning constellations, so we could discuss something together. But I cannot make out any of the real ones. Instead, I came up with different ones on my own. When you look upon the stars next time, do be sure to look for a bunny. Let me know when you find him. Meanwhile, I shall create a tale for him, since every constellation has a legend. My poor bunny cannot be the only one without one, can he?

P.S. Adam has enlisted to work in the office of the Secretary at War. I am praying this means we can get more frequent correspondence from you.

P.P.S. Attaching the sketch of a bunny.

Still your favorite sister,
Sam

January 22, 1806

My Dear Sam,

I've missed you very much and would love to see how much you've grown. Your sketches never fail to put a smile on my face. The bunny, the reindeer, the geese—my soldier mates tease me, saying I am collecting a farm. Do be sure to sketch some pictures for them too. I am certain they are jealous they don't have anyone sending sketches their way.

Not all is cheery at war. Disease swept through the

ranks and many men have fallen. But not I. I am as healthy and safe as I ever was. And I am certain it is because you, My Angel, are watching over me.

P.S. I am afraid the frequency of my letters cannot be attributed to having a brother in the office of the Secretary at War. However, nobody can say for sure. I shall write as often as I can.

P.P.S. As soon as I am back, I shall spend as much time as you like riding with you.

Your faithful charge and soldier,

Ben

July 26, 1807

Dear Soldier,

We are setting off to London soon. This will be Isabel's debut season. She is nervous, but I am certain she will be the diamond of the season, don't you agree? Mama and Papa are very proud of her.

I am joyful we'll get to see Adam too. We haven't seen him much since he joined the War Office. I just wish you could be here with us. I miss you terribly. I shall take my duty as your guardian angel seriously, so that we see you back soon.

P.S. These are the last sketches of the countryside for a while. In the next correspondence, you will get London scenery.

Forever,

Your Angel

October 12th, 1807

Dear Sam,

I wish I could be there to walk Isabel into her first ballroom. Please, send me a sketch of her in her ball gown. I've missed so many of your events. Perhaps I shall be there to escort you to your debut ball.

My comrades are jealous of your frequent bulky correspondence. They say they wish they had an angel watching out for them too.

Love,

Ben

March 9th, 1812

Dear Soldier,

Tomorrow is my come-out ball. I am all nerves and sweaty palms. It is a good thing wearing gloves is a must, or I would be absolutely embarrassed.

Isabel has been a diamond of the first water ever since her come-out. I don't think I can live up to her success. She was constantly lauded by the patronesses of Almacks, now she is being courted by the Earl of Stanhope. Everybody in the family is certain he will propose by the end of the season. I am happy for her. She deserves the best. But I can't help but feel obligated to do just as well. I am afraid to disappoint Mama and Papa if I don't marry an earl at the very least.

P.S. I am attaching the sketch of a bee for you. So you are as agile and elusive as a bee on the front lines. Also, adding some flowers for your comrades. I shall be happily looking out for them too. I have enough power to guard everybody.

Forever,

Your Angel

April 25th, 1812

My Dear Angel,

Whether or not you make an advantageous match does not matter to me or to Mama and Papa. You know this. All we want is for you to be happy and find a gentleman for whom you will indeed be more precious than a diamond.

Perhaps it is best I am not there. I wouldn't let any beau near you. You are far too precious for any of them. I shall write our brothers a separate letter, urging them to not let you out of their sight and only allow the worthiest of men at your side.

P.S. Your sketches have been collected by the other soldiers. They are waiting for more.

Love,

Ben

May 9th, 1812

Dear Soldier,

It's been two months since I've made my come-out, and I am happy to report that I am not a complete failure. I even managed to attract a couple of suitors. I dislike the stuffiness of ballrooms, and I do not feel at ease adhering to the thousands of rituals and rules of proper social behavior. However, this is a necessary part of appearing at court, is it not?

I haven't embarrassed myself yet, but only because our siblings have been keeping a constant eye on me. I don't know what I would have done without them. Unfortunately, that also means that they do not allow me to have any fun. I am not allowed to gallop around the Serpentine, nor to discuss any interesting subjects with the gentlemen. I am not to bring my sketchbook to the ball, although drawing a ballroom scene is my fervent wish. Here's a rough sketch of Lady Royston's ballroom. Perhaps it will bring you closer to peace.

Forever,

Your Angel

No answer.

June 19th, 1812

Dear Soldier,

It has been a few weeks since your last correspondence. But I am not worried, I know you are strong and fast and very capable. I know you are just recuperating from a long battle and don't want to pick up a quill and write. Or perhaps the letters are just lost somewhere on the way.

I just wish to hear back from you. I must have sent you dozens of letters since we last heard from you, and I am running out of things to say.

Remember, you told me you watch the stars often at night? Well, I hope the stars will guide you home. Attaching a sketch of a glowworm. If a star fails to bring you home, let this little bug light your path.

Forever,

Your Angel

No answer.

September 6th, 1812

Dear Soldier,

I have been reading the papers every day, and I am anxious for you to come back. Mama and Papa try to shield me from it all, but I want to know the news of war; that way I feel closer to you. We haven't received a missive from you in a while. I hope it just means that the lines of communication have been broken and we shall receive a stack of letters from you once they are patched up.

I want you to know that you are loved and that we are all waiting for you here. I am watching the night sky every night. Mostly, it is covered with smoke. On the rare nights I see the stars, I remember the silly constellations and legends I came up with when I was little. Do you remember the one about a lone soldier? Well, there's a cluster of stars on the other side of it. It is his family, waiting for him to come home.

Until then, I shall be looking out for you from here.

Forever,

Your Angel

No Answer.

November 14th, 1812

Dear Soldier,

As I write this, I realize that this is the last letter I shall ever address to you. It is silly, truly, and nobody understands my determination to have this one sent out. I know you will not receive this missive, neither will you ever read it. Nor have you read any of the letters I've sent you in the last three months. You are gone, and no amount of correspondence is going to bring you back.

But I feel like I can't move on without saying these last words to you. The last farewell. I've been writing these letters to you most of my life. What shall I be doing now in the dead of the night when I can't sleep? Who shall I be describing the trivialities of my life to? For whom shall I be drawing my silly little sketches?

I've failed you.

All this time, you've called me your Angel, but what kind of Angel loses its charge? What kind of Angel keeps sending optimistic letters into the void when her soldier is long gone from this world?

The ache in my heart from missing you will never truly heal. But with these last words, I let you go. You called me your Angel, but I could not bring you home. Now, as you watch me from the skies, can you tell me: What do the real angels look like?

Forever,

Your Angel

Chapter 1

November 14, 1817

T he only sounds in the room were that of a ticking clock and the matching tap of a quill striking the open ledger on the desk. The study was small and almost empty. John Godfrey, the Baron of Ashbury, had sold off all that he could sell in the past six months since the death of his father. He'd sold all the family heirlooms, unentailed properties, the horses, and anything remotely valuable. He'd worked very hard to make his estate profitable and invested in ventures that were regarded as highly promising by reliable sources, but that wasn't enough. Not according to the family solicitor, the gray-haired, bespectacled old man, sitting—or rather slumping—on the other side of the desk.

"So, what you are saying is…?" John started gravely.

"I am saying"—the older man cleared his throat—"that the only way for you to pay off your debts and save the estate is to marry into money."

"Marry an heiress." John ceased the tapping and furrowed his brows. "And where do you propose I find this heiress?"

"My lord." The solicitor cleared his throat for the dozenth time that afternoon. "You are young and attractive. Many a young lady may find your attentions... err... more than favorable. I am confident you will have no trouble finding a well-dowered young maiden during the upcoming season."

Yes, I'm quite a catch. A young, attractive pauper who has violent nightmares and is unable to sleep in his bed at night.

"Right then," John said, standing up. "If that's the only thing you can advise..." He trailed off with a wave of his hand, indicating that the conversion was over unless the solicitor came up with something else to add.

"That's the only rational thing that might work." The solicitor stood. "Your investments, even if they do pay off, will take some time, and you need money urgently. So, please, take that under serious consideration." With that said, he bowed and sauntered out of the office.

"I shall," John said thoughtfully to the closing door. His hand automatically went to his breast pocket. He tapped it in a thoughtful gesture that came as a habit more than anything else at this point.

There nestled the last letter he'd received from the Angel. The mysterious young lady whose correspondence he'd received by mistake. A lady he had never met and had no hopes of ever meeting but whose letters had given him a reason to keep fighting during the agonizing months he'd spent in the army hospital.

He had been sick at the time, confused and delusional. It was only natural to feel sentimental about the correspondence that helped him regain his focus. He had this ridiculous romantic dream that upon returning from war, he would find her, tell her that she saved his life, propose his hand in marriage, and live happily ever after.

He scoffed. Perhaps he'd needed that dream at the time. A beacon of hope, a motivation to survive the harsh war when he had nothing to look forward to. It sounded foolish now that he was safe and healthy, back in his native land. But he still couldn't quite let go of the image.

Rationally thinking, this Angel, whoever she was, was probably already married. If she was as funny, kindhearted, and unique as her letters made her out to be, he had a hard time believing that she'd stayed unwed all this time. After all, that last letter had arrived five years ago.

Five years. Had he held on to the foolish dream for so long? Well, he couldn't anymore. He needed a wife. Now. And not some mystical Angel, but a living, breathing, well-dowered young lady.

John looked down at his desk. There lay an answering note from a person he'd avoided for seven years now. A person he had no logical reason for avoiding anymore. And the only person who would be able to help him with hunting for a bride—his former fiancée.

* * *

Julie, or rather the Countess of Clydesdale, stood in the middle of the room, quietly conversing with her husband. John studied her as he entered the light-blue sitting room on the heels of a haughty butler. She had changed since he last saw her seven years ago.

John had known Julie all her life. They were lifelong neighbors, friends, and later sweethearts. They'd planned to elope and escape their respective unfortunate households but had been torn apart when John was forced to leave for war.

Seeing her now, he barely recognized the formerly frightened young girl she'd been. Her face had become rounder and softer, the corners of her eyes held laugh lines, and she was relaxed and at ease. She hadn't been like this back at her father's estate. Becoming a wife and a mother clearly agreed with her. John was certain he had changed since then, too. But in the opposite way. Apart from physical scars, his appearance had certainly suffered from sleepless nights, stress, fatigue, and the horrors of war.

John looked around the spacious and bright room. The walls were decorated with paintings of serene landscapes. In contrast to the calm elegance of the room, the floor was littered with sketchbooks, pencils, and children's toys. The room had obviously only been recently vacated by its small occupants.

The butler announced John and exited the room, leaving him and his hosts alone. John lifted his eyes and managed a polite smile for the benefit of his oldest friend.

"Julie, how do you do?"

Julie smiled back. When she smiled, her whole face lit up and made her incredibly beautiful. John would have traded his soul for one glimpse of her smile during the years he'd been at war. Then came the inevitable memory of her letter. The one where she'd said she'd been forced into a marriage with another man. And the devastating day when he came back from war, *for her*, only to realize that his Julie wasn't

4

his anymore. Not only was she married, but she had also managed to fall in love with her husband. That was the moment John had gone back to the army, and he hadn't seen Julie since.

Clydesdale put his arm around his wife's shoulders, and John followed the action with his gaze.

"You are the one who stole her from me, Clydesdale, not the other way around. I have no desire to steal her back," John said with a smirk.

"Not that you could, Mr. Godfrey," Clydesdale answered and bowed in greeting.

Julie raised a brow at her husband.

"It's Ashbury now," John said and mirrored the bow.

Julie disengaged herself from her husband's side and walked toward John with both arms outstretched. "I am so very glad to see you again."

John took her hands in his and placed a dry peck on her cheek. As he raised his head, his gaze collided with Clydesdale's icy one.

"Please, John, do sit down." Julie indicated a seat and rang for tea and biscuits. She settled into a settee with her husband as John lowered himself into a chair in front of them. "How is life back in England?" she asked softly.

"It's... complicated. I would rather not bore you with the details. How are you, and how is Mary? How are the children?" He looked around the toy-littered room.

Julie smiled fondly at the mention of her favorite people. "Mary is in York. She is working as a nanny in the asylum."

"She is? How did that come to pass?"

"Well, after years of the miracle work Clydesdale and Mr. Tule went through with the place, they've turned it into a sanctuary for lunatics and simpleminded people. People whose families cannot care for them. Now we even welcome small children. We went to visit the place several times with Mary, hoping it would help her heal. Imagine our surprise when she displayed a willingness to stay there and help the nurses. She now works there several weeks a year."

"That's... it's incredible news. So her health is better then?"

A shadow passed over Julie's face, and Clydesdale covered her hand with his. Mary was Julie's younger sister. She was simpleminded and thus had been sent to an asylum soon after their mother's passing. Julie had been able to get her out with the help of her husband, but the doctors weren't kind regarding her prognosis.

"She is... She still has chest problems, and I am afraid she is not as strong as she was when she was younger. But she doesn't allow me to fret over her—"

"Which you still do," John interrupted with a smile.

"That's what I do best." Julie smiled. "She doesn't travel much lately, but you should come to the Clydesdale estate. She'd love to see you!"

"Yes, please, come," Clydesdale echoed unenthusiastically, and Julie darted a reproaching glance his way.

John grinned. "I shall definitely put it on my itinerary. However, I have more pressing issues at hand." He cleared his throat. "That is why I am here."

"Of course," Julie said, searching his face.

"Well, this is the awkward part." He smiled self-consciously. "As I said in my note, I am in need of a wife. I am not very good in social situations, and I don't know many people. And no matter what transpired between us, Julie, you are my oldest friend. You know me very well. So I was hoping you would make several introductions to young ladies who you think would suit me."

"Let me get this straight, you want *us* to find you a bride?" Clydesdale leaned closer to John.

"Well, it's only fair considering you stole my last one," John answered with a raised brow.

"We shall be happy to help. Won't we, Robert?" Julie chimed in with a smile.

"I think I'd rather go shoot at something, possibly even myself, than be bride hunting for your dear *friend*." He turned back to John. "No offense."

"Do not fret, Clydesdale. I wouldn't take your advice anyway. So, you are forgiven and excused from my bride hunt," John agreed in what he considered to be a benevolent tone of voice.

John had met the earl just once before, and it wasn't under the best of circumstances. Considering Julie had been forced to marry him while John was at war, John didn't have warm and affectionate feelings toward the man. Still, he had to give him credit where it was due. He made Julie happy.

"Thank God," Clydesdale muttered under his breath. He kissed his wife on the cheek and stood. "I'll go check on the children and do some work before supper. Will you be fine here by yourself? Since Ashbury has moved on, I assume I can safely leave you here alone with him?"

Julie giggled and swatted playfully at his thigh. "Go on with you now!" She smiled at him until the door closed. A heavy feeling settled in John's chest. Julie was obviously in love with her husband. He was glad for her, but he doubted he would have the same relationship with his future wife.

At that moment, a maid came in with a tea tray, arranged it

on a table between them, and bowed out.

Julie turned toward John and settled more comfortably on the settee. "I have to tell you, I am still not a welcome guest in many drawing rooms, so my reach is not as vast as you might like. The scandal with Mary happened many years ago, but the *ton* is not forgiving."

"It is still more vast than mine." John smiled sadly.

Julie nodded. "So tell me, what are you looking for in a wife?" She studied John from beneath her lashes as she poured each of them a cup.

John frowned, not quite certain how much truth to divulge to his friend. Eventually, he decided on telling her everything. It wouldn't help to keep secrets.

"I am in financial straits. I sold off all the unentailed properties, the art, the horses, everything I could get my hands on. I worked hard to put the estate back in order so it could turn a profit, but my old man gambled everything away." He paused a little, gave a weary sigh, and continued, "The solicitor tells me he was devastated when Joshua passed, but once Jeremy died as well, he stopped caring about anything. Since I was left to inherit it all, he decided there wasn't much reason to preserve anything. You know how he felt about me."

Julie nodded and gave him a reassuring smile. She knew the state of his household like nobody else in the world.

"I was a soldier for most of my life. I do not know anything about running an estate. I tried to learn but…" He shook his head. "Now my solicitor tells me the only way out of this is for me to marry into money. I know it's a hell of a reason to marry—"

Julie scoffed, "I married for a title, remember?"

"I remember," John said quietly, almost inaudibly, a sad

8

smile on his face.

"And it all worked out, didn't it?" Julie asked.

John nodded, but he started to lose track of the conversation. The quiet of the room was pressing on his nerves. Too quiet was never a good thing in a war, and the eerie silence always made his skin crawl with unpleasant anticipation. He had to get back to the conversation before he drifted away from his thoughts and was back on the front lines.

"So." Julie stood, breaking him from his reverie. "We shall find you a perfect bride, one you can fall in love with, who has a sizable dowry," she said cheerfully.

John also stood.

"Let me get a quill and paper—" Julie began, but John interrupted her.

"Actually, not to sound rude, but can you possibly do that without me? I don't know any of the ladies anyway, and you can just let me know who you came up with the next time we meet. I need to...." He cleared his throat. "I have a... another appointment soon."

"Oh, absolutely." Julie looked at him apologetically. "We can meet during one of the pre-season events. There's a dinner party at Lady Pelham's next week. Do you have an invitation?"

John stared at her numbly.

"Never mind, I shall ask her to extend an invitation to you. We can discuss the prospects there and go over my list."

"Thank you." John started walking to the door but paused with his hand on the door handle. "There's one more thing I wanted to ask you." He turned his head in her direction. "I know it's a strange question, but do you happen to know anyone who made their debut in 1812?"

"No. That's the year Mary's scandal happened and then I

9

spent most of 1812 and 1813 in Bromley, in confinement. So, I'm sorry. I don't really know who made debuts that year. Why?"

"No reason." He made to turn the handle and paused again. "I am sorry I wasn't there for you... I know you probably needed a friend and you went through some rough times at the beginning of your marriage. We have been friends for too long. I shouldn't have cut you out like this."

"It's fine. I understand," she said quietly.

He nodded and left the room.

John exited the house and took a deep breath. He'd done well. He'd kept the panic at bay. It hadn't been easy, but he'd done it. Now there was a dinner party next week. A room full of suffocating crowds of people, loud noises, thundering music, and lots of stares. He could do it too. He didn't have to stay long this time either, he reminded himself. He would go right up to Julie, let her introduce him to a couple of ladies, and bow out.

Next, he could pay them a visit and invite them for a ride in the park. He always felt better outdoors. He mounted his horse and proceeded toward his house in a slow canter.

And as for his Angel, well, he wasn't holding out hope that Julie would help him find her, anyway. How many young ladies had made a debut in 1812? Dozens. Maybe more.

Perhaps it was for the best. Better to never find her and keep her in his dreams. Because if he did find her... What did he expect would happen? With flaws the size of Mount SnowdOn, finding any wife would be an issue, never mind a perfect lady like his Angel. Yes, he thought wryly, better to keep her in his dreams.

10

Chapter 1

* * *

Samantha woke up with a start. She looked around the familiar room in the moonlight. Ah, yes, she was still in her room at the Gage townhouse. *Thank God!* She kept having this horrible nightmare that she'd gotten married and was getting shipped off to some Godforsaken land north of Yorkshire.

After spending the last season in mourning, she had been welcomed back into the *ton* with open arms. She was no longer a debutante, and even when she had been, she was never considered a diamond of the first water. Now, when she was coming perilously close to spinsterhood, she was courted either by lords who were old enough to be her father—and sometimes her grandfather—or by randy young lords in need of an heiress. After every ball, or other social engagement, she had nightmares that her family was tired of her and sent her away with the first suitor who offered for her.

Of course, that was never going to happen, but dreams were irrational, and the guilt she felt for not making a fit match for her family added fuel to the fire. It wasn't as though it was her fault. She'd met plenty of young lords, danced and flirted with them, but she felt nothing beyond a simple interest. And even then, the spark wasn't enough to turn their relationship into a friendship, much less a marriage. Her parents had a love match, and her best friend was spouting nonsense about true love and how a marriage without it was empty and hollow.

Sam groaned loudly, put a pillow over her face, and toppled back into bed. *I am not going to feel guilty about this. I am not going to feel guilty about this.*

Isabel had sacrificed her chances of making a good match so that their brothers, and most importantly Sam, didn't

11

have to worry about anything. Isabel was the one who had looked after their ailing father. She was the one who helped their brother, Richard, accept his responsibilities as the new Viscount Gage after their father's passing. With numerous estates, somebody had to be the hostess, and Isabel assumed that role all too young. Wanting to spare Sam the same fate, Isabel never married and remained a constant mother figure to the family—even to their elder brothers.

Obviously, there was another reason Isabel had never married—a broken heart.

She had never admitted that to anyone. But Sam knew better. Isabel had been bright-eyed and happy during those long-ago days when she was being courted by the Earl of Stanhope. She knew how excited Isabel had been about the prospect of running her own household. And Sam also saw how broken-hearted Isabel had become when all that courting came to naught once Stanhope disappeared right after their mother's passing. She hadn't accepted a suitor since.

Maybe if Gage wed, then Isabel wouldn't feel so responsible for this family and would be more open to finding her own happiness. Samantha scoffed. Gage, married? She didn't think those two words would ever be uttered in the same sentence. At least not since Richard had inherited the title.

As a matter of fact, none of her brothers was in a hurry to shackle themselves to a wife. Except for Benedict. Ben had wanted to marry and have children of his own. He had written to Sam about all this in his letters.

A peaceful life.

Sam had to shake her head from the maudlin thoughts.

Realizing that the restless thoughts were not going away, she sat up and squinted at the clock on her fireplace mantel.

It was close to dawn.

Well, if I am not getting any sleep, I might as well get some exercise out of the way. With that thought, she climbed out of bed and resolutely walked into her dressing room.

Putting on her pale green riding habit by herself was no simple task, but she didn't want to wake her young maid. Gina was not an early riser, and it would take Sam longer to rouse her than to dress by herself. After donning her riding attire, she went down to the servants' hall and knocked on the farthest door.

"I'm up, Miss," came a sharp voice from behind it. Then the door unlocked and a tall young footman appeared in the doorway. "Are we riding today, Miss?"

Sam nodded and smiled.

Chapter 2

J ohn had enjoyed early morning rides for as long as he could remember. First, they used to be his escape from his household. Later, when he returned from war, he resumed his habit to calm his restless mind. He enjoyed the fresh morning air, the speed, the smell of horseflesh, and the sound of hooves. No eerie silence of the early mornings inside his house, no people to ask him about his war experiences, no walls suffocating him.

Since he'd sold all the horses along with other possessions in an effort to pay off his debts, he was left with no transportation for a while. That was until he acquired a young and inexperienced green-broke horse that nobody wanted because of her bad temper. John had broken more than one horse in his lifetime. Being an officer, he'd spent most of his adult life atop a horse. He knew how to treat them, and he understood his mare perhaps more than he understood people. She was just like him. Easily spooked, nervous, on guard. They both disliked crowds of people and enjoyed galloping. She was perfect for him. Besides, he didn't have much choice due to his limited funds, and he was in need of transport.

Early mornings in the park usually meant solitary rides, and that's how John and his mare preferred it. The aristocracy was not out until after noon, and the park was quiet and empty. John made several measured laps around the Serpentine before urging his horse into a gallop.

The wind beat on his face, and the sun peeked out from behind the clouds and baked his hat. John felt strong, free, and alive. The wind almost took off his hat, and he caught it hastily. However, at the same moment, the horse slipped on the dirt, gave a loud squeal, and reared. John tightened his knees and tried to press his body closer to her neck, but it was too late. Gravity forced him down, and he fell to the ground with a loud thump before rolling several times and stopping in the grass next to the path.

"Perfect, just bloody perfect," he muttered to himself. He groaned and sat up gingerly then looked down at himself. He was covered in dirt and grass. His hip ached from where he'd landed on his left side, and his arm was bleeding. He brought the injured arm closer to his face, squinting at it. How in the hell he'd managed to tear through his jacket, shirt sleeve, and scratch his arm deeply enough to bleed, he didn't know. He only knew that in addition to dirt, he was now covered in his own blood. His valet would be delighted, he was sure.

John sat in the dirt, contemplating whether to clean off in the Serpentine or gallop home for a full bath when he heard another horse's hooves advancing in his direction, a small rider glued to the back of the horse.

"This day is just getting better and better," John muttered

to himself again and put his hand over his forehead so he could see better against the shining sun. The rider stopped a few feet away from him and dismounted. John tilted his head and squinted again. The rider approached him, the skirts of her riding habit swishing about her ankles. The sun was at her back, so he couldn't see her face, but the few tendrils of her hair that had managed to escape out of her bonnet were glowing gold, and the sun at her back gave the appearance of a halo over her head.

"Are you injured?" she asked, coming close to him. Her voice was angelic too, a bit husky and low, yet somehow extremely feminine.

"What?" he asked, bewildered, too distracted by her angelic visage. The last thing he'd expected from his solitary and extremely early ride in the park was company. Especially divine company.

"Are you hurt?" she asked again.

She kneeled before him, her head blocking the sun so that he could make out her facial features. She had extraordinary whisky-brown eyes fringed with dark blond lashes, a lush mouth, and a dainty nose. Her golden hair continued to glow in the sun, highlighting her angelic face.

"Oh, I see you are," she exclaimed as she noted his bleeding arm. "Let me help."

She took a handkerchief from the pocket of her skirt and extended her hand toward him. John instinctively pulled his arm closer to his body.

The young lady looked at him with what looked like astonishment for a moment before laughter replaced the emotion in her eyes. "Do not worry," she said slowly as if talking to a spooked horse or a child. "I don't bite."

16

"And how would I know that?" John muttered under his breath. He got up, ignoring her outstretched hand and her handkerchief. He was looking down at the ground, acting like a wounded animal.

He truly had no idea how to conduct himself in social situations. Wasn't there a rule saying he couldn't converse with a lady unless they had been previously introduced? Maybe that didn't count if said lady witnessed your undignified tumble off of your horse.

The young lady with golden locks seemed to sense his uneasiness and extended her handkerchief again. "Here, take it. Press it to your wound, so you don't bleed out."

John looked up and saw the lady was smiling at him and waving her handkerchief like a white flag. He took it and pressed it to his injured arm.

"I'm sorry, I'm not good at"—he cleared his throat—"interacting with people," he finished lamely.

"Me either," she replied cheerfully and gestured to the solitary path. "Hence, early morning rides. Usually, there's no one around here."

John nodded and turned the kerchief bloody side up, pressing the clean side to his wound. The young lady's eyes widened as she saw the amount of blood soaking the white linen.

"Oh, my!" She hastily drew another handkerchief from her other pocket like a magician and thrust it toward him. "You seem to be bleeding profusely."

"It's nothing," he said gruffly.

She raised a brow at him as if disbelieving his words.

"I've had worse," he added at her look but took her proffered piece of linen. "Although, I should probably head homeward."

"Oh, of course, do you need help mounting your horse?" She was watching him innocently, as if ready to assist him if he said yes.

"And what will you do if I say I do? Boost me up?" He smiled at her, and she laughed.

"No, of course not. But my footman, James, might. He's over there." She pointed at a tall young man a few yards away, watching them carefully.

"Thank you, but I'm fine." For proof, John mounted his horse in one fluid motion. "Oh, and"—he turned to her, drew out his own clean handkerchief from his pocket, and extended it with his uninjured arm—"thank you for the bandages." He dropped the linen and without looking to see whether she caught it or not galloped away.

* * *

"Look at that beautiful emerald silk," Sam's friend, Evie, or more appropriately, Eabha Montgomery, the Duchess of Somerset, called to her across the room. "A pity I cannot order a gown of this color until I am wed. It is silly, don't you think, that even the color of one's wardrobe should be dictated by one's marital status?"

Sam came closer to look at the shimmering silk her friend was holding in her hands.

"That's a simple solution to a problem, wouldn't you say, dear?" Lady Clydesdale asked gently. She was Evie's distant cousin and was chaperoning them on this outing to a modiste before the season began. "Just marry and you'll be able to wear whatever you want."

Evie laughed and spread the fabric wider, holding it against her face. "Of course, if I were a man, I'd be free to choose whichever color I wish." She let go of the silk with a sigh.

"It would perfectly bring out your eyes, Evie." Sam smiled up at her friend, and Evie beamed right back.

This year would mark the sixth season since Sam and Evie had made their debuts.

Even though they'd both missed at least three years due to mourning, it was extremely hard to believe that a beauty like Evie was still on the marriage mart after all those years. She was not only beautiful, good-natured, and polite, but she was also a duke's granddaughter with an extremely large dowry. And now, she was a duchess in her own right. Hers was one of the extremely rare titles that had a clause allowing women to inherit the title, if only nominally.

Which meant that every fortune-hunting male in the country would be trying to woo Evie into marriage. Not that she wasn't an incomparable year in and year out without it. She had to beat her suitors with her slipper to get rid of them, so to speak, and yet season after season, she remained unwed. Because just like every Montgomery before her, she wished to marry for love.

Evie airily waved her hand at the subject. "It does sound rather simple, does it not?" she said, still sifting through the other fabrics. "Go off to a ball, meet a nice, young gentleman, fall in love, and voilà!" With the last word, she pulled out a bright cherry-red gauze and placed it against Sam's neck. "You're married."

Both girls laughed, and from the corner of her eye, Sam saw Lady Clydesdale shake her head with a smile.

"It turns out that it's a little more complicated than that, does it not?" Sam asked as she took the fabric from Evie's hands and walked to the looking glass.

"You are lucky you can pull off colors like that," Evie said with a pout. "With my hair, I cannot ever wear anything so bright."

Sam looked pointedly at her friend's bright red locks. "Dear, with your hair, you could wear a gown the color of manure, and nobody would notice."

"Hopefully, I shall never have a reason to test your theory," Evie said with a chuckle. "And I don't know why love has to be complicated." She returned to their previous topic of conversation. "It wasn't for my parents, nor for my grandparents. Theirs were love at first sight. It seems I am the only Montgomery who requires over one season to find a match." She grimaced. "Or six."

"Your grandfather was eight and twenty when he wed, wasn't he?"

"Correct," Evie answered wryly. "My grandmother wasn't even a debutante. She was a chaperone at a house party, and she managed to snag a duke."

"And your father, was he about the same age as your grandfather when he wed?"

"Six and twenty if I remember correctly. But my mother was a debutante."

"To be precise," Evie's cousin said as she leafed through the catalog with a bored expression on her face. "Both your father and grandfather were older than you when they wed. And *they* were the Montgomeries; your mother and grandmother just married into the family."

Evie's lips parted slightly before she let out a laugh. "You don't mean to say I am to wait until I am eight and twenty before I get to marry?" She threw a pin cushion at Lady

Clydesdale in mock outrage.

Her cousin shrugged as she deflected the cushion. "If you're comparing yourself to Montgomeries, might as well do it right."

Sam crossed to her friend and put one arm around her shoulders. "Come, Lady Clydesdale, you're not implying that her husband should be a debutante, are you?"

Evie's shoulders shook with mirth, and she turned her laughing eyes at Sam. "Since I haven't met him as of yet, it only stands to reason he is not yet out in society."

All three of them burst into laughter before Evie wiped at her eyes and took a deep breath, turning somber. "The truth is the Montgomeries before me weren't even looking for love when they found it. And yet here I am, on the brink of a sixth season and nary a love match in sight."

Sam turned away from her friend and resumed sifting through the different fabrics with a wistful sigh.

"Speaking of your marital problems," Lady Clydesdale addressed Evie and put the catalog on the table. "I might have a solution."

"You do? Don't tell me you have a suitor up your sleeve?" Evie said with a chuckle.

"No, not exactly." Lady Clydesdale shifted uncomfortably in her seat. "John is back from the army, and he is seeking a bride."

"John?" Evie looked confused before her eyes widened in comprehension. "Your John?"

"Well, he is not *my* John…" Lady Clydesdale grimaced. "Yes, my John."

Sam stepped closer to observe the interaction with undisguised interest.

"You want me to marry your John?" Evie continued incredulously.

"Why not? I love you both. I think you will suit perfectly."

Sam looked from one lady in front of her to the other. "Who's John?"

"Julie's neighbor and friend. The one she was supposed to marry before... Well, before she married Clydesdale," her friend finished lamely.

Sam didn't know the details, but she knew that Lady Clydesdale and her husband's marriage had started as one of convenience. They were blissfully happy now, but at the time, it was a messy affair. Lady Clydesdale had been in love with her lifelong friend, and Lord Clydesdale had only married her to placate his father.

"He is coming to Lady Pelham's dinner party next week. And I am to introduce him to prospective brides. Unless you are interested, of course."

Evie looked like she was about to protest, but she pursed her lips at the last moment. "Fine. Couldn't hurt to meet one more person. I mean, I know I've met him before, but I do not remember him. I was a child back then, and so was he. So were we all." Evie's expression darkened for a moment before she turned a bright smile to Sam. "How about you join us? Perhaps John will be to your liking?"

"No, none of my gowns will be ready yet. Besides, Gage avoids all social events unless strictly necessary, and I'll not even speak of my other brothers." One side of her mouth kicked up in a half-smile. "It's not like they need husbands."

"I shall probably be attending every event starting with the dinner. Montbrook seems desperate to get me married too. He has a few suitors lined up for me, I believe." She turned back to the racks of fabrics. "Everyone is desperate to have me shackled."

Sam studied her friend's pinched features. "You don't seem very happy about that."

"Oh, no, I am." Evie turned to her. "If I don't marry this year, next year the both of us will be wearing spinster caps and sitting with the dowagers instead of dancing."

"Ah!" Sam slapped her friend playfully on the arm. "Speak for yourself, Your Grace. I am getting married this season with or without you."

"How about a wager? Whoever is not married by the start of the next season is the one to wear a gown the color of manure to her wedding."

"You wouldn't—" Sam narrowed her eyes at her friend.

Evie quirked her brow. "I would."

"Ladies do not wager," Lady Clydesdale said in a pretentious tone of voice behind them. "At least that's what the dowager would say. I shall officiate the wager," she added with a grin, and they all laughed.

At that moment, Madame Deville came in from the back of her shop. "Did you ladies choose your styles and fabrics?" she asked in a light French accent.

"Yes," they answered in unison.

* * *

Lady Pelham's dinner party wasn't as crowded as John had thought it would be, and he thanked the Lord for that. All he needed was to have one of his fits in a house full of people. Divided into several groups, lords and ladies were lounging in a sitting room waiting for supper to start.

23

He noticed the Clydesdales right away, and after greeting and conversing with his hostess, he moved toward them.

"Here, I brought my list with me as promised." Julie got straight to business after the pleasantries were out of the way. "More than half a dozen beautiful and well-dowered young ladies. Of course, most of them are still in the country, but as soon as the season starts, you should be—"

"I don't want to wait for the start of the season," John interrupted her briskly. "I want to be married and done with it before the season begins. Courting with the entire world watching doesn't seem like a good idea to me."

"Best way to do it too." Clydesdale smiled down at his wife.

Julie shook her head lightly before addressing John again. "Very well, if that's your wish. That shortens our list considerably since not everyone has arrived in London yet, but still…" She paused, looking around. "There's Lady Penelope Hardgrave. In a pale pink dress, standing by her father, the Earl of Royston. As an earl's daughter, she has a sizable dowry; she also enjoys riding and is a nice conversationalist."

"Hmm…" John studied the young lady in question. She stood separate from the crowd, trying to blend into the shadows. Perhaps she was the perfect bride for him.

"There's Lady Aurora," Julie continued, narrating her list. "The Marquess of Bainbridge's daughter. She's sitting on a blue settee in a pale yellow gown. She is young, has only had her come-out last season, and she is rather popular with the gentlemen."

"Why isn't she married then?" John asked, looking at the lady in question.

"I don't know. I've heard she had several offers, but her family probably thought them not worthy enough," she answered thoughtfully.

"And they'd think me worthy?" John raised an eyebrow at his friend.

Julie grimaced in thought. "Perhaps not. Very well, I have the best pick for you right here," she said and gestured for John to turn. "There's Evie. You remember her, don't you?"

"Evie?" John turned in the direction Julie was pointing. "I don't believe I know an Evie," he added thoughtfully.

Then he saw the young lady in question. She was beautiful, with vibrant red hair and a bright smile. She was surrounded by a group of young gentlemen, all vying for her attention, while she spoke and laughed, regarding everyone with the same amount of attention, turning this way and that. John didn't remember the last time he'd exuded so much energy.

"She's my cousin. I was certain you would remember her. But it was quite a while ago when you last saw her and she would have been but a child. She is the granddaughter of the late Duke of Somerset. And the current Duchess of Somerset in her own right."

John turned to Julie with a questioning look. Titled ladies in their own right were a rare occurrence, to say the least.

"One of those rare titles with a clause to allow females to inherit," she explained. "Still, she won't be able to sit in the House of Lords; her husband will get that privilege. Neither does she have access to her full inheritance yet."

"A duchess." John turned back and looked at the lady in question with a frown. He didn't remember the girl, but then again, as Julie pointed out, she would have been a babe when he saw her last.

"She will be granted the full power upon turning five and twenty, or upon marriage. Until then, her guardian, a distant cousin, Lord Montbrook, is running her affairs. But her inheritance is quite a hefty one, including horses, capital, and seven estates," Julie went on while he studied the young lady's form. "More importantly, she is vivacious. I think she would be very good for you."

"But she wants to marry for love. Or so she's said about a thousand times," Clydesdale interjected. "She is a romantic, from a loving family, spoiled by her grandfather. She needs a gentle hand, a coddling husband. *Not a soldier.*"

John was looking at the radiant duchess, surrounded by an army of suitors. Clydesdale was probably right. He would be the worst possible match for a dreamy young girl. But he didn't much care. He needed a wife, and soon. A lady with a large dowry accompanied by her own estates? She would be perfect for John. Even if it made him a cad.

"I think I've made my choice." John turned back to Julie.
"Which is?"
"The duchess," John said, smiling at Clydesdale.

Chapter 3

S am sat in front of her vanity and brushed out her hair. Tonight was the first ball of the season. She was looking forward to it and dreading it at the same time. She was nervous like she was a debutante. Surely, it should have gotten easier by now?

When in London, she usually spent most of her time with Evie, but this year, it was different. Evie wasn't going out as much, and she had a thin veil of grief ever-present in her eyes. The passing of her beloved grandfather and the changes in the household had all taken a toll on her. She was also being courted by Lady Clydesdale's John. Sam hadn't met him yet, and she didn't know how the courting was progressing, but the amount of time Evie spent with him pointed toward serious intentions on both sides. Sam wondered if she'd have to go through the next season alone, or perhaps even this season if Evie decided to marry quickly.

Sam expelled a breath. She wasn't really good in social situations. Not like Evie. Sam had grown up in a big and boisterous family, but those were the people she knew and loved. She could banter with them all day long. Talking to strangers, however, was a different beast altogether.

Sam looked at her own reflection closely. She pulled her eyebrows higher above her eyes, then pinched at her cheeks. She wasn't prideful or vain, but she knew she was pleasing to look at. Perhaps she was a little too serious and she wasn't good at small talk, but these were inconsequential issues, weren't they? Nobody chose their wives based on their ability to talk about weather and gowns, did they? Then why hadn't she found a suitor yet after six seasons? Or perhaps the problem wasn't that the gentlemen didn't find her attractive. The problem was she hadn't found a single gentleman worthy of her affection.

She frowned at the thought. Had Evie's ramblings about love managed to cloud her judgment as well?

A knock at her door interrupted her musings, and she swiveled her head to stare at it.

"Please, come in!" she called. Evie entered and closed the door behind her. "Evie! I didn't expect a visit from you today." Sam hurried to hug her friend.

"I know, but I needed to speak to you. Isabel said I would find you here."

"Is anything amiss?" Sam asked, gesturing for her to sit down.

"No, all is well." Evie sat in a chair to the left of the vanity, and Sam settled in front of the looking glass again, taking back her brush and continuing brushing out her hair.

"I'm sorry we didn't get to see much of each other before," Evie said with an apologetic smile.

"Do not be silly, Evie. I know you have a lot on your mind."

"Yes, I suppose." Evie paused. "You are coming to the Bainbridge ball tonight, aren't you?"

"Of course, I am." Sam paused in the act of brushing out her hair and looked at her friend, who couldn't seem to meet her gaze. "Is something amiss?"

"No." Evie shook her head for emphasis. "But I want you to meet someone tonight."

"Truly, who?"

"Lord Ashbury."

"Who is that?" Sam frowned.

"Julie's John, the gentleman who is courting me."

"Oh." Sam placed the brush on the vanity and turned fully toward her friend. That was a strange way to put it. Not at all like a woman in love talking about her suitor. "You want me to meet him because he is courting you?"

"Yes, well, he seems to be a decent man." Evie stood and started pacing the room. "I think we would suit well together."

"But you've only known him for several weeks," Sam started carefully. "And you said you wanted to marry for love. Evie, do you love him?"

Evie halted mid-stride and turned to Sam. "Love can grow. It did for Julie. And he is very respectful. And he doesn't talk too much, which works out well, because I do. He likes to ride and spend time outdoors. I like the countryside."

Evie was trying so hard to convince Sam that Lord Ashbury suited her that Sam wondered whether it was Evie herself who needed convincing.

"I am certain he is an amiable person. You have great taste in people. You are friends with me, aren't you?" Sam asked in as light a tone as she could muster.

Evie smiled at her friend's attempt at a jest and settled back in the chair. "I can't marry him if you don't like him," she said, and it warmed Sam's heart.

"Of course, I shall like him. I shall love him." Sam hugged her friend tightly.

"Thank you," Evie said before she stood. "Now I need to get ready for this ball tonight. I'll see you there." She smiled and walked out of the door.

* * *

The crush at Bainbridge House was unbearable. John had only just entered and already he wished to leave. But he had duties to attend to: greet his hostess, make idle chit-chat with the lords, and dance with the Duchess of Somerset. After that, he would be free. He had promised Her Grace he would be present at the ball. She was adamant that he attend, and he couldn't very well refuse, lest she think he was not interested. And he *was* interested.

The duchess was beautiful, spirited, lively, and a delightfully entertaining conversationalist. More importantly, she was an heiress and from what he gleaned from their conversations, she was more than ready to be wed. But she was a duke's granddaughter, a duchess. She loved the parties, soirees, and balls. She thrived in a social setting, on the dance floor, among crowds of people. Everything he loathed. What kind of life would it be for a young exuberant girl, locked away in the country with a grumpy old soldier, a hermit with nightmares and occasional hallucinations?

That was the problem: He actually liked the girl. If he didn't care for her, he would probably be content with ruining her life forever. But watching the life drain from her eyes was not something he wanted to see in someone so happy and full of vigor. Much less did he wish to be the reason for it. Clydesdale was right; she was used to a good life, loving parents, and a grandfather who would have gotten her the moon if she would but ask. John was not what she needed, and having another regret was not something he needed either. And he knew without a shadow of a doubt that if he married her and ruined her life, he would add one more sin to his collection.

Nevertheless, there he was, in a ballroom, waiting to meet her, dance with her, and propose marriage.

He'd come in a bit later than was fashionable so that he wouldn't need to wait for his intended to show up. He didn't want to linger while the guests were still arriving, and the quicker he could go about his business, the quicker he would be back in his dank old room, staring at the empty walls.

However, finding anyone in this beehive was impossible. He needed to concentrate on his breathing and hope that the sound of blood rushing through his veins would drown out the noise of the ballroom. After maneuvering through the crowd, he finally noticed his flame-haired bride-to-be. When he came over to greet her and ask for a dance, it turned out her dance card was already almost full. *Almost.* Because she had saved him one waltz. John was pleasantly surprised. Another clear sign that she welcomed his attention.

Why, he couldn't tell. She was always surrounded by a sea of beaux.

The waltz, however, was three sets away, and he had to occupy himself somehow in the meantime. He'd decided to walk toward the card room when a heavy hand settled on his shoulder.

"John," said a familiar voice. John turned and saw the large frame of an old military friend. "Didn't expect to see you here. Or should I say, Ashbury? You've certainly moved up in the world." A deep rumbling laugh followed the declaration.

"Ramsey," John greeted his friend. Ramsey was several inches taller and several stones heavier than John. His hair was bright orange and his eyes the color of the sea during a storm. He was amiable as always, smiling at his friend. Ramsey and John had not served together, but they'd crossed paths regularly during the war.

"I don't think I've seen you in ages. It's as if you crawled under a rock once you sold your commission. Last I heard, you were getting your title, and then you disappeared. Civilian life's treating you well, huh?" Ramsey patted John on his shoulder and laughed loudly.

"Well enough," John answered succinctly. "How about you?"

"Well, I sold my commission years ago, married, and have three little brats now. At home with them, I feel like I am back at war." He laughed jovially. "Sometimes I even think I'd rather be back. Commanding two hundred officers is nothing compared to three little babes." He patted John on the shoulder once again and continued his one-sided conversation.

"By the way, I saw Lieutenant Colonel Harris recently. We got to reminiscing. Remember Badajoz? That's where we all met for the first time. Bullets flying, horses falling on their arses, and there you were..." Ramsey continued his good-natured narrative, but John couldn't hear him anymore; he couldn't hear anything over the loud buzzing in his ears. He had trouble drawing a breath and suddenly felt like collapsing. *Oh, Lord, it is happening again,* was all John could think before bolting toward the doors closest to him.

Ramsey tried to stop him, or at least, John saw him stretching an arm toward him. But John darted away and made his way through the crowd. He was trembling and sweating profusely. He had a feeling he would cast up his accounts right there on the ballroom floor. John hastily opened the first door on the left, closed it, and stood leaning against it for what could have been minutes or hours.

When his breathing slowed, he ventured farther into a spacious room that was sparsely illuminated by the full moon outside. John found a lone candle and a tinderbox beside it. He lit the candle and collapsed on the chair closest to it. He leaned on his elbows and lowered his aching head into his hands.

Would he ever get rid of these headaches and nightmares, or was it his destiny to suffer through them for the sins he had committed during his years as an officer? He closed his eyes and concentrated on the muffled noises coming from the ballroom. *I am back home, there is peace, I am not going back to war. I am home, I am never going back to war,* he repeated over and over to himself.

* * *

Samantha had never been a wallflower, but the age and looks of her partners had changed for the worse proportionally to the number of years she'd been out on the marriage mart. She almost looked forward to the next year, when she could finally sit with the spinsters and dowagers, no longer expected to dance with the gentlemen, unless they were her relatives.

Her brothers always danced with her if they were present,

but they rarely were, having the unfair advantage of being male and skipping the whole charade of the season unless they deemed it necessary to find a wife. And none of her brothers was looking to take on that responsibility.

Alan was still young, but he was only three years younger than Sam. She did not think it fair that he was excused for being too young, while she had been here on display for years.

The suffocating heat in the ballroom made her itchy. To top it all off, her new stockings kept sliding out of her garters. It was fine as long as she was sitting, but once she started dancing, her left stocking kept inching away. She could just imagine it—during a waltz with some stocky old lord, her stocking would slide right off her leg and plop to the floor. *That* would be an embarrassment to remember for years.

As soon as the reel finished, she walked quickly in the direction of the powder room to fix her stockings. The progress she made in that direction was minimal since she had to plow through the sea of bodies to get there. She would have to cross the ballroom to reach it, and with a crush such as this, it would take forever. Sam slipped into an empty hallway instead. She entered the first room on the left and sighed in relief.

The room seemed unoccupied, although a lone candle stood on the table in the far right corner. She walked a little farther into the room, turned her back to the candle, and hiked up her skirts to fix her garter.

"What are you doing?" a masculine voice demanded from behind her.

Sam gave a high-pitched yelp and whirled around. A shadow moved closer to the candle.

"I didn't mean to frighten you," the shadow said. "But I was hoping for some solitude."

Sam opened and closed her mouth several times before she could get her voice out. Her face heated from mortification. Of course, it was rather dark, so there was a possibility the gentleman hadn't seen her with her skirts up to her waist.

"Solitude," she finally repeated, regaining her wits. "During a ball, in a house full of people."

"Yes, solitude. In a dark, empty room away from the ballroom. So, if you please?" He gestured toward the door.

"And what if I don't please? I have as much right to be here as you. So how about *you* go, and I stay?" Sam knew she was courting trouble being in a room alone with a gentleman. But his highhandedness mixed with her embarrassment made her stubborn.

"I was here first so…" He trailed off.

"Oh, what are you five years old?" she asked indignantly.

"Listen, Miss, I am having a bad day, a blasted headache, and haven't had a minute of peace," he said angrily. "I really wish you would leave me alone."

"If you were a gentleman, not only would you not be hiding out in a dark room all by yourself during a crush of a ball, but you'd concede a room to a lady," she said pointedly, although she'd already picked up her skirts and turned, ready to leave.

"If you were a lady," he said in a dark tone behind her, "you wouldn't be hiking your skirts up to your waist in front of a gentleman."

Sam gasped in outrage, while her cheeks burned in mortification. The cad had seen her with her raised skirts, and she wished she could fall through the floor at that moment. "Y-you, i-it is very dark in here, so you couldn't have seen anything," she managed with as much dignity as she could muster.

"Oh, believe me," he said slowly, "I saw plenty. Beautiful calves, by the way. You must be a graceful rider."

Samantha drew in an outraged breath, but for the life of her could not say anything in response. That's when she heard a weird choking sound and realized that the insufferable man was chuckling. He was laughing at her.

"You are the most impossible man I have ever met!" She whirled on her heels and stalked out of the room.

Chapter 4

John was still laughing at the antics of the young lady who'd so innocently flashed her beautiful legs at him. Her expression had changed from frightened to shocked to dignified and finally angry in a matter of moments before she'd finally stalked out of the room. The headache forgotten, he settled comfortably into his chair. She was right; it had been too dark for him to see anything clearly, but the moonlight had outlined her perfect little calves beautifully, and he wished he could have seen more of her. It suddenly occurred to him that it had been years since he'd seen a woman in any state of undress. He was a cad for even contemplating such thoughts about a proper young lady. No doubt unmarried and innocent. Fantasies didn't hurt anyone though, did they?

She had a lovely voice too. A familiar voice, he noted, but then he'd met plenty of ladies in the past couple of months. It could be any one of them, and there was little chance he'd ever find out who she was. *Does it matter who she is?* He was going to offer for the Duchess of Somerset and put an end to this social torture very soon. He thought about the duchess's radiant face, her jovial laughter. It didn't send a spark through him the way this young lady's voice had. But that was for the best. If he didn't care for her, he had a better chance of leaving her to her own devices. And that would ensure that she was safe from him.

John rose from the chair and walked out of the room just in time to hear the first strains of the waltz. He hastily entered the ballroom and saw his intended bride looking around. He hurried his step and a few moments later entered the dancefloor with her on his arm.

They danced in silence for several moments. She was a graceful dancer, and even though John hadn't had the opportunity to practice, he didn't feel clumsy around her.

"Your Grace," he finally said. She turned her forest-green eyes on him. "I would like to call upon you tomorrow if you don't mind."

He'd come to this ball with the intention of proposing to her, but something in him balked at the idea of doing it so publicly. He didn't think it would be very romantic to ask her while they were dancing unless he stopped and dropped to one knee. In which case, it would be over-the-top romantic and obviously out of place, since neither of them was in love with the other.

"I would like that," she answered with a smile.

"We can go for a walk in the park," he added.

"That would be lovely," she offered shyly. She cleared her throat before continuing. "Actually, do you mind if I invite my friend to come with us? I wanted to introduce you to her tonight, but she seems to have vanished."

"Of course." He didn't want anyone else being there when he proposed to her, but he supposed he could steer her away from her friend for a couple of minutes for a private conversation. Besides, it would be rude to decline. "I'd be delighted," he added with a strained smile.

* * *

"Samantha!" Evie jumped from her settee as Sam entered the drawing room.

"*Samantha*? I think this is officially the first time you've ever called me by my full name," Sam answered, smiling and hugging her friend.

"I'm so glad you are here," Evie said, settling back down on the settee and drawing Sam with her.

"Of course, I am. You asked me here. How could I refuse?"

"Well, you disappeared yesterday without meeting Lord Ashbury. I was afraid you would be unavailable today as well, and I have this feeling that he is going to propose," Evie said in a rush.

"You do? He is?" Sam asked, her eyes widening. "What makes you think so? You barely know each other."

"Yes, I know, but he had this very concentrated look on his face when he said he'd call on me today. Oh, God, I cannot accept a marriage proposal until you meet him."

"Evie," Sam said slowly, "I think it is going to take me a little longer than one meeting to ascertain whether a gentleman is suitable to share his life with my friend. And if he indeed is going to propose, I am going to get in the way."

"No, Sam, please, I need you with me today. I shall feel better if you are nearby, and even if you won't know it, I shall know right away whether you like him or not."

"Very well," Sam conceded. "If you say so. But, Evie, as much as I appreciate your desire for me to be the judge of this whole situation… How *you* feel about Lord Ashbury is what matters."

"I am a jumble of nerves," Evie said, twisting her hands on her lap.

"Why the rush to marry him? Is something wrong in the household? Is your uncle not treating you right?" Sam whispered the last sentence, watching her friend intently.

Evie let out a huff of breath. "No, it's none of that." She airily waved her hand. "My uncle is a darling… Except—"

"Except what?" Sam scooted closer to her friend.

"Well, his wife arrived a few weeks back. She let go of my chaperone and started making changes around the house. Montbrook is different around her too, and he lets her do anything." She shook her head. "This house doesn't feel like my home anymore, and I just want to get out. And… Well, Lady Montbrook is very against Lord Ashbury and she has been pushing me toward some… questionable prospects."

"Questionable how?"

Evie wrinkled her nose. "She arranged for several dinners in the past few weeks and invited titled but old gentlemen. Every time she seated me next to Lord Lansdowne."

"Lord Lansdowne?" Sam echoed, aghast. "That's who she is pushing you to marry? How in the world does she think you'll concede to that?"

Lord Lansdowne was an old marquess in desperate need of an heir. He was probably eighty years old, with rotten teeth and a lecherous gaze.

Evie bit her lip. "I do not know. But she did hint that he's the kind of man... The kind of title I should aim for. She has lined up a couple of other suitors for me. But none of them look promising to me. I would have chosen none of them for myself."

"And you would choose Lord Ashbury?"

Evie took a deep breath. "Lord Ashbury is not exactly my choice either. But at least I can be certain of Julie's motives."

"Hmm..." Sam pulled a thoughtful grimace. "Perhaps we should ask Lord Clydesdale to investigate the Montbrooks. There must be a reason Lady Montbrook is pushing you to such a nasty arrangement. Unless, of course, she just wants you to suffer. Or I can ask Gage, I am sure he will—"

"No." Evie shook her head. "No need to involve your family, I shall talk with Julie. I am sure her husband will be more than happy to assist me."

"Besides, it would be easier for Clydesdale being an heir to a dukedom," Sam agreed.

"Well, enough about me," Evie said, rearranging her skirts. "Before Lord Ashbury arrives, I need you to tell me something."

"What?"

"Where did you disappear to last night?"

Sam groaned. "Please, please, please don't remind me." She closed her eyes and lowered her head onto her upturned palms.

"What happened?" Evie's voice held a note of astonishment.

"I made a complete fool of myself in front of some unknown gentleman," Sam said, her words muffled against her palms. "And I was so embarrassed that I convinced Isabel to leave right away. It was such a crush, I couldn't find you quickly, and we had to make a hasty exit."

"Well?" Evie prompted.

Sam uncovered her face and looked up at her friend. "I flashed my legs at a gentleman in an empty room."

"What?" Evie nearly jumped off the settee.

Sam proceeded to tell the story in very excruciating and embarrassing detail. How her garter kept falling off and she was afraid her stocking would end up in a pool on the ballroom floor. How she entered a dark room and hiked up her skirts in order to retie her garter. How the rude stranger made fun of her and how childishly she behaved to cover up her embarrassment.

By the end of the story, both girls were choking with laughter.

"Well, to be fair," Evie said between fits of laughter, "you do have beautiful calves."

"Oh, please." Sam was holding on to her abdomen, laughing. "It was the most embarrassing moment of my entire life. Thank the Lord it was dark enough that he probably didn't even see my face."

"What about you? Did you recognize him?"

"No, I mean, his voice did sound familiar, but I don't think I'd recognize it out of one hundred others. Besides, I sincerely hope I shall never meet him again."

She wiped her tears with a handkerchief. At that moment, Evie's butler, Rogers, entered the room and announced with a flourish, "Lord Ashbury for Her Grace, the Duchess of Somerset."

* * *

John entered a spacious drawing room decorated lavishly in

golden hues and decided that he'd made a perfect choice in his bride. Saying the room was spacious didn't do it justice. His townhouse's entire ground floor would fit in this room. The furniture and walls were styled in the renaissance era, with expensive paintings complementing the room. His gaze was instantly riveted to the two young ladies standing next to a settee in the middle of the room.

"Lord Ashbury." His intended made several steps toward him.

He took her offered hand and bowed over it. "Your Grace."

"Let me introduce you to my friend." She gestured to a beautiful blonde girl. "Miss Samantha Lewis."

John turned toward the lady and froze. He knew the young lady. She wasn't surrounded by a halo this time, but her features were unmistakable. The same dainty nose covered with a few freckles, the same whisky-brown eyes. His gaze lingered on her full and plump lips for a moment before he forced his gaze to return to her eyes.

"Miss Lewis, a pleasure." John bowed over her hand.

Miss Lewis stared at him as if he'd grown horns. She then turned to the Duchess of Somerset and raised her brows. John looked at his intended, then back to her friend, but by this time, Miss Lewis had composed herself and smiled at him sweetly.

She curtsied low then cleared her throat. "Pleasure to meet you. And please, call me Miss Samantha. Miss Lewis is my elder sister."

That voice. That sweet, husky voice was too familiar. He already knew they'd met, but he was certain it wasn't just one time.

"What a rare and beautiful name," he said, smiling. "But I

43

believe we've already met."

Miss Samantha seemed to blanch at the statement. Her mouth parted slightly, drawing his gaze to her lush lips once more.

"You have?" his intended asked in astonishment.

"Yes, indeed. But don't feel bad for not placing me, Miss. I believe you caught me at a disadvantage." He looked back at Miss Samantha then returned his gaze to his intended. "You see, my horse threw me on my morning ride, and I am afraid I tumbled into a puddle of mud. So, I probably look a little better groomed at the moment."

"Oh, yes, that's… yes, that's where we've met," Miss Samantha said with a tight smile.

"Oh, my!" The duchess laughed.

She did it a lot, he noticed. Laughed, that was. The sound was pleasant. But would he get used to hearing it in his house every day, or would it die down soon after their marriage?

"I can assure you I am a far more graceful rider than I seemed then too," John said, and Miss Samantha seemed to choke on air. She coughed into her fist.

"You didn't tell me this story, Sam!" the duchess exclaimed.

Miss Samantha still looked a little dazed, blinking from John to the duchess.

"Well, it was a tiny incident, hardly worth mentioning, I imagine," John continued, looking at her. "Although it did smart my pride quite a bit."

"No need for that. Happens to the best of us, I can imagine," Miss Samantha said in a low voice and smiled at him slightly. And that's when he remembered her sensual voice. She was also the lady who'd bared her legs in front of him during last night's ball!

He swallowed a laugh and studied her carefully. She had beautiful facial features; he'd noticed it from the first. She had a soft feminine figure, the tops of her breasts peeking out above her low bodice. He forced his gaze up.

"I am very pleased to finally meet you," he said with a smile. "I heard Her Grace tried to introduce us last night, but you disappeared."

"Yes, I... um, I wasn't feeling well," she stammered.

"I hope you are feeling better now. If not, a ride in a barouche should put some color in your cheeks."

"A ride in an open carriage sounds heavenly." The duchess weaved her hand through Miss Samantha's and led the way.

When they reached Hyde Park, John left the vehicle in his groom's care and they all proceeded to promenade around the Serpentine. The two ladies were walking hand in hand and chattering away. They were as different as the sun and the moon. The duchess was as bright as her hair, always laughing and animated. She talked of her love of dance, about beautiful gowns, the theater, and art galleries. John couldn't help but think that when they wed, she would suffocate without the city life or they would have to spend most of their married life apart.

Miss Samantha, on the other hand, was quieter, or perhaps compared to the exuberant Duchess of Somerset anyone would seem quiet. He wondered if Miss Samantha recognized him from before. She'd looked flabbergasted when she first saw him, so perhaps she did. Now, however, she just studied him and kept asking him all kinds of pointed questions. It was obvious that she cared about her friend very much and was assessing whether John would be a suitable husband for her. Something that John doubted more and more with every passing minute.

When they finally stopped at the bridge overlooking the roses, John asked if he could have a private moment with Her Grace. They stepped several feet away from Miss Samantha, so they were still in view but could have a conversation without her overhearing.

"Your Grace," John started and cleared his throat. "You must suspect what I came here to ask you."

She nodded silently, and John sighed. "I… In the past few days, I've come to admire your spirit. I enjoy your company very much, and therefore I think it is only fair that we talk openly, yes?"

"Yes, I think it best." She nodded again and smiled politely.

"The thing is… I need a wife," he blurted and waited for her reaction.

She didn't give him any. She was a clever young lady and surely she'd ascertained his intentions from the start, so he continued.

"I inherited the barony about a year ago, and with it, quite a number of debts. I need to marry an heiress to help me settle them."

He cleared his throat and shifted uncomfortably on his feet, waiting for her to acknowledge this. When she realized that he required an answer, she smiled.

"Oh, I know all that," she said. "You see, Julie already told me."

"She did, did she?" John smiled crookedly. "I suppose I should have expected that. Well, regardless of that, there's more… For reasons I cannot tell you, I really am not planning to spend much of my time in the city. I shall not require my wife to follow my example, however. I do not believe

46

that a husband and wife should spend every waking minute together."

"Are you looking for a marriage of convenience then?" she asked thoughtfully.

"Yes, but based on friendship and mutual respect."

"How about affection? Love?" she continued carefully.

"I am not looking to fall in love, Your Grace, and quite frankly, you will find it difficult to feel affectionate toward me most days."

"Why is that?" She cocked her head to the side.

"Let's just say I am a difficult person to get along with. I have a bad temper, although I'd never hurt a lady—any woman for that matter—but… I prefer solitude to company, silence to conversation."

She contemplated that for a while. "What about children? Do you want an heir?"

"I don't need an heir, I don't much care what happens to the title, but I shall not leave my wife childless if that is her wish. Although, do not expect me to be an involved parent. I didn't have much in the way of a role model." He paused. "I know this is not an ideal proposal, especially to one such as yourself. I know you have a bevy of suitors to choose from."

She snorted lightly at that.

"But if you don't object to anything you've heard so far, I would very much like to ask your guardian's permission to have your hand in marriage."

The duchess was silent for some time, her gaze fixed on a single point in the distance. She was quiet and serene. So much so that he was afraid he'd broken her. He had never seen her like this. She was always animated, always in motion. *Oh, God, I would make her life miserable.*

"You do not have to give me an answer right away," he soothed.

"Thank you," was all she said.

* * *

"What did he say?" Sam asked Evie as soon as they entered the house and the door closed behind Lord Ashbury.

"He wanted to ask permission to approach my guardian," Evie said simply, taking off her gloves and bonnet.

"He intends to ask for your hand in marriage." Sam wasn't surprised by that turn of events. She was more curious about her friend's reaction. She took off her own gloves and bonnet and handed them to a waiting footman.

"Yes," Evie said, starting up the stairs. "He also said that he'd only be marrying me for my inheritance, and although he is willing to give me friendship, I shouldn't expect either love or affection from him."

"He did not say that!" Sam exclaimed, outraged.

"Yes, he did." Evie entered her suite with Sam following in her footsteps. "And he said he would give me children if I wanted, but he would not be involved with them."

"Oh, God, Evie, what did you tell him?"

"What could I have told him, Sam?" Evie cried and covered her face with her hands. "I have no choice, do I?"

"What do you mean, you have no choice?" Sam settled on the settee next to her friend. "You can say, thank you, but no thank you!"

Evie laughed a little at that, a familiar twinkle in her eyes. *Good.* Sam had started to think Lord Ashbury had scarred her for life.

"You know I cannot do that, I have to marry."

"But Lord Ashbury? You are surrounded by suitors day in and day out. Why does it have to be him?"

"Because he is honest, young, and our conversation flows naturally. Julie loves him, so there must be something in him to love. Besides, he is pleasing to look at, and be honest, you liked him too, I could tell."

Sam contemplated that for a while. "Yes, it's true, I did like him. But that was before you told me what he said! You don't need to marry *him*. Besides, Lady Montbrook can't force you to marry anyone else, can she? I am certain your guardian will be on your side. You don't need to marry now; you can still find another suitor."

"Perhaps..." Evie gave a little shrug.

"And also, I have something to confess." Sam fidgeted in her seat.

"What?"

"Remember the story about how I met Lord Ashbury?"

"Yes?"

"It wasn't the only time we've met."

"It wasn't?"

"No." Sam stood and started pacing. "I recognized his voice. He was the gentleman in the dark room I encountered at the Bainbridge ball!"

"No!" Evie's eyes widened.

"Yes!" Sam threw up her hands. "I am quite certain it was him, although I don't think he realized that."

"Oh, no!" Evie started chuckling, her shoulders shaking in mirth.

"Oh, you, stop, this isn't funny!" Sam swatted at her friend.

Evie leaned out of her reach. "You have to admit, it is a little funny. My groom-to-be saw your bare legs before he saw mine."

"Oh, God, Evie, where are your thoughts at?" Sam shook her head, grinning.

"Probably not where they should be, or I'd find an answer to my predicament easily."

Sam sobered and said after a pause, "Promise me you will think about this carefully, Evie. You can find someone better. Someone who is not rude and overbearing. Someone who will fall head over heels in love with you."

Evie laughed at that. "The longer I wait for said someone, the more I think he doesn't exist."

"Perhaps he does. Perhaps you just haven't met him yet."

Evie cast her eyes down, playing with the fabric of her skirts.

"Or maybe you should at least look for someone *you* can fall in love with."

Evie looked up with a vulnerable expression on her face. Her gaze was liquid and her mouth in a small pout, and Sam just wanted to hug her and make everything better. *How does one go about falling in love?* Evie had been so confident she would make a love match from the very first that nobody doubted it. Least of all Sam. But now it seemed that even the most precious gemstone of the *ton* would have to settle for a marriage of convenience. And if that was so—as much as she hated the pitiful and self-centered direction of her thoughts—what chance did Sam have for a love match?

Chapter 5

The next morning, Sam ventured out on an early morning ride. This time, she wasn't plagued by nightmares but rather by worry for her friend. She was hoping to run into Lord Ashbury as she had the first morning they'd met, and she intended to give him a piece of her mind.

Her guess proved to be correct, and after a few minutes of cantering, she noticed a rider coming her way at a full gallop. He slowed down as he approached her and stopped when their horses were almost nose to nose.

"Miss Samantha." He touched his crop to the tip of his hat.

"My lord." Samantha inclined her head. "Do you always ride at such a breakneck pace?"

"Usually," he answered with a crooked smile.

A dimple appeared on his cheek, making him boyishly handsome. Sam couldn't help but smile back.

"Care for a race?" he asked with a smile. "Until the next bend."

Sam bit her lower lip in thought. This wasn't why she'd come out this morning. Still, a short race wouldn't hurt anyone, would it? "With pleasure," she answered.

He inclined his head and turned the horse to face the same direction as Sam's. The next moment, they were both galloping side by side. Sam's horse was about one pace ahead of Ashbury's mount. She craned her neck to look at him and saw that he was watching her intently. Sam turned forward and spurred her horse on. As they neared the bend, Ashbury passed her and won by about an inch.

"Ahh!" Sam exclaimed. "It was ungentlemanly of you not to let me win!"

"Was it?" He grinned at her. "I didn't think you'd care for a dishonest victory."

"If I was a spoiled lady prone to hysterics, you might have won yourself a fit." Sam grinned right back.

"I didn't think you were that kind of lady. In any case, now I owe you a rematch." They started their horses in a slow walk along the Serpentine. "So I was correct in my assessment," he said conversationally after a brief pause.

"About?" Sam looked at him curiously. When she'd met him before, she hadn't really paid attention to his face. Now, she had a chance to study him at her leisure. He wasn't handsome. His face was angular, his nose crooked, and he had an angry scar on his right cheek. But he had beautiful hazel eyes, fringed by thick brown lashes.

"That you are a graceful rider," he said and grinned at her.

It took Sam a moment to understand the reference. She gasped when she did and turned on him wide-eyed. "You did recognize me then!"

"I did. Just didn't want to say anything in front of the

duchess."

Sam sputtered but found she had nothing to say.

"In my defense, I had a blasted headache, and I wasn't quite myself. Your appearance actually took my mind off the pain. So I owe you not only my apology but also my gratitude."

"How about we forget it ever happened instead?" Sam felt heat rise up her neck.

"I shall give it my best effort." He smiled wolfishly and looked ahead. "Do you ride here often?"

"Quite," Sam said and nodded. "It helps me clear my head. I prefer to ride in the country, of course, since I love to gallop. And the only time of day I can do that in London is around dawn. Usually, there is no one else here."

"Except for me." He smiled at her again.

Sam had to bite back her own smile. She found it a difficult task.

"Except for you, yes," she agreed.

"I am not much for town life either. In fact, I don't plan on coming to London that often. I'm here this year only to find a wife. After that, I shall retire back to the country."

"Ah, the wife," Sam drawled.

"The Duchess of Somerset told you about my proposal," he stated rather than asked.

"She did." Sam nodded, staring straight ahead. "And I have to say, it was not the most romantic proposal I have ever heard."

He huffed a breath of laughter. "And you've heard aplenty, haven't you?"

"No, not plenty. Not as many as Evie in any case."

"Why is she still unmarried then?" He finally looked at her. "Why are you, for that matter? Why hasn't some duke or marquess swept you off your feet and brought you to his castle?"

Samantha laughed at that. "Evie was waiting for true love," she said softly, and then chuckled as she saw Lord Ashbury grimace.

"In that case, I really did muck up the proposal, didn't I?"

Sam heaved a sigh. "Evie comes from a very tight-knit family. They are all gone now, but both her parents and grandparents married for love. She grew up listening to their love stories before bedtime. That is the only way she ever saw a marriage. And that's what her family wanted for her. But then, life intervened. Her parents passed away, ending her first season prematurely. She was in mourning for two whole years before she braved the *ton* again."

"Is that so?" Lord Ashbury asked, frowning.

"Yes." Sam nodded. "With her grandfather gone last year, she's been left all alone… Don't you think she should at least have a husband who loves her? Whom she loves back? Or at the very least someone she can grow to love and who can grow to love her in return."

Lord Ashbury swallowed and closed his eyes. "Then she shouldn't marry me," he said quietly.

They continued a slow trot in silence, each lost in their own thoughts. That wasn't the confrontation Sam had expected to have with the baron. She'd expected him to be more selfish, to not care about Evie's feelings, or to pretend to care in order to get what he wanted. But he seemed sincerely pained that he would not be able to give Evie what she yearned for.

"What about you?" he finally asked.

"What about me?" Sam asked, frowning.

"Why aren't you married?"

"Sometimes I think it is our family curse." She turned to him with a cheerful smile. He looked puzzled. "You see, none of my siblings are married yet. And most of them are older than me."

"And how many siblings do you have?"

"One sister and three brothers."

"Are you all looking for love too? Because I have to tell you, it seems like the odds are against you."

She thought about the answer for a while. "I don't think my brothers are looking for anything," she finally said. "At least not yet. And my sister… Well, it is a long story, but she's been burned by love once before. I think she decided it was not worth the risk. Besides, she has other concerns to occupy her thoughts. And as for me… no, I don't think I am looking for love. I just have trouble connecting with people, especially gentlemen."

"I find that very hard to believe," he answered earnestly.

"Thank you for saying so." She smiled. "However, I am not flirtatious or coquettish. I prefer a good book to a boring conversation, and I am not really interested in how many hounds or horses one owns or how large one's estates are, something gentlemen seem to constantly want to tell me."

"They want to impress you." He laughed.

"Well, it's not working." Sam was tempted to roll her eyes. "I do not need some grand love or all-consuming passion. All I want is someone I can have a decent conversation with. Someone I can spend quiet evenings with, either reading or playing board games. Someone to go out riding with each morning. A friendship."

Lord Ashbury was quiet for a while. They rode in silence, side by side, each engrossed in their own thoughts. Sam maneuvered her horse to avoid a puddle and brushed her knee against Lord Ashbury's. A curious jolt hit her from the contact, and she smiled at him apologetically.

"I used to want those same things," he finally breathed.

Sam blinked at him.

"From marriage. All the things you've described." He shook his head. "But much like your sister, I've been burned by love. You might know this since you are very close to the duchess. I was in love once too."

Sam nodded. "With Lady Clydesdale."

Lord Ashbury huffed a laugh. "Julie—yes. I dreamed of such companionable evenings with her. The friendship, the love, all in one relationship. She knew me like no one else ever did. When she married… I think I lost a part of myself. A peaceful part. Then the war did the rest. Or war came first, I don't remember anymore. In any case, I am far too damaged to offer any kind of comfort to a lady now. And if you are worried about your friend, you have reason to. I am not going to be an easy person to live with. If she's open to a marriage of convenience, to a marriage where husband and wife lead separate lives, then she will be getting exactly that. If she wants anything more, she will be sorely disappointed."

* * *

Sam returned home without having eased her mind, and if she was honest with herself, with an even heavier weight on her shoulders. She liked Lord Ashbury. She truly did. Despite the impression he'd made at the ball, he wasn't rude or callous. She wanted him to solve his financial issues and to have a companionable wife but not Evie. Evie deserved a lot more than that. She deserved a marriage built on love and passion, just as she had always dreamed.

Evie was so distressed by grief for her grandfather and worry about her guardian's wife's schemes that she was not thinking clearly. Hence her willingness to accept the first proposal she received no matter how unsavory the idea seemed to her. Lady Clydesdale's influence was palpable, too. Marriage was forever, and in this quest to cover her pain, Evie was forfeiting her own happiness.

Well, if her friend was in trouble and in need of a hand, Sam would offer her one. What she needed to do, Sam decided, was to find a suitable gentleman for Evie to marry, and she needed to do that before Evie acquiesced to Ashbury's proposal.

After a short bath, she came downstairs to find her family at the breakfast table.

"You are back late today," Isabel said in lieu of a greeting.

"Good morning, Isabel," Sam answered with a bright smile. "Richard, Adam." She inclined her head toward her brothers, who stood as she entered.

"Where have you been?" Richard furrowed his brows at her.

"A morning ride," Sam answered and settled in her chair.

"I don't remember giving you permission to go on a morning ride. Who was with you?"

"James. James is always with me, you know that," she said with a weary sigh. "And what else am I supposed to do in the mornings?"

"I don't know… embroider?"

Sam narrowed her eyes at her brother.

"She is safe with James," Isabel intervened, and Sam sent her a grateful look.

57

"I don't see how she can be safe with a footman—"

"Richard." Isabel sent him a reproachful look, and he grumbled something under his breath.

"I received a letter from Alan today," Adam said into the tense atmosphere.

"Truly? What does he say? Did he send me a separate note?" Sam asked, watching her brother in anticipation.

"No, he did not. You know how he is, very laconic. He just lets us know that he is enjoying his trip to the Continent and urges us not to worry," Adam answered around a bite.

"As if it is as simple as that," Isabel said and let out a snort. "Is he enjoying his travels so much that he can't find the time and write a proper correspondence?"

"You have to ask him yourself, Isabel," Richard chimed in. "He is alive and healthy. He hasn't forgotten how to hold a quill, so that's all that interests me at the moment. Let him have his fun. When he comes back, he won't have much time to traipse around the world anymore. He will be busy helping me around the estates."

Sam rolled her eyes. "Alan is younger than me, and he gets to travel the world without accounting for his every action. Yet if I am delayed on my morning ride, you take my head off."

"You are a lady. It is different."

"Because I can't take care of myself?"

"No, because there are far more people looking to take advantage of you," Adam interceded. "Come now, sister, you know that. Nobody thinks of you as defenseless, but this world was just not built in favor of ladies."

"When does Alan say he is coming back?" Sam endeavored to change the subject.

"He doesn't. Not for another year, I gather."

Sam chewed her food silently.

"Do not worry, sister," Richard answered with a smile. "If he dares to tarry, I'll go to the Continent myself to bring him back kicking and screaming."

Sam smiled crookedly. "I am not angry at Alan for traveling. Perhaps I am just contemplating the unfairness of it all. Why do I have to suffer the rigors of the marriage mart year in and year out, while neither of you is looking to marry?"

"As I said, the world is not fair to ladies."

"That may be true," Isabel interjected. "But that doesn't mean you shouldn't start looking for a wife. Either of you or perhaps both of you. We need the Gage line to continue."

"How about we delegate the duty to Alan?" Gage retorted. "He has a lady waiting for him as far as I remember. Royston's daughter."

"They are just friends." Isabel waved the issue away. "And don't change the subject. You are the heir. It is your duty to beget children."

Samantha looked thoughtfully around the table, her mind ticking, working out a plan, while her siblings kept arguing as was their usual breakfast custom.

Why hadn't she thought of her brothers? They were all handsome enough, clever, or even brilliant if she were completely honest with herself. True, Gage was harsh and demanding, but that was because he was the oldest with the most responsibilities. Adam, on the other hand, would suit Evie perfectly. He was closer to her age than Richard and more open but just as responsible. *Yes, he would be perfect.*

"What are you smiling about?" Isabel asked her suspiciously, successfully bringing her back from her thoughts to the breakfast table.

"Nothing," she lied. "Just wondering if we should invite Evie for supper sometime. She is not very happy in her current household situation. I would love to offer her some support."

"That's an excellent idea," Isabel agreed. "A small family affair would be perfect to lift her mood."

And a perfect setting to bring two people together.

Chapter 6

E vie sat beside Sam and Lady Clydesdale in the drawing room. Isabel was talking with the housekeeper, while Sam's brothers, Lord Clydesdale, and his friend, Viscount St. Clare, conversed by the hearth.

This was supposed to be a quiet, intimate dinner with just Sam's family and Evie, but Evie had needed a chaperone, so Lady Clydesdale had accompanied her with her husband, and St. Clare tagged along in her wake. Extra people were unnecessary distractions for Sam's plan, especially with Lady Clydesdale present, since she was the one pushing Ashbury's suit.

Sam wasn't worried, however. All she needed to do was to seat Evie beside Adam and once their conversation flowed, a spark would develop. She was certain of it.

As the dinner bell rang, Gage invited everyone inside. Since they were the hosts, her brothers had to show their hospitality and seat the lady guests next to them. Which meant that Gage accompanied Lady Clydesdale, while Isabel took Lord

Clydesdale's arm. Sam nudged Adam toward Evie and took St. Clare's proffered arm.

Sam smiled smugly as she sat across from Evie and Adam. Now her plan could unfurl.

As everybody settled, the conversation started flowing around the table. Only not in the direction Sam was hoping for. The gentlemen were discussing their estate issues, Isabel and Lady Clydesdale discussed something among themselves, while Evie quietly sat chewing at her food. Adam barely looked her way.

"So," Sam said loudly, interrupting the animated conversation around the table. "Evie, don't you just love city life? I sometimes envy that Adam gets to live here all year round."

Adam threw her an incredulous look, while Evie just frowned at her. Sam wasn't fooling anyone. She preferred the country to the city and the people closest to her knew that.

"It's absolutely boring," St. Clare said. "Seeing the same people every day." He shuddered theatrically.

"And yet you're constantly here," Clydesdale said with a crooked smile.

"It's not like I have anywhere else to be." St. Clare shrugged.

"Actually." Adam cleared his throat. "I will be leaving London quite soon. I won't be working with the Secretary at War anymore."

"You won't?" Sam was so surprised she forgot all about her ruse.

"Yes, I think I've overstayed my welcome there. Besides, Gage needs help with the lands. I will try my hand at managing the estates."

"When did that happen?" Sam asked in astonishment.

Adam shrugged. "Long time in coming, if you ask me. I've

been thinking of leaving for over two years."

"With the economy as it is, we need to concentrate on farming," Gage agreed. They continued discussing the merits of farming over diplomatic affairs, while Sam contemplated how to get the conversation back on track.

"If what you are saying is true," she said to Gage, "and farming is the future of the economy, wouldn't you rather Adam had his own lands?"

"And where do you propose I get those?" Adam asked around a bite of food.

Sam wasn't quite sure how to answer that without giving her plan away. Fortunately, she didn't have to answer.

"Why would anyone want to own land? An estate is more demanding than a mistress," St. Clare interrupted. "In fact, I will gladly give my land away as soon as I inherit if I have the chance."

"I am sure your tenants would appreciate that," Clydesdale joked.

"What you need, my lord," Evie finally said, "is a competent estate manager to take care of everything for you."

"And how would you know anything about that?" St. Clare asked.

"I am a duchess," Evie huffed.

"Exactly!" Sam chimed in. "You are a duchess with seven estates. Perhaps it is better if you married someone without a title. And *he* would help you run your estates."

Evie peered at her through narrowed eyes, suspicion clearly present in her gaze. "I don't need help. I am certain I can run my own estates. My grandpa taught me well."

"But you won't be able to sit in the House of Lords," Gage said.

St. Clare scoffed. "Now this is an opportunity she doesn't want to miss. Sitting between sweaty old lords arguing about the best uses of manure."

Evie pursed her lips, visibly trying to hold back a chuckle.

"If one wants to make a change, one needs to endure such difficulties as sweaty lords," Gage said darkly.

"Can we please not talk about this at dinner?" Isabel said with a sigh.

"I am inclined to agree with Lord St. Clare," Evie said. "The House of Lords is a frivolity I do not need. If one wants to make a change, one can sidestep the—" she threw a glance at Isabel— "*sweaty* old lords and do things their own way."

"Amen," St. Clare agreed. "I am changing the lives of young women across London daily and nightly just—"

"Gabriel," Lord Clydesdale growled in warning.

St. Clare waved his fork airily. "I digress."

Sam gritted her teeth. This was all going wrong.

"It is ridiculous that ladies are not allowed a seat in the House of Lords. Queens have run countries for centuries, and yet ladies are not allowed to take part in decision-making processes," Isabel chimed in.

Sam lowered her gaze when in reality she wanted to bang her head against the table. This wasn't a conversation conducive to flirtation. And all through the argument, Adam and Evie hadn't exchanged a word. They barely even looked at each other.

When the dinner came to an end and they all retired back to the drawing room, Sam expelled a breath. Surely, she could bring Evie and Adam together in an informal situation.

"How about some entertainment?" she exclaimed as everyone got comfortable in their seats. "Evie is excellent at the pianoforte. Won't you play for us?"

Evie raised a brow at her but didn't protest. "I would love to," she said with a smile and stood.

"Adam, would you be so kind as to turn the pages for her?"

Adam nodded slowly and accompanied Evie to the pianoforte.

Isabel appeared at Sam's elbow then and gently led her to the side of the room.

"Sammy," she breathed. "What are you doing?"

"What do you mean?" Sam tried to sound nonchalant.

"I mean," Isabel's lips twitched in laughter, "that even a simple-minded fool would realize that you are trying to push Evie and Adam together. Why?"

Sam let out an exasperated breath. "They would be perfect together, don't you think? Adam and Evie: a match made in heaven." She smiled tightly, and Isabel just gave her a pitying look. "Ugh, very well, I admit, I haven't thought this through, but I did think they would be perfect together!"

"Why? Because you wanted them to be?"

Sam cast a glance toward Evie, completely absorbed in a melody she was playing, and Adam, standing by her side like a statue, a bored expression on his face.

"Perhaps I miscalculated," she admitted begrudgingly.

"Maybe a bit."

Sam frowned. It was just one little setback. It didn't mean she was wrong, did it?

* * *

Sam stood by the banister in Lady Royston's ballroom two days later. After her scheme during the dinner had failed miserably, she hadn't made any further attempts to bring Adam and Evie together. She secretly hoped they would still come together. Perhaps if they shared a dance?

Sam craned her neck to see Adam dancing with one lady after another, anyone except Evie, and Evie... Well, she was dancing with Viscount St. Clare at the moment.

Sam was tempted to roll her eyes. St. Clare wouldn't be the one to marry her. Why did Evie even agree to dance with a known rake, wasting time she could have used dancing with more viable partners?

Sam studied Evie's flushed cheeks, the genuine smile on her lips, and decided perhaps she'd miscalculated when she came up with her ploy to put Evie and Adam together. They were total opposites. Adam was serious and grave, whereas Evie was lively and fun-loving. She loved to dance, to sing. Well, any activity involving music, really. Both Adam and Ashbury were absolutely wrong for her. She never lit up around them the way she did around St. Clare. Sam frowned at the thought. She was certain it was just his rakish charm, but surely the person she chose for her fiancé should be able to make her light up like this as well?

The moment the dance ended, Sam ventured to her friend's side. Evie, having returned to the side of her chaperone, Lady Montbrook, was fanning herself vigorously.

"It's incredibly hot in here, isn't it?" Evie asked Sam as she neared her side.

"Yes, it is. But what are you doing dancing with St. Clare? Shouldn't you be looking for a suitor?"

"I already have a suitor," Evie answered dryly.

"It wouldn't hurt to have other options."

"What if St. Clare *is* my other option?" Evie asked without looking at Sam.

Sam couldn't help it; she laughed and received an indignant look from her friend.

"I am sorry, Evie, you can charm anybody into marriage, you truly could…" She paused and wrinkled her nose. "Just, perhaps not St. Clare. Not that you'd want to. The man is a rake!"

She received a freezing stare from a lady to her right and lowered her voice hastily. "Come, Evie. Your only options cannot be an emotionally unavailable pauper baron and a notorious skirt chaser."

"Then who do you propose?" Evie asked with an exasperated sigh. "Don't think I didn't notice your efforts to set me up with your brother." Sam opened her mouth to protest, but Evie held up one finger, prompting Sam to halt. "Don't even try to deny it. I know you, Sam. And even my cousin, Julie, noticed your feeble attempts. I appreciate your help, truly. But it is done. As soon as I see Lord Ashbury, I shall give him my consent."

"Evie—"

"No. Sam, you can't know how much I appreciate your friendship and that you worry about me so, but I've already told my guardian. And he gave me his blessing."

Sam's mouth fell open. She lowered her voice to a whisper. "What did Lady Montbrook say?"

"She wasn't happy about it, but in the end, she agreed to help me arrange the wedding at the end of the season."

"The end of the season?" Sam quirked her brow.

Evie took a deep breath. She leaned in closer and lowered her voice. "As long as I have my guardian's blessing, I can marry Ashbury with no issues. And I can change the date, can't I?"

Sam peered into her friend's face. "You are going to lie to them."

Evie swallowed and shook her head. "I want to be free to do as I please. I don't want to be under the same roof as the Montbrooks for long. And Lord Ashbury needs my inheritance now. This is the only solution."

Sam watched her friend's overbright smile and felt a heavy weight settle in her heart. With Evie's grandfather's passing, that was what her life had turned into. Putting on a brave face, a façade in front of everyone. Not having a single person she could be herself with, even in the comfort of her own house. At that moment, another gentleman stepped in front of Evie and claimed his dance. Evie smiled at Sam and walked out onto the dancefloor as if nothing was wrong.

Chapter 7

Sam fanned herself vigorously as she stood on the sidelines watching the ball. Isabel was chatting with the dowagers, her brothers were somewhere in the cardroom, and she was strangely left unchaperoned in the corner of the room. Not that she intended to go anywhere. She was grateful to not have to dance during this heat.

"Riveting performance, isn't it?" a grave masculine voice murmured beside her. She turned and saw Ashbury standing next to her, observing the ballroom scene. "During the war, what I wouldn't have given to see a ball just one more time. Now, I can't stand the crowds long enough to enjoy it," he said, still not taking his gaze off the dancing couples.

Sam turned toward the ballroom as well, watching the scene. They were quiet for a moment after that. She felt comfortable around Ashbury. The silence wasn't daunting either, and she was loath to break it, but she had Evie to think about first and foremost.

"Have you talked to Evie yet?" she asked after a brief pause.

"No, but that's the sole reason I came here." Ashbury shifted closer, and she felt a warm tingle up her arm where his almost brushed hers. A tickle appeared low in her belly and goosebumps traveled up her arm. Sam swallowed.

"You will insist upon an answer," she said quietly.

"Yes, and as much as I admire your enthusiasm in trying to find a replacement groom for your friend—"

Samantha winced at his matter-of-fact tone. Of course, Lady Clydesdale had told him about the dinner and her failed attempt at bringing Evie and Adam together.

"—I need to marry an heiress, and I need to do it soon." He raked his hand through his hair. "Miss Samantha, I actually sympathize with both you and your friend, but you don't know how dire my circumstances are. "

"What if I find you another bride instead?" Sam asked enthusiastically, and he laughed.

"Like you found a groom for your friend? I think I'll have to pass, but thank you."

"Well, I happen to know a lot more ladies than I do gentlemen. And most of them wouldn't care for a loveless marriage. And why are you so against love, anyway?"

Lord Ashbury thought for a while before answering. "I am not against love. I just don't believe myself capable. And even more so, I don't believe anybody capable of loving me."

"Oh, what a pile of rubbish," she said evenly.

"Pardon me?" Ashbury seemed startled by her reply.

"I said, it is absolute nonsense. How can you know if someone is capable of loving you or not? Especially if you don't even try!"

"It's a long story," he sighed.

"It's a long evening," she countered. "Would you care for a

stroll about the room?"

Ashbury looked around at the crowded ballroom, his brow furrowed. "How about a stroll about the garden instead?"

Sam looked out at the French doors not far from where they stood. People were about, and the garden seemed lit. "Very well," she said and took his proffered arm. She felt him tense when she laid her fingers on his arm, his muscles bunching under her touch.

They proceeded through the French doors onto a patio and farther into the garden. Several couples were strolling along or sitting on the stone benches. It was a warm spring evening, and people were enjoying the rare, beautiful weather.

After several paces in silence, Samantha finally broke it. "So tell me this long story."

He looked at her for a long moment before letting out a deep sigh. "I told you earlier about Julie and me. We were in love, but she was forced to marry another. It was an unfortunate circumstance, but because of that, she now has a caring and loving family." He paused. "When all this happened, I was broken and miserable. I had no more reason to live. I went on suicide missions, and I fought like a madman, not caring what happened to me. Then there was Badajoz."

"What happened in Badajoz?" Sam asked quietly. Her heart constricted at the name. That was where Ben had lost his life.

"I got injured. Badly. I spent weeks in a hospital, lying with a high fever, praying for the Lord to finally take me. But I didn't die. I survived. It was the most horrible massacre I've ever encountered in my life. I've never been the same since." He shook his head. "I still dream of that battle, of my comrades dying, of enemies approaching. I have violent tendencies that don't allow me to sleep at night. I've never told this to anyone

71

before, but I feel you should know. I am not fit company to any lady. Nobody can love a man as broken as I am."

Sam swallowed. She appreciated his candidness. No one had ever spoken to her that way about the war. Not even Ben. Everyone was trying to shield her from the horrors, hiding the truth. At the same time, this made an unpleasant feeling settle low in her belly. *If Ben had come back, is this how he would feel?*

"I am quite certain you're mistaken about that," she said. But her voice came out hoarse.

John smiled sadly. "I am quite certain you don't understand what you are speaking about. And you should be glad of it."

"You said you were hurt so badly you didn't want to live. And yet you survived. How did you come out of the dark mood you were in?"

John heaved a sigh. He stopped and tilted his head back, looking at the stars. Sam followed his lead and gazed at the misty sky.

"I was in the hospital for several weeks. There were many soldiers like me. Nobody could differentiate one person from another. I was given someone's letters by mistake. There was a bulk of them," he said with a smile in his voice.

"Did you read them?"

"Yes." He lowered his head and stared ahead. "I was still delirious with fever. I didn't even notice they weren't addressed to me. The letters seemed generic at first... They were addressed to 'dear soldier.'"

Sam looked at him sharply. That was what she'd called Ben. But other people probably called their soldiers that, too.

"She signed her name Angel," he continued, and Sam's mouth fell open. *My letters.* Lord Ashbury was talking about her letters to Ben. The letters he'd never responded to because he had died without ever having received them.

"That Angel, whoever she is, will never know how close to truth her signature was to me," John continued, oblivious to her turmoil. "She saved me when I had nothing to look forward to. She described peace and penetrated my heart with her words. Gave me a reason to—" He finally looked at Sam and stopped mid-sentence. Sam's face was probably ashen.

Sam licked her lips. "Those letters. Did they come from the office of the Secretary at War, by any chance?"

"Yes." He looked at her intently. "How do you know that?"

"Because I wrote them."

John's eyes widened as he tried to make sense of her words. He seemed frozen, paralyzed. Sam couldn't say anything either.

"Sam?" They both turned as they heard a masculine voice, accompanied by footsteps moving in their direction. "Here you are, I've been looking all over for you!"

The tall, dark figure of her brother Richard stepped in front of them. He looked from Sam to Ashbury and back again. "What are you doing here?" he thundered.

"Please, stop yelling, Richard. We were just talking." Sam slid a discreet look at her companion and was relieved to see that he had composed himself.

Ashbury inclined his head. "Ashbury, a pleasure to make your acquaintance."

"Gage." Richard sketched a brief bow. "Now, if you'll excuse us." With these words, he took Sam by the arm and steered her back toward the house.

* * *

John stood alone in the empty dark garden, staring at the brother and sister walking away from him. He couldn't believe what had just transpired. Had it really happened or was it his imagination? It couldn't be possible that it was a mere coincidence and that someone else had written the letters, addressed them from the Secretary at War's office, and signed her name *Angel*.

He tried to remember everything he'd read about her in her letters and compare it to everything he knew about Miss Samantha. How could he have been such an idiot and not seen it earlier? There was no way he could have known, but he had felt a strange pull toward her since the first day they'd met. He couldn't believe it.

Is it really her? The question flew across his mind before he heard a familiar buzzing. That wasn't supposed to happen. Her letters were the only things that could keep the blasted headaches at bay. Her letter. He reached into his breast pocket and extracted it, smoothing the familiar lines with his fingers. His vision blurred, and the sounds receded into the background.

He knew he had to get out of there as soon as possible. He couldn't have one of his episodes, not now, not here. John pocketed the letter and hurried through the French doors, across the ballroom, and out of the house. He reached his carriage shortly, hopped inside, and settled in. His head was pounding… or was it his heartbeat? He couldn't tell anymore. He was alternating between feeling hot and cold. His hands were shaking. He heard the gunshots and could smell the gunpowder, the blood.

Chapter 7

"Bloody hell!" Another splitting headache.

He didn't know how long the journey home took. By the time he scrambled into the house, his headache hadn't subsided even a little. He came into the hall, and somehow handed his valet his jacket, gloves, and hat. He shuffled up the steps into his room and collapsed on his bed.

Chapter 8

S am stood outside the Somerset townhouse with her maid the next afternoon. She'd received a note from Evie earlier this morning, asking her to come to her with all haste. She wondered if something was amiss. Her heart was pounding loudly, and her palms grew wet from perspiration. After the strange and emotion-filled talk she'd had with Ashbury the night before, she hadn't seen him. Had he proposed to Evie? Was that why she'd asked for Sam to come? Sam wasn't quite sure how she felt about that. Her maid, Gina, had barely knocked on the door when it flew open, and there stood Evie's butler, Rogers.

"All deliveries go through the servants' entrance," Rogers said loudly, winked at her, and closed the door in her face.

Sam blinked. Had he really just winked at her? She saw Gina's outraged face as she was about to knock on the door again, ready to give the elderly butler a piece of her mind.

"Gina, stop." Sam tugged her maid toward the other side of the townhouse and the servants' entrance. "Rogers wasn't mistaken. He knows me very well. He must have had instructions to lead me to the servants' entrance."

The side door opened before they reached it and Mrs. Lambert, the housekeeper, greeted them from inside. She quickly closed the door behind them and led them to the kitchen.

"Miss Samantha, how glad we are to see you." The motherly-looking housekeeper, plump and rosy-cheeked, enfolded Sam in a hug, something she had never done before. *The state of the household must be dire indeed.* Mrs. Lambert indicated for Gina to take a seat and instructed her to stay there, while she drew Sam out of the kitchen and toward the stairs in the servants' quarters.

"Her Grace is in her chambers," she whispered to Sam, mounting the steps. "The new masters are in another wing of the house, so no need to fret that you will be discovered. I shall send a maid in with a tea tray," she added as she pulled open the door that led to the hall.

No need to fret that you will be discovered. Why did her visit need to be so covert? Sam frowned as she stepped into the family quarters. She had never used the servants' stairs in the townhouse, but she was familiar with this hall, as she had visited Evie's suite on numerous occasions before. After reaching her destination, she knocked on the door softly.

"Enter, please," answered Evie's quiet voice.

Sam came in and closed the door behind her.

Evie was sitting at her desk scribbling something furiously.

"Evie." Sam delicately cleared her throat. Her friend looked up, and when she saw Sam, her eyes lit up.

"Oh, Sam!" Evie all but flew out of her chair and into her friend's arms. "I am so glad you came!"

She drew out of Sam's arms and looked her over. "Come, let's sit," she said, already dragging her toward the armchairs and a settee arranged in a semicircle on the other side of the bed. "I'll ring for a maid to bring us some tea."

"It's not necessary," Sam said hastily, putting a staying hand on Evie's shoulder. "Mrs. Lambert already took care of that. Sit, please."

They both seated themselves in the armchairs facing each other.

"I'm so glad you are here," Evie repeated quietly.

"Of course, I am here," Sam said vehemently. "I came here as quickly as I could. Although, if I had known I was going to use the back entrance, I wouldn't have waited for the appropriate calling hours." She smiled at her friend.

"Yes, well…" Evie huffed a breath of air. "This is a matter of utmost urgency. I didn't have time to explain everything in the note."

"What is wrong?"

"Oh, Sam, you are not going to believe this!"

Sam leaned in closer to her friend.

"One of the maids overheard a conversation between Lady Montbrook and Lord Lansdowne last night. She said… Oh, Lord!" Evie covered her face with her hands. "She said she would make me marry him! Lord Lansdowne! And in return, all their debts would be cleared."

"Pardon?" Sam's eyes widened. "Are you certain about this? Are you certain the maid heard her right?"

"The household staff is still devoted to me. They wouldn't tell me this if they were not certain."

"Did you talk to your cousin? Did Lord Clydesdale investigate Montbrook?"

Evie grimaced. "No, I didn't think it pertinent at the time. But after this… There is nothing Clydesdale can do, even if he confirms that the Montbrooks are indeed in a strained financial state. The only thing for me to do is to marry. Otherwise, I am solely at their mercy."

Sam knew it to be true. An unmarried lady was defenseless in this society. Evie still had nine months before she reached her five and twentieth birthday, and she wouldn't be able to outlast the Montbrooks if they decided to marry her off.

"But what about your uncle? Surely he would intercede on your behalf?"

"I can't be certain that he does not support his wife. Ever since she arrived, he's been different." She bit on her lower lip.

"What do you want me to do?"

"I want you to talk to Julie and Lord Ashbury," Evie said resolutely. "I want you to help arrange my elopement. As soon as we can."

Sam's eyes widened. "You want to elope. With Lord Ashbury."

Evie nodded. "Is it too much to ask? You know there's no one else who would do this for me, and it's not like I can do it myself under the watchful eye of Lady Montbrook. But if you are uncomfortable with this—"

"Me? Uncomfortable?" Sam tried to sound cheerful. "Don't be ridiculous. This is going to be an adventure."

Evie chuckled and shook her head. "I am glad my life is providing you with entertainment."

"I shall have it done. Do not fret about anything." Sam stood. "Now, I better leave before your relatives realize I am here."

* * *

John woke up covered in a cold sweat, groaning and twisting his bedsheets in his hands. He opened his eyes and squinted against the bright morning sun. He sat up, looking around. He was in his bed, on the covers, and not at his usual sleeping place on the floor. *Interesting.*

More interesting, however, was the fact that he'd slept through the night without waking. He must have been exhausted.

He looked down and saw that he was still wearing his evening clothes. And that's when he remembered. He'd had one of his nasty headache spells in the garden at Lady Royston's ball. He hadn't had one that bad in a while. When he was in the country, he rode to his heart's content, working in the fields with his farmers. Physical labor always tired him out enough that he rarely woke during the night. Sometimes it kept the nightmares at bay.

But he couldn't go back to the country yet. Things were dire at his country seat; the house was drafty and in need of repairs, and the villagers did not have enough provisions for the winter. He needed to get the money, and he needed it fast. That was why it was pertinent he enticed the Duchess of Somerset into a betrothal. Once he did that, he could go back to country life and perhaps his nightmares would subside too.

But those plans had been developed before he found out that the duchess's dearest friend, Miss Samantha, was in fact his Angel. The lady whose letters had kept him sane for the last years of the war. The one who had gotten him through the most troublesome months in the hospital bed.

When John received the correspondence he had been dosed

with laudanum and he'd been out of it for several days, but he was certain there was no one left in the world to write to him. Still, he opened the letters and read their contents. And for a while, the world righted itself. A sweet young lady was writing the letters, and it was as if she was addressing him in her correspondence.

Dear Soldier, she'd written. *The spring is beautiful in England this year. I wish I could share it with you.*

He would become engrossed in her world of frivolities, her first season, and smile to himself. He'd read them over and over again for weeks as he lay in that hospital. Still hurt, still injured and tired, but not hopeless. But then, the last letter came. John reached instinctively for the breast pocket of his coat and patted it with his hand. *It's still there.*

It seemed impossible. It seemed like a dream. Had he truly found her? And then that blasted headache had hit him, and he'd had to retreat to his home before he disgraced himself in front of the *ton*, and more importantly, in front of her. He'd spent so long dreaming about finding her, about holding her, and telling her how much she meant to him. And there she was, standing in front of him, and all he could do was gape at her and then run away.

He got up and stretched. His muscles protested at the movement, his joints cracked, and his body ached. The years of sleeping on cold, hard ground, breaking his bones, and collecting injuries made themselves known. He ordered a warm bath and soaked for a while before finally venturing downstairs.

It was past noon. A lot later than he usually came down from his rooms. However, he had no wish to exit the house that day. He needed to come up with some sort of plan. How would he approach Miss Samantha? What would he say to her?

He entered his dining room and saw his breakfast, cold on the dining room table. Luncheon wouldn't be ready for hours yet, and he had to eat. He sat and poked at the cold eggs and bacon. After years in the army, cold eggs and bacon still seemed like a heavenly feast.

The butler entered the room and bowed. "A letter arrived for you, sir."

John wordlessly stretched his arm out, and the butler put the missive in his hand. John opened the envelope as he chewed and read.

> *Lord Ashbury,*
> *Please meet me on the morrow at dawn near the Serpentine. You know the spot. It is of extreme importance. I shall explain everything there.*
> *Regards,*
> *Miss Samantha.*

His heart raced, and his breathing accelerated. John stared at the piece of paper for a long mute minute, wide-eyed. What did she want to talk to him about? Was she curious about the letters? Should he admit his pathetic feelings toward her and stop this charade with the duchess? Was it possible she was interested in him as well? Millions of thoughts rushed through his head. He'd waited years to finally find her, but it seemed impossible to wait one more day.

Chapter 9

Lord Ashbury met Sam in the same place she'd met him the first time, where he'd fallen off his horse and they'd raced. James trailed behind her, a discreet distance away. Discreet enough so that he could not overhear their conversation but not so discreet that he couldn't still see them at all times. Sam had explained the predicament with Evie and that she needed to talk to her friend's fiancé. James, ever a loyal servant, agreed to help out his mistress and keep their clandestine meeting a secret. No matter how understanding her siblings were, they wouldn't allow her to meet a gentleman alone in the park. And she couldn't very well call on him at his lodgings.

"I am so glad you agreed to meet me, my lord," she said as soon as she reached Ashbury's side.

"It seems to me I did not have a choice. You did say it was urgent," he answered. "And... can you—?" He broke off as if he thought better of his words. Sam looked at him inquiringly. "I just, I don't quite like my title. Would it be fine with you if you called me John?"

Sam stared at him wide-eyed.

"At least when we are alone," he added hastily.

Sam thought about refusing, but he looked so uncomfortable that she decided to humor him. "Certainly," she paused uncomfortably, "John."

He looked at her with a startled expression on his face, as if she'd surprised him. Surely not. He was the one who'd asked her to call him by his Christian name after all. She decided not to dwell on it. More important things were at stake.

"Let's proceed toward the path." She gestured with her hand and turned her mount in the direction of Rotten Row. There was little possibility that anyone would see them here in the dead of the morning, but on the off-chance that someone did, she wanted it to look like they'd come upon each other by accident. They followed the path for a little while before Sam finally spoke.

"When were you planning on speaking to Evie? You said you were going to insist on an answer last night, but you disappeared and—"

John cleared his throat, looking suddenly uncomfortable. She was being too blunt. That was not the way ladies behaved. Sam heaved a sigh.

"I apologize for my directness. It's just that I spoke to Evie this morning, and she is desperate to be wed as soon as possible," Sam continued.

Lord Ashbury turned to her sharply. "She is? Has something happened?"

Sam quickly relayed the problem with the Montbrooks and the need for Evie to elope and marry without her guardian's knowledge.

John frowned in thought. "I didn't think you thought me a suitable husband for your friend."

"It's true, I was against your suit." Sam nodded as she collected her thoughts. "But that is not of any importance now, is it? I wish her only happiness, and I know she has a greater chance of having it with you than with Lord Lansdowne." Sam shuddered at the thought.

"I wouldn't be so sure," John muttered under his breath.

Sam expelled a breath, exasperated. "You have too low of an opinion of yourself," she said, a bit sharply. "You are caring and responsible as well as intelligent and perhaps with more capacity for love than you give yourself credit for. Evie will be honored to call you her husband, and I... I'd be honored to call you my friend."

He gave her another of his queer looks. She was frustrated that she didn't know what he was thinking. She didn't think for a moment that he would refuse to help Evie, but something in her proposition had made him pause. Sam had no idea what that could have been. After all, he was the one who'd proposed marriage to Evie.

"I feel secure that you will take care of her. I trust you to keep her safe," she continued after a short pause. "I don't know much about you, but I believe in fate. Meeting you at the time she did... I can't help but think that it was meant to be."

She heard his muffled laughter, and she looked at him sharply. But he wasn't laughing in mirth; he had a bitter look on his face. She decided to disregard his interruption and plunged ahead.

"You proposed to her at the exact moment she needed it most. You were honest about your intentions. Many of her suitors are after her inheritance, but they pretend they are not. If she can't have love or mutual affection in marriage, she will at least settle for honesty. I think it an even trade," she finished with a slight grimace.

"Miss Samantha—" he started.

"Sam," she interrupted him hastily. "If I am to call you by your Christian name, it is only fair that you do the same."

"Sam, then," he continued with a nod. "I think both your friend and you give me too much credit where it is not due. You should not trust me that easily; you do not know me. I've spent a huge part of my life at war. My life up to this point has been devoid of beauty and peace. I saw things, I lived through things that are too gruesome to even speak about in front of a lady. When I came back, I brought all that ugliness with me. And you have no idea how it will affect a person who is going to share a life with me."

"If that's the case, then I stand by your marriage even more than before. I believe Evie can help you. She can bring beauty into any household," she said with authority. "She is one of the most cheerful and optimistic people I know. Granted, she is going through a rough time now herself, but maybe you can heal each other."

"It is not something that you can heal with smiles and laughter, even love," he said a bit too sharply. "I don't want you to have any false hopes regarding my union with the duchess. I do, however, intend to keep my end of the agreement. You don't need to sell the idea of marriage to me. I proposed to Her Grace, and I have no intention of letting her go. As for the elopement… I shall take care of everything. I give you my word."

Sam swallowed through a lump that suddenly formed in

her throat. "That's all I wanted to hear," she said quietly, her throat suddenly dry. That was what she wanted, right? Then why did she feel so bereft?

They cantered on ahead for a while in silence. Then he rummaged for something behind his saddle and turned to her, a bundle of letters in his hands.

"I thought this was the reason for your note today," he said and handed her the correspondence, his fingers brushing against hers, sending a shiver down her spine. Sam didn't have time to contemplate the strange feelings his mere touch evoked in her. His next words cleared all thought out of her head. "These are all the letters I received by mistake in the army hospital. I believe that your brother and I were admitted at the same time and our identities got mixed up... I do not remember seeing him. I... I don't even know his name."

"Ben..." Sam gingerly took the bundle and placed it on her lap. "His name was Benedict."

I do believe in fate, she'd said to John just a moment ago. John receiving these letters by mistake, Sam now learning of them and having them back... It must have been some sort of sign, but she couldn't decipher it at the moment.

"Now, *Sam*," he said with extra emphasis on her name. "If you don't mind, it seems like I have business to tend to." He tipped his hat at her, turned his mount, and thundered away.

* * *

As soon as he got home, John put himself in order and ventured out to his intended's home. Something about Sam's mood and the way she talked about the duchess's fate bothered him. Montbrook looked as if he approved of the match. He had been pleasant every time John saw him. But if what Sam told him was true, there must be more to Montbrook's deceptions than that.

John wanted to make certain the duchess was not in jeopardy. After all, she was going to be his fiancée. He heaved a sigh.

A few hours earlier, he'd been ready to dissolve their agreement and propose to Sam. It was a fanciful dream. Sam didn't have any feelings toward him. Granted, neither did the duchess, but he was ready for a marriage of convenience, was he not? And hadn't he decided that subjecting his angel to a marriage with him was a fate worse than death?

Whatever the case might be, the duchess now depended on him in a way that nobody had ever depended on him before. And he wasn't about to fail Sam's trust.

As he neared the Somerset townhouse, he tossed his reins to the approaching footman and reached the front door steps. Several moments after he knocked, the door opened and a tall, gray-haired butler appeared on the doorstep. His face was impassive, but something akin to relief danced in his eyes the moment he read John's card.

"Welcome, my lord," the butler said with a bow, then showed him into a drawing room and left.

This was a different drawing room from the one he'd seen before but equally spacious and expensive. John looked over the room slowly. His gaze fell to a portrait above the hearth, and he moved closer to study it. It was a portrait of a young blond man and a smiling, red-headed young lady. For a moment, John thought he was looking at the duchess, but there was something different about her eyes.

"My grandparents," the duchess said from behind him.

John stiffened and turned slowly. It had been a while since someone was able to sneak up on him. The expensive, thick Persian carpets muffled the sound of footsteps very well. The duchess was looking at the portrait with something akin to sadness in her eyes, or maybe, reminiscence.

"Theirs was a love match," she continued, still looking at the portrait. "And a scandalous one at that. She was a merchant's daughter; he was a newly titled duke. You've come to see my guardian?" She trained her gaze on him at her last sentence.

"Your Grace." John inclined his head, and she sank into a graceful curtsy. "Yes. But also, I am here to invite you out for a ride in the park."

Surprise registered in her eyes for a moment before she masked it with a smile. "I shall be delighted." She drew her hand toward her hair as if to make sure her coiffure was still intact. "I shall go and put myself in order then."

John couldn't fathom what she meant to do with her appearance. She already looked ready for court. The duchess turned her overbright smile at him, and he inclined his head.

At that moment, Lord Montbrook entered the room. He was a heavyset middle-aged man, and he was breathing heavily, as if walking from one room to another was too difficult of an exercise. "My dear," he said, addressing the duchess, "you shouldn't be alone with a gentleman."

He then turned to John and inclined his head.

"The door was ajar, Uncle." She smiled at him and walked toward the door. "Lord Ashbury asked me to go for a ride. I hope you don't keep him occupied for too long," she threw over her shoulder and hurried out of the room.

The moment she left the room, Montbrook's gaze hardened. "Your betrothal is not official yet. I wouldn't want rumors surrounding my niece."

"That is why I am here, to make the betrothal official. With your consent, of course."

"I don't have a betrothal contract ready yet. We shall need to reschedule when my solicitor is present. I shall send you a note."

"But we do have your consent, yes?"

Montbrook grunted in answer. "Until the betrothal contract is signed, you need a chaperone present with her at all times."

"Surely, it is not necessary for today? We shall be riding in an open barouche."

"You do not seem to care for her reputation." The man puffed out his chest.

"She will be my wife soon enough," John answered stonily.

Montbrook's nostrils flared. "Until she is, take care to act with complete respect. No rendezvous behind closed doors. And stay in full sight of the *ton* during your outing. If there's even a whiff of impropriety—"

John raised his brow. Was Montbrook trying to threaten him?

"I know you overeager types," the man continued. "There will be no hasty weddings. She deserves a grand celebration."

"I assure you. My intentions toward Her Grace are more than respectful."

Montbrook grumbled something under his breath and turned on his heel. "Have a pleasant ride."

* * *

Several minutes later, the Duchess of Somerset turned up

on the front steps of her house. She had changed her gown to a pale green one that complemented her eye color and smoothed her hair. He walked her to his barouche and helped her up.

"Thank you for taking me out on a ride, my lord," she said once the vehicle lurched into motion.

"Not at all, Your Grace." John inclined his head. "Sam told me about your predicament with the Montbrooks, so I wanted to make myself known," he said good-naturedly and realized his mistake a little too late.

"*Sam* said?" She looked at him quizzically.

John cleared his throat, feeling uncomfortable. "She is worried about you," he said with a nod, trying to sail past his slip. "And since she can't do anything about it herself, she enlisted my help."

Evie smiled fondly at that. "Samantha is the best friend I could ask for. I don't know what I would do without her."

"How long have you two known each other?"

"Oh, ages." She laughed. "If you count bumping into each other at balls and soirees almost every week. We made our come-out the same year, but I had to withdraw because of my parents' passing." She paused as if to collect her thoughts. "We officially met at her birthday ball. We haven't been friends for that long, however. It is hard to get to know people at these social events, as you might imagine. Especially since the goal is to attract members of the opposite sex."

"How did you two become friends then?" He wasn't good at making conversation, so he decided it was best to keep her talking. Besides, he was genuinely curious about Sam and wanted to find out all he could about her.

"One summer, my grandpa took me to one of his properties

in Hampshire. He made certain to visit all of his estates for at least a short time every year. But Hampshire is beautiful, so he decided to spend all summer there. I met Sam during one of my rides. It turned out that their property borders our own. She was in mourning at the time, her father had passed, so I decided to fill the void." She laughed merrily. "She didn't stand a chance."

"I believe that," John answered honestly.

"We've both lost too many people," she continued. "But we've found each other, and it's truly a blessing."

John fought not to squirm in his seat. Finding Sam felt like a blessing to him, too. Being married to her best friend, though, had the promise of becoming a curse.

Chapter 10

John looked at Sam as she rode beside him, a smile playing about her lips. He had come out for a morning ride not because of his usual habit, but in hopes to see her again. His hopes were not in vain, so here they were, riding side by side once more. He didn't think it possible, but she was getting even more extraordinarily beautiful every time he saw her. Like at this moment, sitting on a gleaming brown mount, her profile to him, a few tendrils of golden blond hair blowing in the breeze, her back straight as a lance, her delicate feminine figure so fragile, yet so strong. Atop a horse, she looked like a Goddess.

After a good gallop, she was rosy-cheeked, her golden-brown eyes glowing with happiness, her beautiful, lush mouth looking sinfully attractive. His gaze lingered on her mouth as he imagined licking and nipping at her lips, learning her taste. The sudden thought gave him a start. What a horrible way to feel about one's fiancée's best friend. He had to shake himself out of his reverie.

"What a great way to start a morning, isn't it?" she called happily.

It was. If he had his say, he would start each morning like that, looking at her happy face. He looked away. That wouldn't last. He would crush her with his wounds, his moods, his temper. It was probably a good thing he was marrying her friend and not her. He would ruin her life, but he could save the duchess's.

It would be a marriage of convenience. He would give her freedom, her rightful inheritance, and they would remain distant yet friendly. He would save his lands as well, and the farmers living on those lands. Everyone would get what they needed.

But none of them would get what they wanted. The duchess would be stuck in a loveless marriage, he would be married to his Angel's best friend, and his Angel... Well, she'd probably soon be married to someone else. His stomach churned at the thought of Sam in someone else's arms. He shook his head again, trying to rid himself of the unwanted images.

"Is there any news regarding your marriage to Evie?" Sam asked.

"Yes, and no."

Sam looked at him with a raised brow.

"The betrothal contract is still not signed. Montbrook is stalling. But I've talked to Clydesdale," he said carefully. "He made some inquiries into Montbrook's affairs. It turns out it is even worse than we thought. Not only does he have gambling debts, but both of his sons do, too. His heir is the biggest wastrel this world has ever seen and probably owes half the *ton*."

"Evie didn't tell me anything about his sons," Sam said with a frown.

"She probably hasn't even met them. They both live in Scotland. I assume Lady Montbrook exiled them there so they wouldn't be shot in a duel for not paying back their debts. She is the Iron Lady of the house. Or that's what everyone seems to call her. Lord Lansdowne is one of the people they owe. I do not have details on how much, but I can assume it's not a small sum if the Montbrooks are willing to sell their niece for it."

"The scoundrels!" Sam exclaimed, her nostrils flaring.

"That's not all," John continued.

"Of course not," she said with an exasperated sigh.

"Somerset's previous solicitor, the man who is responsible for taking care of Her Grace's inheritance, said that Montbrook had tried several times to wager against it. Since he is her guardian, he has a legal right to use the inheritance and make investment decisions. So, at the moment, he is happily squandering her fortune away. He can't spend all of it. Fortunately, there's a clause in the contract only allowing a certain percentage. But after that is gone, the Montbrooks will only get more desperate. We can't let the duchess spend any more time with them. We don't know what they are capable of. Montbrook doesn't seem to want to hurt his niece, but we don't know what he'll do if he's cornered, and we don't know his wife's motivations."

"He doesn't want to hurt her? What do you think selling her to Lansdowne is?"

"I just meant hurting her physically."

Sam scoffed. "Fine. But what are our solutions?"

"We marry," John said with a heavy heart. "As soon as possible."

Silence hung for a moment between them.

"You need to get a special license. Can you do that?" Sam finally asked.

"I am a simple baron." John shook his head. "But Clydesdale will be able to. Since Montbrook gave his blessing to our betrothal, this shouldn't be difficult."

"Thank you for keeping me informed." Sam smiled sadly. "I can't imagine what it's like for Evie. It pains me that it's come to that. She has become a beacon of light in my life ever since I met her; I don't want that to change. I am so glad you are the one she's going to marry."

John just smiled and nodded. What could he say to that?

"Did she tell you how we met?" Sam smiled in reminiscence.

John cleared his throat. "Yes, she said you were in mourning when she stumbled upon you riding in the field or some such."

Sam turned her bright smile in his direction. "That's correct. I think I spotted her bright hair before I ever realized who was galloping toward me. She rides like a hellion, you know."

"Does she?" John wouldn't have imagined a sophisticated lady like the duchess ever being described as a hellion. Trotting along the Rotten Row during a fashionable hour, yes, but galloping through the fields, he couldn't contemplate.

"Oh, yes," Sam continued, lost in her memories. "She never mastered a sidesaddle as a child, and her grandfather taught her to ride astride instead."

"You don't say." John shook his head with a smile.

"Indeed. Many a gentleman would be rather surprised to learn that little fact about her. She pulled me out of my grief and misery that summer, and she's been a great friend to me ever since," she concluded.

"What about you?" John asked after a moment of silence.

"Have you ever ridden astride?"

Sam laughed merrily, and he delighted in the sound. "Evie tried to teach me several times, but such a scandalous activity is not for proper ladies," she said with a purposefully pretentious accent.

John laughed alongside her. All his worries moved to the background.

"I love to ride as much as anyone," she continued. "But I mostly do it because I have trouble sleeping sometimes."

"Do you?" He was surprised that they had one thing in common.

She gave a sound of acquiescence. "When I am in the country, though, my rides usually have a destination. There is this boulder by the creek. I like to sit on it and sketch." She gave a self-deprecated little laugh. "Not that I am any good at sketching, I just like to do it."

"You don't think you're good? Oh, I beg to differ." He laughed, and she raised her brows at him.

"Oh," she said once she realized what he meant. "That's right, you've seen my sketches."

John gave her a crooked smile. Her expression changed every time he brought up the letters. He wished he hadn't mentioned them.

"I just mean, from what little I've seen, you are very good."

"Thank you. That is very kind of you to say." She smiled and turned her face to the sun.

"Isabel would say not to do it," she said after a moment, her head still turned up and her eyes closed. "She'd say that it would give me freckles. But what are a couple more freckles?" She was speaking as if to herself, not requiring an answer from him, and he couldn't give her an answer if he tried.

He was distracted by the expanse of pure white skin she exposed to him by tilting her head back. Her soft, creamy neck, so enticing and succulent, just begged for his lips to touch it. For his tongue to—

She opened her eyes sharply and looked forward. "Oh, Lord," she exclaimed. "The sun is so high already. My family will be looking for me soon. I better get back."

All John could do was nod. Sam flashed him a quick smile, and he watched her disappear behind the bend.

* * *

Sam rode home lost in thought. Evie was going to get married soon, to John. The thought was accompanied by a slight pang in her heart. She couldn't comprehend if this was because she was slightly jealous of her friend for getting married before her, if this was because she worried Evie was making a mistake, or if it was because Evie was marrying John.

She scoffed at how easily she thought of him as John and not Lord Ashbury. She felt safe with him, at ease. There was a peculiar feeling in the pit of her stomach every time he was next to her; sometimes it would make her breathless. She couldn't interpret that feeling, and perhaps it was best that she couldn't.

She liked him. She knew that much. She liked spending time with him, talking with him, and riding. Even standing still and silent seemed pleasurable in his company. But her physical reaction to him was something else. He wasn't handsome, not in a classical sense. At least she hadn't found him handsome when she first met him. But the more she saw him, the more appealing he became. *How did that happen?*

She could look at his unfathomable hazel eyes for eternity. His hard mouth lured her lips to his. And she had a fickle urge to trace the scar on his cheek with her tongue. She almost laughed out loud at the thought. She'd never thought about licking a person before. She wondered what he'd taste like. She closed her eyes and had to shake her head. Hard. He was Evie's future husband. Evie—who was her best friend. And so was he. A friend. And nothing more.

Sam dismounted as she neared the front door and scaled the steps. The butler opened the front door, and she saw Isabel coming toward her. Sam smiled at her sister as she came in and started taking off her bonnet, gloves, and pelisse.

"You are awfully late from your ride," Isabel said as she reached Sam's side.

"I like the exercise," Sam answered, not looking at her sister. "Why, were you looking for me?"

Isabel regarded her quizzically. "No, it's nothing. I just worry about you, that's all."

"Worry?" Sam looked at her sister then. "Why would you worry?"

"Well…" Isabel gestured for Sam to proceed up the steps. "We haven't really talked for a while. You seem to be quite busy lately."

"I am never too busy to talk to you, Isabel." Sam smiled over her shoulder. They were silent until they reached Sam's bedroom. Gina was waiting for Sam inside, as per usual, but Isabel dismissed her and started helping Sam out of her clothing herself.

"I just mean," Isabel continued, unfastening Sam's riding habit, "you have so much going on with Evie, her odious cousin-guardian, her brute of a fiancé—"

"Brute?" Sam looked at Isabel, her lips twitching.

"Didn't you say something to that effect? That he's rude, and he told her he wouldn't love her or even feel affection toward her? Anyway, what I wanted to say is, if you feel like you have too much weight on your shoulders, you can always count on me to share the burden."

Sam looked up at her sister with love in her eyes. Isabel had always been her confidante, her champion when their parents were alive, and even more so after their untimely demise.

"I know, Isabel, and I love you for it." She smiled weakly. "I suppose I do have a heavy burden on my shoulders. But I need to figure out what it is before I can share it with you."

"Good," Isabel said, finishing up with the stays and leaving Sam in her chemise. "That's all I wanted to know. I ordered you a bath. It should be here any moment." Isabel smiled at Sam over her shoulder and left the room.

The door barely had a chance to close after her sister when Gina stormed in holding a piece of paper.

"The butler told me to give this to you with all haste," she said with a belated curtsy.

"Thank you, Gina." Sam looked at the signature and expelled a breath of relief. It was from Evie. She smiled as she opened the missive, but the smile died on her face the next moment. Her eyes widened, and her mouth went slack before she gathered her wits and screamed at the top of her voice, "Isabel! I need you!"

* * *

"This is going to be hell," John muttered to himself as his valet stepped back to admire the job he'd done on John's cravat.

100

"It is just a ball, sir," the valet answered.

John grimaced. It was a ball. There was nothing *just* about it. He'd have to rub shoulders with the crush of bodies again. Endure the smell of sweat, the loud noises, and the incessant crowds that gave him shivers. It was like being in the thick of the battle again.

But he needed to see Sam and tell her their plans. She had sent him a note, saying that the Montbrooks were planning to leave London in two days. Since the duchess was betrothed to him, they saw no reason for staying in London, while she could be learning about running the estate, preparing for their wedding, and taking over the dukedom. A noble reason, if he'd ever heard one. Only he doubted it was the main reason they were taking her away, especially since the betrothal contract was still unsigned.

The Somerset estate was located in Carlisle, not an hour away from Gretna Green. Since the betrothal to John hadn't been made public, Sam assumed, and John agreed, that it would be easiest for the Montbrooks to force the duchess to marry whoever they wanted in the quiet of the North and return to London unscathed.

John went to Clydesdale right away, and they made plans of their own. Now, he needed to relay those plans to Sam and prepare everything so it would work out without a hitch.

"Your mount is ready, my lord," his valet shouted from downstairs.

John took a fortifying breath and exited the room.

A half an hour later, he was entering Gage's townhouse. He stood in the receiving line, trying to block out the noises, the smells, and the suffocating heat. He concentrated on the fact that he was about to see Sam again. Her angelic features always made him feel calm. And that's when he spotted her. She was standing flanked by her brothers and a sister, greeting the arrivals at their ball.

She looked like a beacon of sunshine in this suffocating manor. She stood out among the crowd, even her family. There was almost no familial resemblance at all. All of her siblings were dark-haired and had vivid blue eyes, while his angel was glowing like gold. For a moment, John wondered if perhaps they had even more in common than he'd initially thought. He watched her as he approached the hosts. Her gleaming golden hair was swept up in an intricate coiffure, her lips pursed in a thoughtful pout. She was wearing a high-waisted soft lilac gown, with an off-the-shoulder cut, white pearls around her neck, and long white gloves. She looked adorable. No, she was absolutely beautiful. He couldn't seem to take his eyes off of her.

She looked at him then, caught his gaze, and smiled. His eyes softened in a smile as well. It seemed the only time he truly smiled was when he was with her, or saw her, or was near her. He reached Sam's side, not paying any heed to the crush of bodies he had to weave through. His headache, the jitters, and anxiety were nowhere in sight. Could it be that this young lady was the cure to all his troubles?

Sam's sister cleared her throat, and he realized that he stood there simply staring at Sam. She was blushing profusely under his intense gaze. He raised his eyes to her brother then and encountered an icy, dark gaze.

John sketched a bow. "Lord Gage."

"Ashbury." The man sketched a bow so short it was practically a nod. "My brother Mr. Lewis and my sisters, Miss Lewis and Miss Samantha Lewis," he said, indicating each of the siblings.

"A pleasure." John bowed over the women's hands and winked at Sam. She unsuccessfully tried to suppress a smile. "We'll talk later?"

Sam nodded. "Wait for us by the French doors. We'll come find you after we are done with the receiving line."

John grimaced as he looked at the crush of people he had to traverse to reach the French doors but didn't protest. He nodded and started weaving his way toward the indicated place. People were literally rubbing elbows with each other, so packed was the ballroom. He heard a familiar ringing in his ears.

Damn, not now. He hurried his step, although this made him even more awkward, bumping into people on his way. What seemed like an eternity later, he reached the French doors and burst through them onto the balcony. The fresh, frigid air hit his face, and he breathed in a lungful. He braced his hands on the railing and shut his eyes tightly.

John didn't know how long he stood like that. He didn't feel the bite of the cold or the sounds coming from the ballroom. His eyes were shut so tight he saw tiny stars in them.

"Ashbury." A faint female voice cut into his subconscious. "Ashbury," the voice said more forcefully this time, intruding on the fog in his head.

"John!" Someone touched his sleeve.

John opened his eyes, looked at the hand covering his arm, and then looked up at the worry-filled honey-gold eyes.

"What's wrong?" Sam asked, furrowing her brows.

"I'm fine," he said and covered her hand with his. At that moment, male hands yanked Sam out of his reach.

"That's enough of that," Gage snarled.

"Richard!" Sam looked at him sternly.

"Come now, it's not proper behavior and you know it!"

"He is ill, can't you see?" Sam reached for John again, but Gage tightened his grip on her arm. Miss Lewis was watching them with an incredulous look on her face, and Mr. Lewis just raised a brow.

"That's fine," John said, turning to them. "I'm fine," he said softly and smiled at Sam. She gave a slight nod and stepped back.

"Let's get right to business, shall we?" John continued, looking at the men.

"Yes, let's." Gage was frowning at him ferociously. If John was a lesser man, he probably would scatter at the look. But John had seen worse looks in his lifetime, and he wasn't easily frightened.

"I talked to Clydesdale this afternoon. We've come up with a plan."

"What is it?" Sam interjected impatiently.

"The duchess and I shall marry before they leave for the Somerset estate."

He saw Sam's eyes widen, her mouth slightly opened, and she seemed shocked and confused. John saw vulnerability in her eyes and something that looked like hurt or sadness. Or had he imagined that? Perhaps he had seen his own feelings mirrored in her eyes.

"When do you plan to do it and how? Montbrook is keeping Her Grace under lock and key before they leave," Gage noted.

"We've thought of that too. There will be a ball this Friday at the Marquess and Marchioness of Wakefield's home. The marchioness will personally invite the Montbrooks to attend. She will call on them on the morrow and extend a personal invitation. Seeing how the Montbrooks crave to be a part of the elite circle, they won't be able to cry off." A personal invitation was the highest form of honor. Ignoring it would show a great insult. And considering the Wakefields' position, the Montbrooks were not likely to risk offending them. "And... We can marry that same night."

He looked at Sam, but she refused to meet his gaze.

"Clydesdale will get us the special license before the ball. The marchioness already agreed to throw us a small celebration to honor our wedding. "

"Why would Lady Wakefield help us? Allowing a wedding at her ball, extending a personal invitation to the Montbrooks? This seems too much," Miss Lewis chimed in.

John grimaced. "She didn't want to... But Clydesdale's friend, St. Clare, managed to change her mind. He has a way with ladies."

Sam looked at him, confused, while her brothers shifted uncomfortably and cleared their throats.

"After that, whether the duchess leaves to the Somerset estate, some other place, or stays in London will be up to her."

"And what about you?" Miss Lewis asked.

"I'll go back to the country. I don't believe any harm will come to the duchess after that. She will be powerful in her own right."

"Is there anything we can do to help?" Mr. Lewis asked.

"Yes." John nodded. "As soon as the Montbrooks enter, I need you to detain the man in the card room until the announcement is made. You"—he turned to Sam's sister—"and Lady Clydesdale will have to occupy Lady Montbrook's time. We don't want them leaving before everything is taken care of. And... prepare for the wedding."

Chapter 11

Sam watched her reflection in the vanity as she pulled on her gloves. Physically, she was ready for the ball. Mentally... Well, her thoughts were in chaos and her stomach was twisted in knots. She was worried for Evie and nervous about the whole ordeal they'd have to go through, but something else nagged at the back of her mind. *Evie is getting married to John.*

She couldn't quite understand why that fact bothered her so, but it did.

"Are you ready to go?" Isabel yelled as she walked past Sam's room.

"Yes, just a moment." Sam's voice came out hoarse, so she had to clear her throat.

Isabel slowed her pace before she retraced her steps and entered Sam's room. "Is everything well?" She tilted her head to look Sam over.

Sam turned and smiled at her sister. "Yes, all is well. I am just a little nervous. I don't know why."

Isabel bit her lip and walked farther into the room. "Do you want to talk about it?"

"No, there's nothing to even talk about." Sam gave a short laugh. "I am just being a ninny, it's nothing."

"Are you certain?" Isabel sat on the corner of the bed and patted a place beside her.

Sam heaved a sigh but sat next to her sister.

"Good." Isabel smiled. "Now, how about you tell me how it feels to have a gentleman you're attracted to marry your best friend."

Sam's head shot up at that. "I am not attracted to him," she said instantly.

Isabel gave her a pitying look.

"I'm not!" Sam said more emphatically.

Isabel licked her lips and took a deep breath before speaking again. "You do know that James tells me everything you do on your outings, do you not?"

Sam's mouth opened in shock. *That little weasel. Fine, a large traitorous weasel!* She felt her face heat like a rock under the sun. She was embarrassed that she'd gotten caught like that, but it wasn't as if anything improper had happened on their outings. At least nothing that would prompt Isabel's assumption that she cared for him.

"Don't be angry with him. You know he only has your best interests at heart," Isabel said softly. "So, is there something you want to tell me?"

"Yes," Sam grumbled. "I am never taking James anywhere with me again."

Isabel raised her brow. "And?"

"And nothing! I am not attracted to him. I've met him several times to discuss the situation with Evie, nothing more."

Isabel chewed on her lip. Sam didn't like the way she was looking at her. "Sammy," Isabel finally said. Sam hated when her sister called her that. She only did that when she was trying not to offend her while saying something extremely condescending. She failed every time.

"I am not blind. I saw you with him at our ball. You care for him. And he cares for you too."

Sam stiffened at the words, her cheeks heating even more. "Even if that were true, the point is moot. He is marrying Evie."

"Does Evie know?"

Sam expelled a long breath. "No."

"I didn't think so. She is too good a friend to let you suffer through your feelings and marry the only man you've ever shown an interest in. She'd notice too, I am certain, but she is too preoccupied with her own drama."

"Yes, and her drama is more serious than mine."

Isabel looked at her intently. "Perhaps you should let Evie decide that."

"I wouldn't want to disturb her—"

"She is your best friend," Isabel interrupted.

"She is," Sam agreed.

"She deserves to know that you are hurting." Sam started shaking her head. "Do you think she will forgive you that easily when she does find out? And she will find out, you know. You are her best friend. Knowing that she is the reason for your misery, she will hate herself, and eventually resent you for lying. You don't want this to come between you, do you?"

Sam heaved a sigh and tilted her head back, looking up at the ceiling. She found no answers there either.

"What choice do I have?" she said through her teeth, then looked back at her sister. "If I say nothing, she will hate me. If I do say something, she will suffer, and *I* shall hate me."

"I think she deserves to make that choice for herself," Isabel said evenly. "What if things were reversed? Wouldn't you want to know?"

Sam blinked. She'd never thought of it that way. Of course, she'd want to know. She'd never marry anyone Evie was attracted to. And once she found out, she'd be furious at Evie for not telling her. But what if the attraction was not mutual? John would have said something to Sam, wouldn't he? Although he couldn't break the betrothal, even if he wanted to. He'd ruin Evie, and under current circumstances, he wouldn't come out unscathed from the scandal either. Then she remembered their morning rides, his intense gazes, their conversations. She couldn't be sure about his feelings, but Isabel was right. She owed Evie the truth.

"You don't need to be the martyr here," Isabel continued. "You can either save your friend just to lose her, or you can discuss it with her and come up with a solution together, like partners. Friendship is a partnership."

Isabel was right. But it wasn't as simple as that. Evie had too many problems as it was; Sam shouldn't be dumping her problems on top. But what if she realized her feelings for John were more than a simple attraction? What if they grew out of control when he married Evie? *Well, there is only one way to find out.*

* * *

The ball was a crush. The scents of flowers mixed in with

burning candle wax and people's sweat made Sam nauseous. The nerves weren't making it any easier for her either. She tried to speak to Evie several times, but every time, they got interrupted. Sam wondered if it was even worth speaking to her friend. This was nothing but a slight infatuation. She was certain it was going to pass. Should she endanger Evie just because of that?

She saw Evie weaving her way through the crowd back to her. She'd finished a dance with yet another suitor, smiling and acting as if nothing was amiss. Isabel and Lady Clydesdale were chatting up Lady Montbrook nearby, her brothers were somewhere in the card room, and John was nowhere in sight. Sam thought this would be a perfect moment to talk with her friend.

"I shall be happy if I don't dance anymore tonight," Evie said as she reached her side. "It is too hot in here. Why doesn't Lady Wakefield open the doors and make it habitable?" She fanned herself vigorously.

"I think people will start to swoon quite soon."

Evie gave a short laugh. "I am sure of it. Where is Lady Wakefield? I don't think I've seen her in a while."

"I don't know, perhaps she is the first victim of the heat of her own making."

Evie smiled at her. "You are in a sour mood. It is my wedding tonight, not yours; you are still happily unattached."

Sam gave her a queer look. "Are you regretting the decision?" Perhaps the talk with her friend would go easier than she thought.

"No." Evie shook her head. "Yes... Maybe."

Sam widened her eyes and looked at her friend in inquiry. Evie heaved a sigh. "I've been re-reading the letters from

Grandpa. He left me a string of them in his will, something to read when I am feeling down." She paused and fiddled with the fan in her hands.

"What did the letters say?" Sam leaned in closer to Evie.

"The same things as he always said." Evie smiled tenderly. "That he loves me, that he wishes me only the best. That love is more important than anything… Do you know that he was buried in debt and in need of an heiress too when he inherited? Just like Ashbury. He chose love instead and everything worked itself out." Evie said the last almost to herself, her gaze distant. "Perhaps I should take a leap of faith. Maybe if I follow my heart, it will lead me to happiness."

Sam took a deep breath. This was it. It was her chance to speak up. Perhaps they could both set each other free.

"Evie." Sam bit her lip. "There's something I need to tell you."

"Truly?" Evie looked up at her. "Because there's something I wanted to tell you too. But please, you go on."

Sam took another deep breath. "I th—"

A high-pitched scream followed by something breaking interrupted Sam's speech. Evie and Sam both looked at each other before following the crowd that had now assembled outside of the ballroom.

"You dirty old harlot, how dare you? He's mine!" The words flew across the hall. Sam and Evie exchanged a startled glance before weaving their way through the crowd. Sam craned her neck to see what was going on. She squeaked as she ran into someone and realized she'd bumped into Evie's back. Her friend stopped short in her tracks and stood there motionless. Sam craned her neck again to see what Evie was looking at.

Inside the room, two women were yelling and hurling

fragile items at each other. The next moment, one of them lunged and grabbed the other by the hair. Sam's jaw dropped open. She had never seen such open hostility, in front of so many onlookers, no less. *Is it Lady Wakefield?* She had to give herself a shake. Her gaze shifted a little to the side where Viscount St. Clare stood in the corner, nonchalantly buttoning up his falls as if the entire ordeal didn't involve him at all.

Sam's cheeks burned in shame for whatever had gone on in the room, for the abominable behavior by the high-born ladies and the shameless viscount.

A shadow loomed in front of her, and she tried to evade it and see inside the room again.

"What are you doing here?" Gage asked with a menacing scowl. "It's not a place for a young lady." He took her by the arm and started leading her away.

"But—"

"No. What were you even thinking, going in there?"

"Evie—"

"And where's Isabel? Isn't she supposed to be watching you?"

"Richard—"

"If you see scandal brewing, you walk away from it, not toward it—"

Sam dug in her heels. "Richard, Evie is still in there!"

"Damn it," Richard muttered under his breath. Sam raised her brows at him. "Pardon. I'll go fetch her, but you... Stand right here, do not move."

Sam threw up her hands. *Where would I even go?*

* * *

Sam stood in place for several long moments. People started returning to the ball. Even the orchestra resumed playing, yet there was no sign of her family. *Where did everyone disappear to?* She heaved an impatient sigh.

"Care for a stroll?"

Sam turned and saw John lingering by her side. She smiled but shook her head. "You have to ask my chaperones. Only none of them are anywhere in sight."

"They are dealing with the mess made by St. Clare. There was a threat of a duel and your brother had to intervene along with Clydesdale. And your sister is with the duchess. I believe she isn't feeling well."

"Evie? Oh, I must go to her." Sam turned, but John placed a hand on her shoulder.

"I think your sister is capable. They will just freshen up before our wedding can take place and I... Well, I wanted to talk to you."

"Oh." Sam lowered her gaze.

He offered his arm, and they ventured onto a patio in silence.

John heaved a long sigh as soon as they stepped over the threshold. "Crowded ballrooms and tight spaces are not my favorite things in the world."

"Evie loves it," Sam whispered.

"Yes, it's one of many reasons why we are not compatible. But that's not the point, is it? *Ton* marriages are rarely made based on compatibility."

"Do you ever wish you could go back and marry Lady Clydesdale?" Sam voiced her sudden thought. *Does he still love her?*

John looked at her, startled. "No. Not even once. She is

better off with her husband. On some level, I always knew that, and that's why I never bothered to fight for her."

Sam frowned in thought. "What did you want to tell me?" she finally asked him.

"I... I just wanted to say a proper farewell."

Sam swallowed.

"In the short time since we met, I have appreciated our friendship more than you can ever imagine, and I hope we shall continue being friends after tonight," he continued with a slight frown. "The truth is... Ever since I received your first letter, I've wanted to experience this. With you. To dance with you in a ballroom, to talk to you about your life. You saved my life, I hope you know that. And I shall always be grateful to you for that. I owe you my life."

Sam swallowed, not quite certain how to react to his words.

He rummaged through his pockets before extracting a small object. He then took Sam's hand and placed it in her palm. "I realize it isn't proper to gift things to unmarried ladies, but since we are friends... Well, I just wanted to give you a parting gift," he said, his face dark with some emotion.

Sam uncurled her fingers and looked at her present. It was a tiny pendant with angel wings and a halo. She looked up at him through tear-filled eyes. *An angel.*

"It's not just because of the letters," he said with a sad smile. "The first time we met, when I was flailing in the dirt, you leaned over me and the sun cast a glow around your head like a halo. For a moment, I thought I'd died and gone to heaven. I thought you were an angel."

Sam gave him a strained smile. "My brother, Ben... He was the one who came up with the nickname." *And I failed him. Perhaps I am failing you too.*

"Well," he said, after a moment's pause. "Farewell." He turned to leave then, and Sam stopped him by grabbing his arm.

"Wait," she said, before rising on her toes and bringing her lips toward his face. She was intending to give him a quick peck on the cheek, but at the same moment, John turned and caught her lips with his. His lips were soft and warm, not at all as hard and unyielding as they seemed. His scent reached her senses, surrounding her in a mindless fog. He smelled like clover leaves and horses, and something else, likely his own wonderful masculine scent. She closed her eyes, breathing in the sensation, not wanting to let go.

"You shameless wanton!" came a loud shriek from the doorway.

John and Sam drew apart, startled. Sam placed the back of her hand over her mouth. Lady Montbrook stood in the doorway, a menacing smirk on her lips.

"I knew you were cavorting with this fellow, behind my niece's back too! Well, you are not getting your hands on her inheritance. Either of you!"

A crowd started gathering behind Lady Montbrook, and Sam's vision blurred in front of her. Her cheeks heated, and her hands covered in perspiration. Just beyond Lady Montbrook's shoulder, she saw Evie's surprised gaze.

Chapter 12

Richard Lewis, Viscount Gage, was livid with anger and barely holding on to his temper, so much so that Sam thought he was going to burst.

"I can't leave you alone for one damn second! What were you thinking?" He stalked the length of the drawing room like a caged beast.

After being caught with John by Lady Montbrook, Sam was quickly bundled up in a carriage and Isabel took her home. Gage had still been dealing with St. Clare at the time and didn't know what had happened. What a surprise it was to him when the whole ballroom was abuzz with a second scandal on the same night. A scandal featuring his dear sister.

"Haven't we hammered into your head the importance of propriety and not stepping out anywhere alone with a gentleman?"

"Richard, that's enough. Can't you see she's upset?" Isabel sat next to a defeated Sam, holding her hand.

"Oh, she is upset, is she? Well, she should have thought

before acting so foolishly!" Richard let out a growl. "I'm going to kill Ashbury!"

"No!" Sam lifted her eyes to her brother's for the first time that night. "Please don't do anything to him."

"What the devil are you talking about, sister? He's ruined you! If I don't restore your honor, how will I be able to look upon my face in the looking glass?"

"My honor?"

"You are not talking of a duel, are you?" Isabel asked. "Not after spending half the night talking Stanhope out of it."

"Stanhope?" Sam turned to look at her sister.

"St. Clare's other paramour." Isabel grimaced.

"The woman who was fighting with Lady Wakefield was Stanhope's wife?"

Isabel nodded. Sam was shocked, but Isabel seemed unperturbed. Of course, she'd witnessed the whole event and had had plenty of time to compose herself. Still, having the wife of her ex-fiancé make a spectacle of herself over another man must have provoked some emotion in her. Sam decided she'd ask her later. After Gage was done scolding her.

"It is different," Gage said irritably. "Those women knew what they were getting themselves into when they agreed to a tryst with St. Clare. You were tricked!"

"I wasn't tricked," Sam protested.

"He seduced you. There's no other explanation."

"Richard!" Sam let out an exhausted sigh. She knew he was trying to protect her, or perhaps cast Ashbury as a villain, but his logic was faulty at best.

Isabel put a staying hand on Sam's arm. "Promise me, Richard, you won't do anything rash. Not when you're in a temper."

"I am not in a temper!" he yelled.

Isabel raised her brow.

"Fine! I shan't do anything rash. But don't you think I am letting Ashbury get away with this. He's either going to marry you or die."

Sam's jaw went slack.

"Besides, I don't think the duchess is going to marry him after that," he added quietly.

Sam lowered her gaze, her stomach tied in a knot. She felt like she was going to cast up her accounts. How could she have done this to Evie? Tears started falling from her eyes and onto her skirts.

"It's all Adam and Ben's fault," Gage muttered under his breath. "I've tried to discipline you the best I could, but they spoiled you and allowed you everything you wanted. They still took you out to the lake with them, taught you to swim, and even climb the trees!"

"What does this have to do—?"

"Don't interrupt me!"

Sam and Isabel exchanged amused looks. Gage always tended to go off-topic with his tirades.

"And you"—he pointed to Isabel—"coddling her ever since she was a babe. If you were firmer with her—"

"Don't I get to take responsibility for my actions?" Sam asked with a sigh.

"By all means!" Gage waved a hand, before planting his legs apart and folding his arms on his huge chest, looking dark and menacing. "Please do."

"It's all my fault," she said and bit her lip. "I shouldn't have gone outside with John. It's my fault and no one else's."

Gage raised his eyebrow in a condescending gesture.

"Don't you think I know that? Don't you think I feel bad?" she cried. "The look of betrayal on Evie's face." She bit her lip, tears gathering in the corners of her eyes.

"I think that's enough for today," Isabel said, standing up. "We all need rest."

She stretched her hand toward Sam, and she took it. Isabel tugged her up and enfolded her in a warm embrace. Sam let her tears overflow and trickle down her cheeks.

"Fine, but don't think this is over," Gage said, and Sam heard his footsteps retreat toward the door.

"You promised not to do anything rash!" Isabel called out to him as the door closed.

Sam disengaged herself from Isabel and wiped at her cheeks. "He's right," she said on a hiccup.

"About what?" Isabel smiled. "That it's my fault or Adam and Ben's?"

"No." Sam waved her hand with a watery smile. "That I am spoiled and irresponsible."

Isabel gave a short puff. "He never said that."

"Well, he meant it, and he's right."

"He is not," Isabel said emphatically. "You were caught up in the moment. It happens to everyone."

"Does it?" Sam raised her vulnerable gaze to her sister's.

"It does. We are not all as virtuous as we seem. I am sure Gage has conducted a fair share of indiscretions himself."

Sam scoffed. "I doubt it."

"Well, don't. I know *I* have been less than perfect." Isabel lowered her gaze.

Sam cocked her head. "Do you mean with Stanhope?"

"I do." A small, sad smile appeared on Isabel's face before she tugged on Sam's hand and led her out of the drawing room.

They walked in silence for a while until they stopped in front of Sam's room.

Sam's mind traveled from her downfall to Isabel's misfortunes. Sam knew her sister still felt deeply for Stanhope; otherwise, she would have found another man to marry. It served him right that his wife was cavorting with St. Clare.

"You know," she said carefully. "I think Stanhope deserved what he got."

Isabel grimaced uncomfortably. "To be humiliated so publicly. I don't know. I never wished him ill."

"You didn't have to," Sam said smugly. "You have a sister for that."

Chapter 13

Sam got dressed in her riding habit and knocked on James's door the first thing in the morning. The door opened, and the footman appeared, only instead of his usual friendly smile, Sam was greeted with stony features.

"I have explicit instructions not to accompany you anywhere, Miss," he said in an even—if slightly trembling—voice.

"Very well." Sam turned on her heel. "Then I am going by myself."

She heard a long, weary sigh behind her, and she slowed her step.

"I'll be ready in a moment, Miss," her favorite footman finally called behind her.

She turned to him with a sunny smile.

"But if I get booted—" he started.

"I shall provide for you handsomely," Sam interrupted with a smile. She turned back toward the stairs and heard the shuffling noise of James's footsteps.

Several minutes later, she stood at the servants' entrance to

Evie's house. She knew she wouldn't be welcomed inside if she came knocking on the front door, not with Lady Montbrook standing guard, but she needed to speak to Evie, desperately.

The door opened, and Mrs. Lambert appeared on the doorstep.

"Miss Samantha." She curtsied and ushered her in. "We were hoping you would come to see Her Grace off."

"Off?" Sam stopped, her eyes wide. "She is still leaving?"

Mrs. Lambert nodded and beckoned Sam to follow her. She accompanied her up the servants' stairs to the family wing and left to order tea and biscuits for them.

Sam lingered in front of Evie's door in indecision. Her hand hovered in the air for several moments, afraid to knock. What if Evie was angry with her? What if she didn't want to see her? She took a fortifying breath. In that case, she would have to hear it from her friend. Sam gathered her courage and knocked on the door.

She heard a faint answer to come in, entered the room, and stood in the doorway, uncertain if she'd be welcome.

Evie sat on the windowsill reading a book. She hadn't looked Sam's way as she heard her enter. She just flipped the page and continued reading. Sam looked around the room. Several trunks stood by the bed, filled with clothing. So it was true then; she was being taken to the Somerset estate after all.

"Evie," Sam said quietly and made an uncertain step forward.

Evie lifted her head, and a smile appeared on her face as she saw Sam. "Oh, it's you." She stood, walked toward Sam, and gave her a hug.

Sam expelled a breath of relief. She hugged her friend back, tears gathering in the corner of her eyes.

Evie pulled away and looked at Sam's face. "Oh, my God, are you crying? Is something wrong?" She looked at her with a frown of concern etching her face. "Come, sit."

Evie led Sam by the hand to the settee in the middle of the room. Sam felt silly for crying like that in front of her friend, but of all the greetings she'd expected—and thought she deserved—a smile and a hug were not on the list. She should have known better though; it was Evie.

"I'm sorry." Sam wiped at her tears. "I am turning into a watering pot."

Evie handed her a handkerchief.

"I thought you were angry with me." Sam wiped her face and blew her nose into a handkerchief.

"Oh." Evie gave a musical laugh. "Because of Ashbury?"

Sam nodded, biting her lip. "We didn't get to speak after the ball, and you seemed... shocked."

"I was! Well, I am. But not because of what you think. Why didn't you tell me?"

"Tell you... what?"

"That you care for him."

"Oh." Sam chewed on her lip. "I didn't know. I mean, I didn't know if it was a slight infatuation that would pass or if it was something more. Besides, you needed to marry fast to get out from under your guardian's wings. And I didn't want to ruin this by speaking up about something I wasn't certain of. You understand, don't you?"

"Samantha." Evie looked at her sternly. "You've never, in all your years on the marriage mart, had *a slight infatuation* with any gentleman."

"You didn't either!"

Evie wrinkled her nose. "That's irrelevant," she said after a pause. "What I mean is, after all these years, you find a gentleman you fancy and you were going to let me marry him?"

"You know I had to!"

"No, you did not!"

"With what is going on with the Montbrooks, how was I to ruin your chances for a better marriage?"

"I wish everybody would stop making decisions for me."

"But the Montbrooks—"

"We are friends, and you should have been honest with me about this. How would I have felt if I found out about your feelings after I married him?"

Sam grimaced. "Isabel said the same thing."

"Well, you should have listened to her."

"I didn't want to hurt your chances of an escape."

"Yes, but not at the expense of hiding your feelings. If I were a lesser person, you would have lost me," she said smugly and smoothed the wrinkles on her skirts in a prim manner.

Sam laughed. "I am lucky to have you as my friend."

"I know you are." Evie grinned. "In any case, this was the only reason why I seemed shocked last night. I thought you would've told me."

"I wanted to, I really did. I just didn't want to hurt you." Evie raised her brow. "I am so sorry, Evie, dear. I promise I shall tell you everything from now on."

Evie looked down and chewed on her lip. "I don't think I would have married him," she said, still looking at her hands. "You know I was having second thoughts. In fact, I was about to call the wedding off when I came into the ballroom."

"You were? Truly? You are not just saying that to make me

feel better, are you?"

Evie shook her head. "I don't want to spend the rest of my life in a loveless marriage. I shan't."

"But what about the Montbrooks?"

"Escaping one unwanted marriage into another is not a solution. I know that now."

"But... What are you going to do now?"

"I am not helpless, you know. And I have a plan, do not worry," Evie said and gave her a wink. At that moment, the maid came in with the tea tray and Evie proceeded to pour each of them a cup. "How about you tell me what you are going to do now, my dear friend? How does it feel to be a ruined woman?" Evie grinned, and Sam swatted at her.

"I wouldn't know. Not yet, anyway. This is the first outing I've been on since last night, and so far it has been wonderful." She smiled, and Evie laughed. "The only reminder of last night was the paper this morning. Have you read it?"

Evie nodded with a smile. "*A Wakefield ball of immorality?* Yes, I've read it. " She giggled and took a sip of tea. "So our betrothed hasn't come to ask for your hand yet?"

Sam shook her head. "I'd think he'd come to you first."

Evie peered at the clock on the mantelpiece. "Well, it's not calling hours yet, so he probably will." She paused and sipped on her tea. "Sam, do you want to marry him? I mean, a kiss in the moonlight is one thing, but do you want to be married to him forever?"

Sam heaved a sigh. "My emotions are in quite a turmoil. I think I do, but how do you know for certain?"

Evie looked at Sam with a thoughtful expression on her face. "When you think about seeing him every day, waking up to see his face the first thing in the morning... Does it fill you with dread?"

Sam thought for a moment before answering. She hadn't realized this before, but every morning she woke up with the urge to go for a ride and see John. She was excited to see him, and she was loath to leave him. "No, it doesn't."

Evie smiled at her. "Then you're a far better candidate for his wife than I ever was. Will you promise me one thing, though?"

"Anything." Sam put down her cup.

"Promise me to do everything in your power to be happy."

Sam studied her friend's open face. The request puzzled her, but Evie just looked at her earnestly. "I shall give it my best effort if you do the same."

Evie smiled. "Deal."

* * *

The moment John entered Viscount Gage's study, he was greeted with a punch to his face. He staggered, seeing tiny little stars in his obscured vision, but managed not to fall to the floor. Another shot came at him and this time John crashed onto the side table, taking down all of its contents with him. He lay on the floor in a heaping mess, his jaw swelling already.

"You bloody bastard! You have the nerve coming here!" the viscount roared.

The door busted open as Miss Lewis rushed in.

"Leave, this is not your business!" the viscount commanded.

"You said you wouldn't do anything rash!" she said in an exasperated tone.

John propped himself up on his elbows and looked around. He was sprawled in an undignified heap on the floor, bottles and decanters surrounding him, expensive whisky soaking his clothes.

"I didn't hunt him down and kill him, did I?" Gage huffed.

John slowly got up and tried to straighten his clothing, although it was a hopeless endeavor. Two more people filed through the still-open door. Sam and her other brother surveyed the room wide-eyed. John restrained himself from gaping at Sam and instead trained his eyes on the viscount.

"I would beg a private audience with the viscount," he said in an even tone.

Gage looked John dead in the eyes and didn't take his gaze off him as he spoke. "Adam, take our sisters out of this room."

"Richard, please," Sam cried but was quickly ushered away.

"You have thirty seconds to convince me not to throw you out on your arse, accompanied with the invitation to a meeting at dawn." With that, he walked behind his desk, turned the hourglass, and sat, staring at John dispassionately.

"I came to ask for Sam's hand in marriage."

Gage gave him a menacing look.

"Miss Samantha," John corrected himself hastily.

"What about the Duchess of Somerset?"

"She cried off."

"Not surprising," Gage scoffed.

"I know that it seems like the only reason I am proposing is because of what transpired last night. And while it is partially true, it is not the whole truth." John paused to draw a breath. "Miss Samantha and I have gotten to know each other very well in the past few weeks. I came to admire her, respect her, and I feel that there's an affection between us. There is from my side, at least."

"And there is a large dowry from her side," the viscount

noted.

"I can't deny that it is a factor as well. But not the main factor."

Gage studied him narrowly. He then shifted his gaze to the hourglass, which had emptied by then. "As much as I'd love to throw you out on your arse, I am not a foolish man. You ruined Sam last night; she has no prospects now."

John nodded. "Does that mean I have your blessing?"

Gage just sat there staring at John for a while, tapping his finger against his desk. Then he stood suddenly.

"If she'll have you, I have no right to stand in her way. But be warned. Husband or no husband, if you hurt her, we'll come for her," he said menacingly. Then suddenly he smiled, but it didn't reach his eyes. "And then we'll come for you."

* * *

Samantha paced the length of the library. "They've been there a long time, haven't they?" She stopped and stared at Isabel, who was peacefully embroidering in a chair by the hearth.

"It's been too quiet. Perhaps Gage killed him," Adam said in a droll voice.

Sam turned sharply to him. He raised his hands in mock self-defense before raising the paper to cover his face from Sam.

"Why did Richard hit him? Do you think John said something to offend him?"

"I doubt it. The man hadn't been inside for more than a second before I heard the crash. Gage probably didn't give him a chance to speak," Isabel said, not taking her eyes off the embroidery.

Sam resumed pacing. "Then why would Richard hit him?" She heard a scoff from Adam and turned to him.

"Come now, sister. The man defiled you! Did you expect Gage to throw him a welcome party?"

"He did not defile me," Sam said, narrowing her eyes on her brother. "It was one blasted kiss, and that horrid Lady Montbrook had to jump out from behind the fern to catch us at the exact same moment!"

"Oh, if it was just one kiss then it's fine," Adam intoned sarcastically.

Sam heaved a sigh. Now that she thought about it, perhaps Lady Montbrook didn't happen upon them accidentally. Perhaps she'd followed them in hopes of catching them in an indiscretion. Not that she would have any luck if there'd been no indiscretion. It was all Sam's fault, and now the Montbrooks were taking Evie away and could do whatever they wanted with her. She groaned and resumed her pacing.

Finally, she heard footsteps in the hall, and then the door swung open. She was a bundle of nerves, wound up so tight that she jumped in reaction. Richard peeked his head out, then opened the door fully, but kept to the other side of it.

"Oh, good, you're here," he said calmly. "Isabel, Adam, would you mind joining me in the other room? Sam has a visitor." Sam watched wide-eyed as her family silently filed away. Isabel raised both eyebrows at her as she passed and gave her a sly smile.

"I'll be just outside the room," Richard said just as John entered.

Sam blinked at the empty doorway. Had Richard just left her alone with a gentleman after that tirade he'd given her the night before?

"Hello, Sam." John smiled at her, and Sam concentrated her attention on him. He still stood one step from the door. He didn't venture farther into the room, just stood there, looking nervous and uncomfortable. His clothes were in disarray, his breeches and coat soaked in what smelled like alcohol. His hat was crumpled in his hands, betraying his uneasiness. Sam's gaze roamed him from head to toe, not quite knowing where to rest her eyes.

"Yes?" was all she could say.

He smiled at that. "I…" He cleared his throat. "I need to talk to you."

Sam nodded. "Of course. What about?"

"Marriage," he said succinctly.

"Marriage," she repeated slowly.

"I didn't think it would come as a surprise." He frowned. "After what transpired last night."

"No, it's not a surprise." She let out a tiny laugh. "Did you talk to Evie?"

"No, not exactly. Her guardian didn't let me see her, but he made it clear in no uncertain terms that I am not welcome in their household anymore."

"I've seen her today. For what it's worth, she is not upset with you."

"Good." John shifted uncomfortably from one foot to another. "I know this is probably not what you wanted, but I don't think we have a choice in the matter. After the scandal last night, it is only logical for us to marry."

"Just because I am ruined doesn't mean I don't have choices," Sam said miserably.

"I know you do. I am simply giving you another one." John heaved a sigh. "I know it seems like the scandal is the only reason I am here today. But it isn't."

"Isn't it?" Sam cocked her head to the side.

"No." John cleared his throat. "You know my circumstances more than anyone. I need to marry an heiress. You have a sufficient dowry. We've also spent some time together, and I think we understand each other quite well. And after last night, it's only logical..." He paused and grimaced, raking a hand through his hair.

Sam let out a nervous laugh. *How romantic.*

"And then there is the whole business where you saved my life," John continued. "So, it is only fair that I at least shield you from scandal."

Sam looked at the man standing in front of her. This beautiful albeit scarred man, this imperfect creature, but somehow perfect for her, and she wanted to laugh. Mostly at herself. She was infatuated with this man. She'd hoped he might return the feelings too. What an idiot. She shook herself out of her reverie.

"That is the most romantic marriage proposal I have ever heard," she noted dryly.

"Even more romantic than when I proposed to the duchess?" He smiled crookedly and paced to the window. He stood for a couple of seconds looking out into the gloomy garden outside, then turned back to her.

"I know this is not what you deserve. You are beautiful, clever, and funny. And I am certain you could have chosen from dozens of more romantic proposals that came before me, but you haven't." He ran his hand through his hair and tugged on his cravat again. "I am not the best prospect for you, I know that. I am rough, and I am difficult to live with—you don't even know how much. I shall probably make your life a living hell."

"This proposal just keeps getting better and better," she murmured during a brief pause in his speech.

"I am surly, I have no social polish, I have no fortune, and I shan't be coddling you the way your family does." He took a deep breath and looked straight into her eyes. "But… I don't speak a lot. I don't have any hounds, I own but one horse, and I shan't bore you with details about her. My estate is tiny, so I shan't brag. And I'd rather sit in silence than fill it with idle chatter. The last time we spoke, you seemed adamant that these are the qualities you seek in a man."

Sam let out a burst of laughter. She had said that, hadn't she? It warmed her that he remembered. Which gave her hope that he cared for her, even if only a little.

John took several steps forward until he was standing in front of her. He raised his hand and cupped her cheek. Her eyes widened, then she lowered them, staring at his cravat. His heat, his closeness, muddled all her thoughts. Her breathing quickened, and her eyes couldn't find a point to fix upon in the intricate, crisp white folds. Then his thumb started brushing her chin, slowly moving up to her lower lip.

"Are you…?" She swallowed and looked up into his eyes. He seemed to be mesmerized by her lips. She licked them self-consciously and tried again, "Are you proposing a marriage of convenience?"

"Yes." His voice was strangely low and hoarse. "Please, say yes," he continued in a husky whisper, "so I can kiss you again."

"Kiss me first," she murmured before she could think better of it.

He seemed surprised by her request, but he lowered his lips to hers. His mouth was warm and soft on hers. She closed her eyes and concentrated on the warm and pleasant feeling it evoked. He brushed his lips over hers several times. Then he opened his mouth and licked across her lips.

The sudden tingly caress was so unexpectedly delicious that she moaned in response. At that moment, his left arm came around her waist and pulled her up into his embrace. With his right hand, he tilted her head, and he slanted his mouth over hers fiercely, possessively. His thumb was playing across the corner of her mouth, coaxing her to open for him. She gave in under the onslaught, and he thrust his tongue into her mouth.

It was all too much for her untried senses, and she felt as if she was falling. Sam grabbed at his shoulders tightly in order to hold on, and he gave a low growl of appreciation. His tongue was sweeping inside her mouth, over her most sensitive parts. Her hips came to press closer to him by instinct, and his arm tightened closer around her waist. Her insides felt like molten lava; heat pooled inside her belly, and even lower. All her senses reeled with excitement.

She couldn't understand what was happening to her. She wanted it to never stop, and at the same time, she required something more. She didn't know what it was. What seemed like an eternity later, he finally withdrew his tongue and gave her light brushes over her mouth as if trying to calm her down. She whimpered lightly, not willing to let it end yet. Then he put his forehead against hers and just stood there with his eyes closed, holding her and breathing heavily.

Sam was panting too. Her mind was jumbled from the experience. Her hands were still clutching at his coat, so she forced herself to let go and took a step back.

John finally opened his eyes and ran soothing hands over

her upper arms. "I've wanted to do that for far too long," he said with a crooked smile. "You taste like heaven."

Sam felt herself blushing fiercely. What did one say to that? She lowered her eyes and stared at the carpet. John gently pushed at her chin with the tips of his fingers.

"So," he continued, smiling. "Is that a *yes?*"

Sam cleared her throat and gathered her wits, so she could think more clearly.

"Yes," she finally answered. "Under certain conditions."

"Naturally." He nodded and looked at her encouragingly.

"I want children. I am from a big affectionate family; I might want a houseful."

He looked her over from head to toe, lingering slightly on her mouth and breasts.

"That will not be an issue," he finally said.

She nodded, color rising on her face.

"Anything else?"

Sam thought for a while before responding. "You said that you can't give affection and love to your wife."

John nodded.

"Then I want at least friendship."

"Agreed." He stretched out his arm toward her in a request for a handshake. She walked closer to him and pressed her palm into his. John's fingers came around her hand in a tight grip, and then he tugged on her arm. She started forward and crashed into his chest. Sam looked up at him, startled, as his face descended toward hers.

He caught her in a warm, sweet kiss again. He brushed his mouth over hers, then gathered her closer and touched his tongue to her lips. All her senses fired up in anticipation of the same wicked feeling she'd gotten the last time he ran his tongue over her lips. But at that moment, the floor creaked, and she heard a harsh clearing of the throat.

John and Sam both jumped back like guilty adolescents caught in mischief.

"I hope that means you two are betrothed." Her brother's low voice came from the direction of the door. Sam couldn't quite meet his eyes. She nodded.

"Yes, my lord," came John's confident voice.

"I expect a short engagement," Richard barked. "Now, I believe this interview is over. Ashbury, please, proceed to my study so we can draw up a betrothal contract."

John took a step in Sam's direction, took her hand, and kissed her fingers. She looked up at him, still blushing fiercely. John gave her a wink and walked out of the room.

Richard lingered a moment or two in the doorway. "We'll talk later," he finally said and left the room without giving her an opportunity to reply.

She stood there frozen before she collapsed into a chair and covered her face with her hands. It was difficult enough to recover from the heat-inducing kiss her fiancé had just given her. But then her eldest brother had witnessed it. That was absolutely embarrassing. Absolutely. Embarrassing.

Chapter 14

John sat opposite Viscount Gage in the study of the Gage townhouse. They had been going over his estate books ever since the day of John and Sam's betrothal.

Despite Gage's insistence that the wedding be a quick one, he absolutely refused to get a special license. He said that it would invite more gossip and, since there was no real rush, he insisted on banns to be read. This meant that John had to spend more time in London. And as much as he disliked the viscount, he preferred his company to a crowded ballroom. The viscount had agreed to help John with his estate issues and had given some advice on investments John could make with Sam's dowry. John appreciated all the help. He had never gotten advice and education of this sort from his father. Being in Gage's study also meant that Sam was somewhere nearby, and that thought made him feel more at peace.

John tried to visit his bride every day, but he wasn't allowed to see her for over fifteen minutes at a time unless they were out for a ride or a short walk in the garden. Sam was always busy, either preparing a menu for the wedding breakfast, shopping for her trousseau, packing her suitcases, picking out her wedding presents, and God knew whatever else. So when John was at her residence, he spent most of his time in the company of her eldest brother, like today. John threw a glance at the viscount. He had a concentrated expression on his face as he studied the numbers.

"I don't think these numbers are correct either," Gage said after a short while. "I think you're better off finding yourself a new estate manager."

"That is easier said than done. I don't know where to look. And the current manager has been with the Ashbury estate since before I was born."

"And that's the issue. He's grown complacent. None of the numbers match up in the books. Since the late baron's passing, I gather he stopped keeping any records whatsoever."

John heaved a sigh. "Or possibly even before. My father didn't truly care for his estates. Especially after both my brothers died. I doubt he checked in with the manager much in his last years." John didn't want to explain his family situation or why the baron didn't care for him and didn't want to leave him an inheritance worth receiving. Thankfully, the man didn't press further.

"We'll need to go over more of those, but my man of business is arriving soon. So this will have to be it for today." Gage closed the book and stood, indicating the end of the meeting.

John followed suit and collected his belongings as he stood. He peeked through the window behind the viscount. The weather was beautiful, a rare occurrence in London. He squinted at the clock on the mantelpiece as he put on his gloves. It was still visiting hours. If Sam was unoccupied, perhaps he could entice her for a short walk in the garden before he had to leave.

"Thank you, Gage." John tipped his hat. "I appreciate you helping me with this."

"I am not doing it for you."

"I realize that. I am grateful nonetheless." With a final nod, John exited the room.

John walked through the hall and stopped beside the doors leading to the drawing room. A pleasant chatter of female voices drifted to him from inside the room. He smiled to himself, imagining a similar scene. Him coming home from a long day's work about the estates, Sam sitting in a drawing room, greeting him with a smile on her face. He closed his eyes and had to force the image away. If only it were this simple.

He entered and looked around the room. Several ladies were sitting in a circle, drinking tea and chattering away. He recognized some of the guests, but his eyes were riveted on his bride-to-be. Sam smiled as she noticed him, and the chatter immediately ceased.

"Good afternoon, ladies." John inclined his head. "Do you mind if I steal my bride for a walk about the garden?"

"Not at all," Sam's sister answered with a smile. "You should go ahead. We will join you in ten minutes or thereabouts. Won't we, ladies?"

"Oh, we don't need to crowd the young couple," one of the older ladies answered and looked John up and down in a suggestive manner. John's lips twitched in laughter.

"You have to keep an eye out on those young and eager gentlemen," another lady chimed in. They continued debating the issue as Sam bowed out and left the room on John's arm.

They entered the garden in silence. John was just drinking in her closeness, enjoying the feel of her hand in the crook of his arm. The silence never felt daunting around her. He enjoyed hearing her voice, but he'd gladly sit in silence with her too. She didn't seem to mind the quiet either. He liked that she didn't feel the need to fill the silence with mindless chatter.

They walked quietly through the garden until they reached the rose arbor.

Sam stopped and turned to look at him. "How are things progressing with Richard? You haven't killed each other yet, so I am guessing it's not too bad?"

John smiled. "No, not too bad. On the contrary, I appreciate his help. It's obvious how much effort he's put into his own estates. He isn't much older than me, but he has so much more experience."

Sam nodded. "Our father sat down with him when he was but a child and taught him everything he needed to learn. Richard accompanied him to meet the tenants, and the managers. Father always believed that if he were to pass unexpectedly, Richard should know what to do. I am guessing yours didn't have the same view?"

John grimaced. "I am a third son. I was never expected to inherit."

Sam looked like she wanted to ask more, but John decided to change the subject.

"It's a beautiful arbor. I don't think we've ever stopped here before."

Sam smiled and looked around. "I like this little place. Somewhere quiet where I can sit and sketch."

She leaned in to smell the rosebuds. "And it smells lovely

here."

John came up behind her and enfolded her in a gentle embrace. That's all he meant to do, just have her close to him, inhale her scent the way she did with the rose. Only his hands came up of their own volition to caress her breasts. The warmth of her body and the scent of her skin clouded his mind. He would have stopped if she protested, but she leaned harder into him, threw her head back, and closed her eyes. He ran his thumbs over her already erect nipples, she sighed, and he lost control.

He pressed his mouth against the side of her throat and sucked her delicate skin. He scraped his teeth lightly where her pulse throbbed and then soothed it with his tongue. Her hand came up, and she threaded her fingers through his hair. One of his hands slowly traced a path down her ribcage, then her belly, lower... Finally, he cupped her between her legs through her skirt. She sucked in her breath but didn't protest.

Slowly, she turned her head toward his and kissed him on the lips. She tasted so damn good, her mouth hot and welcoming. He kissed her like a hungry man would devour his first meal in days, his tongue tasting her, teasing her, daring her to kiss him back. And when her sweet tongue touched his, he felt lost.

His hand, still caressing her breast, came up over the bodice of her dress, and then he sank his fingers into the bodice. His hand touched her bare nipple, and he squeezed her soft breast. She pressed her bottom closer to his hips, her derriere deliciously grinding against his erection. That felt too good.

He growled in response. John moved his other hand lower and bunched her skirt in his fist. He was riding her skirt up higher when he heard feminine voices in the distance. He immediately remembered where they were—in her family garden, with her family just a few feet away, and guests in the drawing room. *Oh, God, what am I doing?*

John took his mouth from hers and immediately released her. She whimpered in protest and stumbled in surprise.

He put a steadying hand on her arm. "Someone's coming," he whispered.

She whirled around at that. And he was satisfied to see that her eyes were still glazed over and darkened from passion. Her lips were wet and puffy from his kisses, her neck abraded by his stubble, and one beaded nipple was peeking out of her bodice. Oh, how he wanted to take that rosy peak into his mouth and suckle it. But the voices grew louder. Someone was coming closer to their hide-out. So, he re-adjusted her clothes the best he could, then took her arm, and proceeded walking toward the exit of the garden.

* * *

"All done, Miss," Gina said as she bounced a curl dangling at Sam's temple.

She'd dressed Sam's hair in an intricate coiffure, leaving a couple of curls at her temples and one at the nape of her neck. Gina loved fussing with Sam's hair. Usually, Sam took exception to spending hours in front of a looking glass. Today, however, was her wedding day.

Sam turned to a looking glass and studied her reflection carefully. She was dressed in her best lilac gown, with a low bodice and high waist. Several flowers weaved through the curls in her hair. She looked like a bride, but she didn't feel like one.

She hadn't seen John in several days. He'd come to see her every day at first. He touched her and kissed her at every opportunity. She'd even started to believe that he was genuinely attracted to her, but after that passionate moment in the garden, he'd disappeared.

Oh, that passionate kiss in the garden. She remembered his hands caressing her breasts, how heat pooled low in her abdomen. His hair had been crisp and silky under her fingers, his tongue hot and demanding in her mouth. Sam clenched her thighs in response. Just the thought of that moment gave her butterflies in the stomach.

She wondered if John was going to kiss her again tonight. Had he been as moved by that moment in the garden as she, and if so, why had he stopped visiting her? She heaved a sigh. She wished she knew what was going on in his head. She cared for him, but she failed to understand him. She wished, even more, she knew what was about to happen on her wedding night.

Sam was an intelligent woman, and she knew that marital relations did not stop at kissing. There was something more. But a lady's education was so limited that she had no idea as to what that more was. She'd heard from gossip, of course, that this something involved a bed, having a man's pants down, and a woman's skirts up. During that wonderful moment in the garden, John had been pulling her skirts up. Was he about to do whatever it was people did, to her, in the garden? Could people even do those things out of bed?

She closed her eyes tightly and shook her head. Oh, why hadn't she paid more attention to her brothers' crass conversations that Isabel constantly had to stifle with her looks? Of course, Isabel was unmarried and probably didn't know much herself.

"Look at our blushing bride!" her sister called from behind her.

Sam turned around and saw Isabel studying her from the doorway. "Are you ready to go? Our brothers have probably walked a hole in the floor downstairs. They've been waiting for half an hour, I believe."

Sam wanted to answer with a joke, but her stomach was tied in knots and her throat constricted. So she just smiled tightly at her sister.

"Isabel, can we have a talk before we go out there?" she finally managed to push out between her parched lips.

"Of course," Isabel said with a frown. "Please, let us sit."

They both perched themselves on Sam's bed and sat in silence. Isabel was waiting for Sam to speak, but she didn't know how to even start this conversation.

"Isabel." Sam folded her hands on her lap and looked pleadingly at her sister. "I am worried… about the wedding night. Mama is not here, and we don't have female relatives who could help me—"

Isabel grimaced and looked away for a moment. "I am sorry, darling, I haven't thought… In fact, I wondered if perhaps you and John… that maybe he…" She let out a frustrated huff.

Sam just stared at her.

"You don't know anything that's about to happen?"

Sam shook her head. "Do you?"

Isabel looked down at her hands and picked at the tips of her gloved fingers. "I can tell you a little," she finally said quietly. "My experience is lim—I mean, I am not married."

Sam frowned at her sister's choice of words.

"It is a very private experience. You might feel exposed and vulnerable. Perhaps if Ashbury is patient with you, if he's gentle…" Isabel bit her lip. "I am sorry, I can't tell you more. It is going to hurt a bit, but according to gossip, it's just the first time."

Sam laughed nervously. "Thank you."

"I apologize. I wish Mama was here to talk to you about this. Or perhaps, I should have brought one of our aunts."

"No! No aunts. I don't think I'd want their help on this."

Isabel smiled crookedly. "Maybe if you talk with Ashbury instead. You know, I don't have a lot of experience in relationships. My only fiancé fled rather quickly. But if you try to emulate the relationship that was between our parents… They were open and free with each other, at ease. I don't know how they reached that phase, but you can always aim there. I know Ashbury is… he doesn't seem very open, but if you think you can be happy with him, then don't give up."

Sam nodded and stood. After this brief conversation with Isabel, she felt even more confused than before. Before, her thoughts were concentrated on the wedding night. Now, however, she realized she had to think long-term. About marriage.

When they reached the church, John was already inside. Clydesdale met Sam's family outside, with a muttered, "Thank God." Everyone followed him into the church with the exception of Sam and Richard. They lingered briefly on the stairs just outside.

"Sammy," Richard said, turning her to face him. "Today, I shall be giving you away in front of God and our family. Legally, you will be another man's wife." He seemed to have difficulty continuing. His throat worked, but he couldn't get the words out. Finally, he said, "But you were my little sister first, and you will always be my little sister. So no matter what, if you need me—" He cleared his throat and Sam gave him a watery smile.

She and Richard had never been close, but he had been the patriarch of the family almost as long as she could remember. Even as a child, he had been the one to scold her if she got into mischief. He was the one who'd prohibited her from riding too fast or swimming too far into the lake. All of her brothers were protective of her, but Richard was different. Perhaps it was because he was the eldest and felt responsible for his family in a way others didn't. Perhaps it was because he was the heir and later on the viscount.

Ben was her favorite brother as a child; he was always babying and coddling her. She and Alan were closer in age, so they were playing together, causing trouble. Adam was the older brother who allowed her everything, and Richard was just always there. Just like Isabel.

She felt like she was going to cry, and Richard must have sensed it, because he smiled warmly at her, brushed a loose tendril from her cheek, and whispered, "Let's get you married, shall we?"

Chapter 15

The ceremony was swift and businesslike. Sam and John said their vows, signed the register, and proceeded out of the church and to the breakfast table. And that was it; Sam was officially Lady Samantha Godfrey, the Baroness of Ashbury.

The only memorable moment from her wedding ceremony was when the priest asked for the rings and John took out identical bands, simple in their design. Hers had an engraving at the back. John showed it to her before putting it on her finger. It read: *My Angel.*

Sam looked at him, her eyes filling with tears. It was the most beautiful ring she could have ever wished for. No diamond or other shiny stone could compare to the words engraved on her simple wedding band. He'd had the rings specially made for the ceremony, carefully choosing the words engraved. The thought filled her with warmth. The fact that it said Angel made her feel like Ben was present during the ceremony as well and that he would always be close to her heart. John's ring also had an engraving. It was the date of the ceremony and a sideways 8, the symbol for eternity.

Now, sitting in the carriage, Sam was able to study the ring closer, twisting it on her finger, looking at it from every angle. Her husband was riding outside, next to the carriage. They'd ridden out right after the wedding breakfast concluded, an hour before noon. John wanted to get an early start, but it took a while to load all her luggage into the carriages and say their goodbyes.

According to her husband, the travel to his estate would take about twelve hours, so they planned to stop at an inn halfway, rest, dine, and have a good night's sleep. The cook had packed some sandwiches for their luncheon, so they stopped only to change the horses, stretch their legs, and use the privy. John bought her a cup of hot broth or tea at every stop and was generally very courteous toward her. But other than a few polite words, they didn't talk.

By the time they reached their destination, Sam had spent about seven hours in a rocking carriage with her silent embroidering maid. She couldn't read in the poor light, since the sky was dark, and the carriage light was constantly shaking and rocking. She wondered how Gina was able to work with the needle and escape unscathed in such circumstances.

Sam was tired, and her stomach was churning from the travel. They stopped in a small village, at a tiny inn with a wooden sign reading *Quacks and Ducks* above the door. John helped her out of the carriage and slowly walked her to the inn door. He looked at her with worry in his eyes, so she wondered if she looked as bad as she felt.

John talked to the innkeeper, and then he walked her up the

stairs and toward one of the bedrooms. He opened the door for her and waited until she proceeded into the room.

The room was small, with one narrow bed across from the window and a washbasin to the left of the door.

"I hope this room is nice enough for you. I know it is not what you are used to, but we shall be home tomorrow afternoon." He smiled slightly. "It won't be much nicer, mind you. But after this inn, it won't look too terrible either."

Sam just stood looking over the room. She didn't much care about the size of the room or even the stained linens on the bed. The truth was, she was too weary to care; she just wanted a wash and a good night's rest.

"I've ordered a bath for you," John continued as if reading her thoughts. "Supper will be served in the common dining room downstairs. At seven. I'll see you there." With these words, he exited the room.

Sam frowned, wondering where he was going. A moment later, she was even more puzzled when her travel valise was brought up, but his trunks were mysteriously absent. Was he not spending the night with her? Was she going to spend her wedding night alone? At that moment, a bath was brought in and several maids rushed in pouring hot water.

She would worry about her wedding night later, she decided. For now, she resolved to enjoy a nice hot bath.

* * *

John sat at the supper table, waiting for his wife to grace him with her presence. He was tired from a long day's journey. Considering he hadn't slept much in the past several nights, he was in a foul and irritable mood. Add to that the knowledge

Chapter 15

that he'd have to wait one more night to bed his wife, and he was a raging beast. He'd felt on edge and impatient ever since that blasted day in the garden. But it wasn't like he could take her in the dirty old inn either.

He regretted that he'd stopped coming to her a few days before the wedding. But he couldn't endure the temptation anymore. It was getting more difficult, painful even, to keep his hands—and more importantly another organ—off of her.

He didn't want to take her virginity in her garden, on the floor of her library, or in a closet. She deserved better. And in order to safeguard her from himself, he had to cut his visits. His dreams of her were bad enough; he couldn't endure the real thing. Just this morning, he'd woken up tangled in his sheets, drenched in hot sweat, his sheets sticky with his seed. He was as randy as an adolescent.

He looked around the inn impatiently. Where was Sam? Why was it taking her so long to come downstairs? He shouldn't have left her alone in the room. They were married; he should have stayed with her.

We are married. The thought made him smile. Finally, his long-time dream had come true. He couldn't wait to start sharing his life with her. His Angel.

Sharing his life? John scoffed. He had nothing to share with her except for a crumbling manor and his broken body and spirit. What was he doing taking a brilliant young girl from the bosom of her family into a monster's den? His estate was in a horrible condition. He hadn't had the time for proper renovations yet. They would have to live in a half-ruined old manor for a good part of the year before it would start to resemble a comfortable home. Maybe not even then.

John had no idea how to make a home cozy. He'd never had

one. He could only hope Sam would know. He was putting way too much hope on her fragile shoulders. How would she be able to cope with his beastly nature, his injured soul, the failing estate, starved tenants, and crumbling manor all at the same time? This should have been bothering him all these weeks, not his randy cock.

He couldn't worry about that right now either. He ran a hand through his hair and gave a long-suffering sigh. Then he looked up and saw her. And his earlier thoughts and all his problems disappeared.

She was wearing a simple blue day gown with tiny flowers on the hem of the skirt and lining her bodice. Her hair was swept up, and a smile lingered on her lips. She looked pale and her smile was strained, but she looked enchanting, nonetheless.

He stood and drew out her chair, relishing her scent as she swept past him, her hair brushing over his arm as she sat. John lingered a few moments longer behind her, not willing to let go of her closeness yet. She turned to him in question, and he had to reluctantly move to his place across from her.

They ate in silence. Sam was obviously famished because her social niceties had abandoned her, which meant that John had to be the one to carry the conversation. He didn't know how to do that, but he wanted Sam to feel at ease with him.

"Was your journey comfortable?" he asked and grimaced. Nice conversation starter.

Sam nodded. "It was fine."

John chewed, thinking about what could he possibly talk about. "Ashbury Manor," he finally said. "I don't want you to have your hopes up concerning it. It hasn't been lived in properly for quite some time. My father was always in

London, and I... Well, let's just say I haven't exactly nestled there. To be honest, I find it difficult to feel at home anywhere after the war. I spent way too much time in makeshift tents and on the road. I don't know what a home should look like."

"Do not fret," she said good-naturedly. "I'm sure we'll figure it out. I am not exactly an expert hostess, but we can learn, can't we?"

"It's not just the house. The estate itself is abandoned, and the tenants' houses are in bad condition. You'll see why I was desperate to marry when you get there. There's a lot of work to be done."

She nodded mutely.

"Anyway, you should get a good night's rest. The journey won't be as trying tomorrow, but I imagine it won't be easy for you to settle into the house."

"You won't be sharing my room tonight, then?" She didn't look up at him as she asked, just poked at the chicken with her fork.

"No." His voice sounded strangled to his own ears. "You need your rest, and so do I. I don't think either of us would get that if I stayed with you."

She nodded again. Her lips were drawn in her thoughtful pout that he knew so well. He wanted to smile at the gesture and then kiss that pout off of her mouth.

His eyes dropped to her low bodice, the swell of her breasts rising and falling with every breath. At that moment, he wanted to curse his resolve not to go to her tonight. To hell with it; she was his wife. He had a right to her. But he didn't want her first time to involve stained linens in a cheap creaky inn. He was starved and rough. He wasn't sure he would be able to restrain himself enough not to hurt her. So the least he could do for her was provide a comfortable bed.

John forced his eyes to remain on his plate until supper was over. After that, his wife went to her bed, and he stayed at the bar, drinking ale until he was too tired to think about anything. He paid for the meal and drinks, went to his room, plopped a blanket on the floor, and settled next to his bed until he fell into a fitful dreaming state.

Chapter 16

Sam exited the carriage with the help of her husband and looked around. Ashbury Manor loomed before her. It seemed dark and unwelcoming, even abandoned. The lawn was overgrown with weeds; the house was covered in so much moss and trellis that Sam had trouble making out the windows. John offered his arm, and they both ventured inside.

The interior of the house wasn't much better than the exterior. It was dark and dank, no doubt due to the greenery covering the windows. They stepped onto the stairs, and Sam took hold of the banister, but it shook under her fingers. She instantly let go and stared up at John. He didn't seem to notice as he kept walking on, ignoring her stare. Apparently, when he'd said that the manor was crumbling, he wasn't exaggerating.

Sam heard hurried steps and heavy breathing coming from above, and a moment later, a plump, middle-aged woman appeared before them.

"My lord, my lady." She curtsied hastily, still breathing heavily.

"Mrs. Lawson, here you are," John said as they climbed to the first-floor landing.

"My lady Wife, let me introduce Mrs. Lawson, the housekeeper. Mrs. Lawson, Lady Ashbury, your new mistress," he added as the housekeeper curtsied.

"A pleasure." Sam smiled at the woman.

"I've arranged your rooms," the housekeeper said, still looking down.

"Good," John said, "then if you don't mind, please show my wife to her chambers."

"My chambers?" Sam blinked up at John. Were they to occupy separate bedrooms here too? She knew it was a common practice for most husbands and wives of the *ton* to maintain separate bedchambers, but her parents had shared one bedroom and she'd hoped her marriage would be like theirs. Apparently not.

"Yes, I hope you will find them comfortable. I have some things to take care of in the meantime. I trust you'll be fine by yourself?" John asked, already letting go of her arm.

Sam didn't know what to answer to that. They'd just gotten there, and he was abandoning her already?

"Of course." She smiled a wobbly smile, but he was already halfway down the stairs. *Splendid.*

She turned to Mrs. Lawson. "Please, lead the way."

Mrs. Lawson showed her to a spacious bedroom, a mistress's apartments. They were clean and orderly, although it seemed like the rooms hadn't been occupied for decades. Sam stepped inside her room and looked around. The moldy scent was present in every corner of the room, the floors creaked, and the furniture seemed old and neglected. However, it seemed like the room had been aired out and the draperies and sheets on the bed looked new. Well, at least that was good. She walked farther into the room, touching the furniture and running her finger against the walls.

She stepped into the dressing room. It was small, smaller even than the one in her rooms back at the Gage townhouse, but she'd make due. There was a door leading from her dressing room, and she walked toward it to investigate where it led. She suspected that it was a connecting door to John's chambers, and she wanted to see what his room was like. She came closer and rattled the door handle, but the door was locked.

Sam turned to Mrs. Lawson. "Where does this lead to?"

"The late master's chambers, my lady."

"Late master's? Where does his Lordship sleep then?"

"Down the corridor, my lady."

Sam frowned. "Is there something wrong with the master's chambers?"

"Not that I know of, my lady." The woman seemed unsettled by all the questions, and Sam decided not to pursue the issue further. She'd have to ask her husband those questions. If she ever saw him, that was.

"Thank you, Mrs. Lawson. I am ready for the rest of the tour now," she said with a smile.

The tour of the house proved to be very educational, although it filled Sam with dread. The west wing of the house was the worst of the two. It was drafty and even had holes in the walls and the roof in several places. Most rooms were empty, although some had old furniture covered by a dusty white cloth. The east wing was in slightly better condition, but it still lacked furniture, the carpets in the halls were moth-eaten, the rooms were cold, and the walls were bare.

The housekeeper explained that they had been ordered to ready the mistress's chambers, dining room, and the library before their arrival, but the rest of the rooms were to be closed, awaiting their master.

"His Lordship was very clear that we are to decorate the house under your supervision, my lady," the housekeeper said. "But we'll need more servants. The household staff currently consists of me, the butler Mr. Lawson, the cook Mrs. Everly, and her son, young Douglas, the stable boy. And we can't do everything by ourselves in such a big house. We have two young maids and two footmen who come from the village every other day, but I expect you'll want stay-in servants?"

Sam didn't know whether to laugh or cry. She was expected to put this abominable place to rights? And suddenly John's desperation to marry as soon as possible and whoever possible hit her hard. He hadn't needed a wife; he'd needed a mistress for his estate. Sam just wished Isabel was there to tell her what to do.

She took a deep breath. "Certainly. Are there more people on the estate we can hire?"

"I am certain we can find a couple of good workers, my lady. But the village is almost uninhabited. I doubt we can find enough to put this place to rights," the housekeeper said.

Sam's head started to ache. Where was she supposed to find the maids if there weren't many people on the estate? Perhaps she could ask Isabel to send some of their staff. Sam nervously looked around the room. "Is this the last of it?" she asked hopefully.

"There's still a nursery upstairs," Mrs. Lawson said, and

Sam immediately brightened up. A nursery. She'd like to see it very much.

* * *

John entered his bedchamber and took off his coat and waistcoat. His cravat followed, and he loosened his shirt at the collar. Now he could breathe easily again. He was still not used to the buttoned-up, tight civilian clothing, and he wouldn't have worn it if it weren't for his wife. He'd dressed up for supper, *for her*, but his efforts had been in vain. His wife had dined earlier without him. He didn't fault her for not waiting for him; he hadn't told her he'd be late. Perhaps not the best beginning of a marriage, probably better still than an awkward supper conversation.

He'd spent most of his day working with the villagers, helping them repair fences, shoveling dirt, and looking for servants for his estate, and he was mighty tired. *Good*. That meant he'd be able to fall asleep easier too. The day had been busy and productive, but throughout the tasks, he'd kept thinking about his wife. *How can one person occupy so much space in another person's thoughts?*

He wasn't certain she'd be receptive to him after he'd missed supper. She'd seemed pale and weary after the trip, too. He was afraid that she'd be too tired tonight and would refuse him her bed. He'd waited for far too long to keep himself in check, and that meant trouble no matter what happened this night. If she refused him, he'd be angry and irritable the whole day tomorrow. If she didn't, he would probably ravage her like a starved beast.

His cock strained against his breeches just at the thought of her, and he ran his hand over it. He had to curb his lust. Sam was a gently bred lady; she would not appreciate his savage passions. He ran a hand over his cock again and squeezed it. It was probably a good idea to relieve himself before he went to her. He hadn't had a woman in a long while, and even when he had, they were used to the rough treatment of soldiers. A gently bred lady like Sam, he assumed, needed a gentle hand.

John stroked his length and was about to unbutton his breeches when he heard a knock at the door. He jumped and before he could answer, the door opened, and his wife came into the room. She was wearing a pale blue gown with an indecently low bustline and bare shoulders. Her breasts peeked out from her bodice, leaving little to the imagination. It highlighted her tiny waist and accentuated her pretty golden eyes and her pale white skin. The gown was downright erotic. Fine, maybe it wasn't erotic, but in his current state, she might as well have been naked. His cock strained tighter against his breeches, and he prayed she wouldn't look lower.

"May I speak with you?" she asked in a low sensual voice.

"Why aren't you getting ready for bed?" John growled. His gaze lingered on her lush mouth before traveling lower to the swell of her breasts. He decided he wouldn't allow her to wear this gown in public. It was too revealing.

"I wanted to speak to you first," she said.

"About?"

She cleared her throat. "Are you planning to come to my bed tonight?"

For a moment, John caught his breath. Was she about to ask him to wait? He would die before he let that happen.

"Why... Why are you asking me that?" he asked hoarsely.

"Yes or no?" She raised her eyebrow.

"Of course, I am planning to come to you. You are my wife," he said, a little too harshly.

"Oh," she said.

"Oh? That's all?" he asked, half in outrage, half in disbelief.

"Well… Yes." She paused, confused at his expression. "I just wanted to know, that's all. You've been avoiding me for two days now, and even more before the wedding. I wondered if you… well, if maybe you didn't want to…" Her voice trailed off, and she turned as red as a beetroot.

"Oh, I want to," he growled and stalked closer to her. "I want to very much," he said in a whisper. He came so close to her that his breath wafted across her face, fanning loose tendrils of her hair.

"You do?" she asked, breathlessly. "Well, good then."

She nodded slightly and started to turn as if to leave.

"Sam," he whispered, placing a hand on her arm. She looked up at him, her eyes wide and luminous. "As long as you're already here."

He grabbed her by her arms and crushed her body to his.

Her eyes widened, and her lips parted in surprise. Her heat, her scent, was driving him to the edge. He lowered his mouth and took hers in a hard, open-mouthed kiss. Sam immediately went pliant in his arms. She was so warm, so lovely. His mouth slanted over hers, drinking her in, sucking on her lips. He couldn't get enough of her.

Her arms came up behind his neck, and she grabbed onto him tightly, as if she would crumble to the floor if she let go. His hands roamed her body, starting from her sides, up her ribs, then down her back. One of his hands settled at the back of her nape. His thumb caressed her jaw, urging her lips to part. She opened her mouth on a moan, and he took

159

advantage, thrusting his tongue in.

John groaned. She was warm, wet, and tasted like wine and sugar.

He took his mouth off her and stripped off his shirt. Sam stared at him with dazed eyes, not moving, just watching him, her breaths coming in frantic gasps. He slowly reached out and started unbuttoning her gown. Sam tentatively put her hands on his arms and traced them higher along his shoulders. John closed his eyes. Feeling her gentle caress on his skin was something he hadn't even dreamed of. He lowered his mouth and traced his tongue down her neck, stopping to nip on her collarbone. Sam whimpered in frustration. Her bodice sagged the moment he finished with the buttons, then he spun her around and started working on her corset.

Sam ran her hands along her arms, as if from the cold. "John?"

"Just a moment, darling. Give me one moment," he croaked, still working on her corset.

A moment later, he was pushing down her chemise and taking off her drawers. Sam stood there, unmoving, seemingly dazed and confused. She was standing with her back to him, so he couldn't see her expression, and John was glad for it. He was afraid he'd see her frightened look, and he'd have to stop. He wasn't ready to stop; not yet.

John picked her up and placed her carefully in the middle of the bed. Sam immediately started pulling at the bedsheets to cover herself. The moment John put his hands on his falls, she froze, her gaze fixed on his fingers. John closed his eyes and willed himself to slow down, to calm himself, but it didn't seem to work. The beast inside him was awakened, and it demanded he take Sam and bury himself in her warmth. He wanted her. His skin was stretched taut over his thick cock, his breathing was erratic, his hands shaking.

John unbuttoned his falls and climbed onto the bed. Sam's eyes grew round as he towered over her. The fear in her eyes was evident.

"Don't be afraid of me," he whispered.

"I'm not," was Sam's immediate reply.

He knew she was lying, but he was ready to take her at her word. "I want you too much to stop now."

"Then don't stop." Sam placed a hand gently against his cheek.

With a growl, John crushed his mouth to hers, parted her lips, and thrust his tongue inside. He swept over the silky corners of her mouth in a proprietary motion, while his hands roamed her body. He caressed her breasts and thighs, then squeezed her buttocks. Sam froze. John tried to force himself to go slow, but his ravenous body seemed to have a mind of its own.

John spread her legs wider and settled in the cradle of her thighs.

"Sam," he croaked.

"John," came her answering sigh.

He took himself in hand and guided his cock to her center. "Darling," he hissed between his teeth. "I can't wait any longer."

Sam bit her lip and nodded. John willed himself to go slow, to be gentle, but the moment the head of his cock met her warm, wet center, he lost control.

Sam cried out from the sensation and grabbed his shoulders in a vice-like grip. The feeling of her holding on to him like he was a lifeline broke the last straw of his sanity. He was too hot, too hard, his breathing labored. He wasn't going to be able to wait any longer. She was already wet, bathing the head of his cock in her juices, so he settled more comfortably between her thighs and pushed his cock inside her.

She was too tight. Too hot. And the moment he pushed in, she tensed. He didn't go far, only the head of his cock was inside her. Sam shut her eyelids tight and curled her fingers firmer into his shoulders.

"Relax," he croaked out. "Oh, God, please, relax." He couldn't stop himself, and he did not know how to act differently even if he could. All his previous lovers were experienced and enthusiastic. He had never bothered to learn the art of lovemaking.

Sam didn't protest either. She just held him tighter in her embrace. So he kept pushing inside her inch by inch, and after a while, her muscles gave in, and she relaxed as he entered her all the way.

She didn't cry or shout; she was just holding on to him with all her might, her eyes squeezed tightly. She felt so very good. Like heaven. He didn't want to prolong their lovemaking, not that he even could. She was in pain, and he was over the precipice. So, he just let go and sank into oblivion after several thrusts. With a low growl, he spilled his seed inside her and collapsed on top of her.

Chapter 17

When Sam opened her eyes, she was alone in her room. The weak light peeking through her curtains indicated it was still midmorning. She tried to move and felt her muscles ache in strange places. Then she remembered last night and grimaced in pain and embarrassment.

She shifted, trying to gauge where it hurt. It seemed like everywhere. The burning pain between her legs wouldn't go away. She still ached there and felt sore all over. It had felt so good to be in John's arms, so delicious to be kissed by him. But then he'd done *that* to her. That horrible thing.

Oh, God, was it always going to be like that? Would she have to endure that agonizing pain every night for the rest of her life? The thought horrified her.

After the act was done last night, she'd been shaking. At least when his comforting weight was on top of her, she'd felt somehow safe and protected, cherished even as he crooned sweet words in her ear. But then he'd given her a light kiss on the forehead and left the bed. She didn't remember how she'd gotten back to her room after that. Perhaps John had carried her over. But why? Sam was flabbergasted and confused.

She understood now why women referred to the marital act as unpleasant. Although she wouldn't call it that exactly. Uncomfortable, embarrassing, incredibly painful, yes. Unpleasant? No, it wasn't that. Maybe if he'd stayed with her after, kissed her, soothed her, she wouldn't feel so bereft. Still, could she keep letting him do it to her night after night? He said he didn't care for an heir. Children were her idea after all. Maybe he wouldn't mind if they didn't do that at all. That was an encouraging thought. Until she imagined a childless future and her world darkened.

She carefully sat up and moved her pillow so she could lean her back against the wall. If the act was always this terrible, how was she to explain all those women ruining their reputations over a tryst with St. Clare? She frowned in thought. Perhaps a tryst didn't include that; maybe it consisted of something else. Or maybe it wasn't painful for everyone. What if she was the problem? She closed her eyes tightly, trying to shake the thought away. Surely there was nothing wrong with her. What if the problem was with John? Perhaps it didn't hurt with all men. Maybe that's why all women flocked to St. Clare.

Was it fine to ask her husband questions such as these? Would he even know the answers? What if she disgusted him if she told him how she felt? She didn't want to displease him on the first day of their marriage. But she'd promised him friendship, had she not? And that implied being completely honest with each other. She took a deep breath. Oh, if only her mother was alive to advise her about such things.

Sam scrambled from her bed and rang for the maid. A moment later, the door opened and footmen brought in the bath and filled it with hot water. Apparently, her thoughtful husband had ordered a bath to be brought in as soon as she awoke. The fact that he'd thought of her before leaving the house was an encouraging sign. She looked at the hot bath in anticipation. Soaking her tired muscles sounded heavenly.

As soon as the servants left, she stripped off her clothes and lowered herself into the water with a moan. Her muscles relaxed, and the stinging between her legs receded. This felt so pleasant. All of her earlier thoughts disappeared, leaving her feeling languid and restful.

She lay there until the water grew tepid, then lathered her skin with soap as she contemplated whether to breach the subject of the marital act to her husband. On one hand, she wanted to be honest with him. On the other hand, wouldn't it drive a wedge between them if she refused him her bed at such an early stage of their relationship? Sam scrubbed her skin violently in frustration. She had known marriage to John would be complicated; she hadn't known, however, that it would become so from the start.

As soon as Sam went down for breakfast, Mrs. Lawson informed her that her husband had gotten up early, as was his usual habit, breakfasted, and left to work on estate matters with his tenants. He'd conveyed his regrets that he wouldn't be back for supper and asked Sam not to wait for him.

Sam didn't like the news. Was that how John saw their marriage? They would spend their days separately, not even share a supper, have marital relations, and sleep in separate beds after? Perhaps he'd planned on it when he was about to marry Evie, but Sam wasn't about to let that stand.

165

No, this was not the marriage she wanted, and she would tell him about it at the first opportunity. Of course, that meant actually seeing her husband, which she wouldn't have a chance to do until late at night. Perhaps she was overreacting. It was just the first day of them living together; they needed to get used to each other, to adjust to their new living arrangements. He had a lot of work to do, she knew that. He was also used to acting on his own. But he was married now, and he had to change his habits.

There was nothing she could do about it now. However, she could do something about other things. She picked up her notebook, took Mrs. Lawson by the arm, and proceeded to make plans for the manor renovations.

Mrs. Lawson was a lovely middle-aged woman. It turned out that John had hired her, her husband, and the rest of the household staff a week before his wedding. Apparently, the old baron had squandered all of his money away to the point that he had to let go of all the help. He'd lived with his valet and a butler in London and abandoned his estate and other properties. John, upon inheriting the title, sold all the unentailed properties, and everything else he could sell but kept the two remaining servants.

As Mrs. Lawson had told her the day before, there weren't many people left in the village to choose from. When the old baron became impoverished, the tenants suffered greatly. Those who could move away did, which left the place even worse than it was initially.

"I doubt he will be able to find more help to work on the manor from the village," the woman continued. "The young and the healthy moved on months ago, finding work where they could. They had families to take care of. Most of the people who are left in the village are the ones who have nowhere to go, or are too old and don't want to leave their homes."

Sam absorbed the information and shook her head in dismay. There was too much work for such a small amount of people. They would need to work day and night to get things in order. That, of course, would give her husband the perfect opportunity to ignore her. As selfish as the thought was, Sam couldn't help her distress over it.

"So, the village is full of the sick and the elderly?" she asked, another thought eclipsing her self-pity.

"Yes, seems like it," the housekeeper agreed.

"As the new mistress of the Ashbury estate, I think I should get to know the people, don't you?" Sam asked, remembering how she and Isabel would go to their village with food baskets, medicine, and other gifts for the villagers. Theirs was a prosperous estate, but they used to look in on the sick, elderly, widows, or women in confinement. The Ashbury estate was anything but prosperous, which meant that the people here needed her even more. "Can you please order the cook to make some pies and other portable foods? I would like to call on my villagers."

"Of course, my lady," the housekeeper answered. "But you don't mean to head out there alone, do you?"

"I certainly do. Why wouldn't I?"

"Well, you are new here. Mayhap you should wait for your husband to go with you?"

Sam contemplated that for a while. She didn't want to wait for John. She did not know when he would come back, and she didn't want to set a precedence of always asking for his permission.

"No, Mrs. Lawson. This is my village now, and these people are my neighbors. I think I can converse with them without supervision."

Mrs. Lawson just smiled, nodded, and scurried off in the direction of the kitchens.

A couple of hours later, Samantha and Gina were traveling toward the village in a carriage filled with goods. She was prepared to see the ailing estate, but what she saw exceeded her expectations, and not in a good way.

The village was devastated. No crops were growing in the fields, the roads were in an abysmal state, and the only bridge over the river was shaky and narrow. The village itself was small, and most cottages were ruined or abandoned.

Sam saw a rustic smithy and a small bakery shop, but other than that, no businesses were about. She didn't notice a school, or children, for that matter. Most of the villagers were elderly.

Sam got out of the carriage and started knocking on doors. Most of the occupants seemed gloomy and sullen, but their faces lit up once she introduced herself. Apparently, they'd heard that their master had married, and by their hopeful faces, she realized they knew she was supposed to bring capital and prosperity to their households.

She distributed food and talked to as many people as she could, trying to put on a pleasant façade to hide her dismay. Some villagers invited her into their houses, but seeing the pitiful interiors of their homes made her heart die just a little with every new person she met. The houses were drafty; the roofs were leaking. The state of these houses was even worse than Ashbury Manor, although she had doubted it could be possible when she first saw the place. Gina just stood beside her with a frozen smile on her face. As much as Sam had prepared herself for the ruin that was the Ashbury estate, she was still in shock. Her maid, on the other hand, had no idea what she was getting herself into.

When they moved toward the seventh or eighth house, Sam noticed men working on the roof. They were patching the cottage of an elderly couple. She moved closer and shaded her eyes against the sun. The men were working in their shirtsleeves, tirelessly patching the roof. One man, in particular, held her attention. *John.* He'd shed his coat and was working in his shirtsleeves like the other men. It was still cold outside for the beginning of May, but he was definitely over-warm. As she drew closer, he tilted his head up to the sky and wiped his forehead with the back of his hand.

The muscles in his arms were straining against his shirt-sleeves, and his damp shirt clung to his broad back and shoulders. He was filthy but exuded raw masculine power. Sam's mouth went dry just looking at him, and a strange tingle appeared between her legs. Then he turned and saw her. Sam had to swallow. He wore a look of hunger, joy, and something else on his face.

Sam forced herself to smile and waved at him. John exchanged some words with the other men and carefully leaped from the roof. When he reached her, however, he was wearing a dark frown.

"What are you doing here?" he asked gruffly.

"And good afternoon to you too, husband," she replied in mock cheer. "How is your day so far?"

He didn't stop frowning but sighed slightly. "You shouldn't be here alone. It's not safe."

"I am not alone," she answered calmly. "I am with Gina. And why is that not safe, precisely?" She raised an eyebrow at him.

"There are all sorts of men about. They might not know who you are and take liberties."

Sam swallowed her laugh and tried to look concerned. "Truly? Where?" She turned and looked around. "Do you mean Mr. Potter? Because I am certain I can fend for myself against a surly eighty-year-old." Her lips strained from holding a smile. But John didn't find it funny.

"If you wanted to visit the village, you should have told me. I would have taken you with me." He was still frowning, and it began to exasperate her.

"When? When was I supposed to tell you? Last night, at the supper you missed or after you left the bedroom?"

John flinched a little at her question. Good, it meant he knew he was in the wrong. She didn't get more reaction than that, however.

"How about we talk about this later? I have a lot of work to do." He gestured at the roof. "I can introduce you to the villagers later this week if you like. And I can show you the rest of the estate as well."

"That is not necessary, John. I am a capable young woman, and I don't need a chaperone anymore."

"Heed me on this, please. We are renovating the village, and strange men are working on the estate. Men I do not know well. I don't want you in the village alone." He gave her a look, something between concern and anger, and she didn't want to push him further. At the same time, she didn't want her marriage to continue down this path.

"I cannot just sit in the house and do nothing, can I? This is my village now. I want to get to know my people."

"You have a lot of work in the manor as well. Why don't

you do that and we can go meet the villagers later? Together."

"It is not done, John. I am the mistress of this estate. I can't do it later."

John looked away and sighed wearily. "Very well," he finally said gruffly. "We'll compromise. Next time, at least take one of the footmen with you." She smiled at him brightly, but his next words wiped her smile off her face. "Right now, you have to leave."

"But I haven't finished yet." She lifted the basket of food she held in her hand.

"Oh, you are indeed finished." John took her by the arm and tugged her toward her waiting carriage.

Sam tried to twist away from him. "The food will go bad. Besides, I've already met half the village; the other half will be upset if I don't meet them now."

"They won't mind." John didn't release his grip on her.

Sam dug in her heels and tugged her arm free. "I am not going back!"

John finally stopped and lifted his gaze heavenward. "Very well, you obstinate woman. If you're dead set on staying here… I'll help you."

"Thank you." Sam smiled at him and gestured for Gina to join them. The maid was standing several feet away, pointedly looking away, feigning interest in the scenery.

They finished distributing food in a little over two hours. John mostly stood to the side while Sam talked and charmed the villagers. They thanked her for the food, welcomed her to the estate, and expressed their well wishes to the newlyweds.

John looked bored and impatient. He didn't bother to convey the impression of a happy groom. He grunted in answer to congratulations and steered his wife away if she lingered too long at any particular cottage. By the time they were done, his mood had turned completely foul, and he kept looking at the sun as if he was angry that it kept moving too fast for him.

He escorted her to the carriage without a word and handed her inside.

She settled comfortably before deciding to speak up, lest he wander away without another word. "I realize that I've ruined your schedule, but you didn't have to be rude."

He looked at her as if surprised. "I wasn't rude."

"Oh." She looked at him with wide eyes. "That was you being polite?"

"Look, Sam." He lifted the hat from his head and ran a hand through his hair. "I am a soldier. Smiling at people and making small talk is not my thing. I have work to do."

"So, you've said." She turned away without another word and stared out the window. From the corner of her eye, she saw John hesitate by the carriage. He looked as if he wanted to say something but thought better of it and just shook his head. He then gently closed the door and gestured for the groom to be on their way.

* * *

John came home a few hours after suppertime. He bathed without hurry, changed his clothing, and sauntered into the dining room. A cold supper stood on the table, a lone wine glass next to it. Sam was nowhere to be seen. She'd probably eaten hours ago and was now readying for bed.

He was bungling this marriage. John had known he wouldn't be a great husband, but they had been married for a mere three days, and he was already failing. He'd abandoned her alone at the house, and when she'd tried to do something useful, he'd been rude and surly. This wasn't the way he'd wanted their marriage to go. Marriage to Sam was supposed to be easy: lively suppers, long conversations, passionate nights. When he'd dreamed of it, he'd never taken into consideration how inept he was in making someone comfortable. He wanted to make things right, but he didn't even know how to go about doing that.

He wasn't good with words. When he was in the army, he'd used letters as an outlet, writing out his feelings to Julie. But as soon as that communication had stopped, he'd forgotten how to use words for anything other than commands. Simply talking felt like torture to him. What was he to say to her, anyway? That he was sorry for how he'd acted? He was, but it wasn't as if he was going to change overnight either. He didn't want her roaming around the estate alone; he couldn't show her around either. Not until he found more workers. Although where he was going to get them, he didn't know.

Maybe he should have left her in London until everything here was done. He sighed and sipped on his wine. Maybe he needed something stronger tonight. Not that it ever actually helped. It only made everything worse as far as he could remember. Dull the pain for an hour and feel it all over again afterward. And the nightmares would worsen. No, he'd given up strong liquor for a reason, and he wasn't going to subject Sam to his drunkenness. His surliness was enough.

He finished his food quickly and went looking for his wife. He needed to talk to her, come what may.

John found her in the library. The room was cleaner than he last remembered, cozier. Sam was curled up in a chair next to the hearth, a book on her lap. She looked up as he came in and closed the book, marking the page.

"Are you enjoying the book?" he asked, grasping at something to start the conversation.

"I was," she said, pointedly referring to him ruining her enjoyment.

"I am sorry I interrupted then," he said, looking around. Then he walked over to the chair closest to her and lowered himself into it. "Do you think you can spare some time for us to have a conversation?"

"Do you mean an actual conversation or one where I talk and you avoid my questions, concerns, and doubts? Because we've already had that."

"Sam," he breathed and looked at her wearily. "I am certain you've already noticed it, but I have no idea how to be a husband. I should have told you before, should have explained it better..." He paused and shook his head as he stared at the fire in the hearth. "I was a soldier for most of my adult life. All I know how to do is follow orders and kill, how to command soldiers and make them kill. I don't know how to live a civilian life, I never have."

"That is not an excuse, John. You have to learn someday."

"I know. But I can't do it now. I don't have time to sift through my feelings and figure out how to be friendly and outgoing. I have people who depend on me. I need to help them now."

"And what about your wife? Do you mean to keep ignoring me?"

"I am not ignoring you." He frowned at her again. "But I can't be with you all day while the roofs of the tenants' houses are falling, the bridges are collapsing, and the stables drowning after the rain. Until I can find people to do the work, I need to do it myself."

Sam sighed. "Very well. You do the work and keep to your responsibilities. And I shall keep to mine." She raised her book and started reading from it again, ignoring him. Dismissing him. He rested his head on the back of his chair and closed his eyes.

How he'd dreamed of quiet evenings like this during the war. He'd dreamed of his Angel sitting like this with a book, reading to him. Of hearing her angelic voice, being surrounded by her innocence. And now she was here, with him. But he couldn't quite recreate the evening of his dreams. Of course, he could not. For those evenings to turn into reality, he had to be different. Not this broken man, who couldn't communicate with his wife properly.

He stood and slowly walked toward her. She looked up at him when he was a few inches away. He lowered his head and kissed her chastely on her forehead.

"Good night," he said and walked away.

Chapter 18

The sun was shining high over the horizon, the birds were chirping in the sky, and a light breeze beat against Sam's face, bringing the scent of fresh grass with it as she rode among the fields. She knew John wouldn't like it that she was out alone again, but she didn't care. She wagered with herself that he wouldn't even find out.

It had been a fortnight since their wedding, and she'd barely seen her husband. She woke up every day to find him gone and fell asleep before he returned. Sam was puzzled over John's behavior. She hadn't expected him to avoid her, but she suspected that was exactly what he was doing.

Perhaps she hadn't satisfied him in bed, and he didn't want to repeat the experience. The thought depressed her. As much as she hadn't enjoyed the act herself, she didn't want John to be disappointed in her. Or perhaps he hadn't cared for her attitude the other day when she'd visited the tenants. What did he expect her to do? Blindly follow his orders? She wrinkled her nose. That was exactly what he expected her to do. He had been a soldier, an officer, for most of his adult life, and he was not used to people disobeying him. Well, she wasn't one of his inferior officers, and he wasn't at war anymore. She was his wife, and she was not to be ordered about.

The worst part was she had no one she could talk to about this. She was used to settling questions by talking the issues out. Since her husband avoided her and her siblings were far away, there was no one she could vent her frustrations to. She'd even contemplated broaching the subject to the housekeeper once but quickly squashed the idea. Their household wasn't large, but she wasn't certain whether the woman would keep her confidence or if the entire village would know about her issues the next day.

Instead of fretting over her husband's strange behavior, she spent her days making plans for the manor renovations, reading books, and visiting the tenants. The house required a lot of work, and she'd even traveled to nearby auctions and fairs a couple of times to order some new furniture. She enjoyed this part of being a mistress, setting everything up to her liking, spending days shopping or sketching designs for the chambers. She was the most excited to create the library of her dreams. John's library was spacious and would be able to hold as many books as her heart desired.

John didn't seem to notice the changes around the house. Not that she'd had a chance to ask him about it. Perhaps he truly didn't care. Not about her, nor the state of the manor. Sam was resolved to make him notice both, even if she didn't know how yet.

She smiled as she rode through the field, feeling happy and free, when she saw a small form moving amidst the grass.

Next, she heard a scream from somewhere ahead and slowed the horse to a trot. A tiny figure kept creeping up closer to her as she peered at it. It was probably a small animal, except it was moving erratically, as if with no goal in mind.

"Carrie!" A scream pierced the air again, and Sam pulled her mount to a stop. At that moment, a small child emerged from the grass, pitch-black hair waving about, her gown tangled about her legs. Sam dismounted and caught the child by the shoulders. The girl halted with a yelp.

She looked at Sam with wide brown eyes, then tried to wiggle out of her grasp. Sam held fast. A child this small shouldn't have been wandering alone in the field. At that moment, the shouting grew louder, and a woman ran toward them. The woman picked her skirt up to her knees as she ran, stumbling on her way to the child.

"Carrie! You come back this second!" She stumbled again but managed to catch herself before hitting the ground. "Thank you so very much for stopping for her," she said with a thick country accent as she reached Sam's side.

She then knelt and scooped up the child. The woman was wearing an old bedraggled dark brown gown and a white, dirt-smudged apron around her waist. Her hair, just as dark as her daughter's, was collected in a tight bun at the nape of her neck, although several curly locks had tumbled out, probably during her dash for the child. Her eyes were dark, and her face was shadowed either with worry or weariness.

"Carrie is very inquisitive. I can't look away for a moment or she is gone."

"She looks like a lovely child," Sam observed with a smile.

"She is," the woman said, and then added begrudgingly, "when she's sleeping."

Sam laughed at that. The young woman was looking at the girl as if she were the center of the universe.

"Do you live here?" Sam asked. She hadn't seen either the woman or the child when she'd visited the village before; she hadn't known there were any children in the village at all.

"We've just moved here. Oh, where are my manner?" She puffed a strand of hair out of her face. "Linda Anderson, and this is my daughter, Carrie."

"Pleased to meet you, Mrs. Anderson," Sam said with a smile, then turned to the child dangling from her mother's arms. "Miss Anderson. I am Lady Ashbury. But you can call me Sam."

"Oh." Mrs. Anderson's eyes grew wide. "You're the baroness. I should have realized, I suppose. There aren't many pretty young ladies in the village. My brain must have gotten scrambled from running after Carrie." She was shaking her head and straightening her clothing, all the while still holding the squirming child. "Am I supposed to curtsy? Of course, I am—"

"No formalities are necessary. We are neighbors after all." Sam smiled warmly. "Do you mind if I walk with you to your home? I was out for a ride, but I'd much prefer company. There aren't many women my age in the village, as you must have noticed."

"No, there aren't." Mrs. Anderson grinned at her. "I shall be honored if you join me! My Christopher will not believe I just ran into you this way. Well, Carrie ran into you." Her face became shadowed for a moment. "Perhaps better not to tell him that part. He worries for little Carrie very much."

Something warm unruffled in Sam's heart. This little girl's father must love her very much if he was so protective of her. Would John act the same way if they ever had children? He'd said he wouldn't be involved with them, but surely his protective instinct would be greater than that?

"She is very active, and I am not always able to look after her with all the house chores I have to do." Mrs. Anderson grew quiet. Worry lines deepened on her face.

"It's quite understandable. Children aren't easy," Sam said with a confidence she didn't possess. She had absolutely no experience with small babes.

"I suppose," her companion said. "Carrie, be still!" The girl wiggled in her mother's arms, turning this way and that, peering at Sam's horse.

"Where did you move from?" Sam asked.

"Essex. I am from here originally. Lived here with my gran, Anne. But I've stayed in Essex with my in-laws since the marriage." Mrs. Anderson gave Sam a crooked smile, and her face took on a wistful expression. "I was visiting a cousin in London when I met my Christopher. He was in the Depot then, just for a few weeks before he left for the war. After we married, I moved in with his elderly mother in Essex. He thought it best, so she could help look after Carrie."

She paused to let her daughter down but didn't release her hand. Carrie frowned at her mother and kept tugging at her arm.

"You stay with me, Carrie. I am not letting you run wild again."

The child grumbled but settled down for a moment before starting to jump and collect wildflowers, tugging on her mother's arm at the same time.

Mrs. Anderson sighed but continued her story. "When Christopher came back from the war, he was let go from the army. See, he lost his arm, wasn't fit anymore." She shook her head. "He couldn't find much work, and he was also very troubled, you know. He couldn't sleep in a bed, and some nights he would just wander off somewhere. At first, he even couldn't hold his child, so wild he was."

"That must have been very difficult for you."

Sam regarded her companion with sympathy. John was much the same. Although she wasn't certain if he went wandering during the night, she knew he didn't sleep well.

"Did he... Is he better now?" she asked hopefully. If a man who'd lost his arm in battle could get better, then certainly John would too.

"Not a lot. But little by little he is. He loves Carrie, but he fears that something will happen to her." She drew a harsh breath and let it out. "It wasn't just the sleeping and his skittishness."

"He was skittish?"

"Oh, yes. Loud noises startled him. Sometimes he would jump up and act as if he had no idea where he was. But that wasn't the worst part. He couldn't find decent work. Some places were too loud for him, but most places would turn him away because of his arm." She shook her head again. "He risked his life for this country, lost his arm for it, and now nobody wants him." She paused and looked at her rambling daughter. "Except for us, of course."

Sam hadn't even noticed that they'd drawn up close to the village.

Mrs. Anderson gestured to one of the small cottages. "This is our home. We live with Gran Anne for now, but Christopher wants to fix one of the cottages for ourselves. When he learns enough how to do that, in any case. Today is his first day at work," she said so proudly, Sam couldn't hold back a smile. "Gran Anne wrote to me about a sennight ago. Said a new baron came here fixing the land and needed workers. And we decided to try our luck here. We weren't holding out hope. Nobody wants a cripple for a worker, but at least here is home."

"I am confident your husband will get along quite well here," Sam said with conviction. She was certain John was not about to turn away a fellow soldier.

By this time, they'd approached a little cottage.

"Would you like to come in?" Mrs. Anderson asked. "It is not much. The house is small and since we've just moved in, it's in a bit of a mess. I am certain you are used to more orderly accommodations."

Sam laughed. "Oh, believe me, Ashbury Manor is in a much bigger mess than your house."

"In that case, come on inside," the woman said with a smile. "I suppose Gran is not home yet. She likes to spend her time visiting the neighbors during the day."

She put the kettle on for tea as they entered and proceeded to clean up around the tiny kitchen, while Sam played with Carrie. The little girl only had some knitted dolls and a wooden horse but a broad imagination. Sam smiled as the dolls galloped through the entire house, getting in the way of the girl's mother and tangling in the drapes. Sam decided she would buy more toys for little Carrie once she went to one of the fairs again.

"Carrie, don't bother our baroness with your toys," her mother said as Carrie tugged on Sam's arm and was dragging her around the small house.

"It's no bother," Sam answered with a smile. "I quite enjoy

playing with her. She is a darling."

"She likes you," Mrs. Anderson observed. "You have a way with children."

Sam laughed. "I don't have much experience with them, but I would love to have children someday. A houseful." If John ever came back to her bed, that was. She smiled for the benefit of her new friend, but her stomach made a nervous flip-flop.

Mrs. Anderson put two teacups on the table. "You can let Carrie play on her own for a while. Let's sit and enjoy a cup of tea."

Sam nodded and seated herself by the side of the table. "You've done a marvelous job with the house. It is bright and clean. What more does one need?"

"More room?" Mrs. Anderson grinned. "This is a nice little cottage, but Carrie is so active she doesn't have enough space. Christopher promised we'll have a new place by winter."

"Oh, that's good."

"I don't believe it will come true though," she said sadly. "This estate needs a lot of work, and I don't believe we have enough hands to get it all done."

"Yes, John is always away at work because of it. And I am left quite alone in the empty estate. So it is good I finally made a friend."

"I imagine we won't see our husbands for many long days now. I don't presume to complain though. We have a roof over our heads, and Christopher feels useful. He feels needed. It makes such a difference to a man when he is able to take care of his family."

Sam frowned in thought. Did John have the same reservations? What if he didn't feel needed by Sam? True, he had spent most of his days working, but she'd never once waited for him to come back before she retired to bed. Perhaps, to change their relationship, she needed to make the first move.

"You said that when Christopher came back he was skittish, surly, and often in a foul mood," she started carefully.

"Yes, he was suffering mightily."

"When... how did he start getting better? I don't mean to pry, I just... I truly want to know."

Mrs. Anderson stared at the wall as if lost in thought. Then she turned and smiled at her daughter. "It was Carrie."

Sam cocked her head. "How so?"

"Well, when Christopher came back from the war he was like a wild animal. Withdrawn, angry, frightened. He didn't acknowledge Carrie for several months. I think he was afraid he'd hurt her. But after a while... He sought out her company. I think he was tired of everybody talking about the war in his presence, he was tired of adult problems, of nightmares. He just wanted to be surrounded by innocence again. He would play with her daily, collect flowers with her, and take her out on walks. He never wanted to spend any time apart from her."

Sam contemplated that silently. Perhaps John was the same way. She knew he avoided gatherings, and he didn't like to be surrounded by people; maybe he too needed a drop of innocence. Peaceful, quiet moments. *Can I provide that for him?*

"Why do you ask?"

Sam shrugged lightly. "Christopher is not the only soldier with these symptoms I gather."

"Oh, no. He met many in London. They were all discarded like so much garbage after the war ended. The Secretary at War advocated for some benefits, but whatever work they found in factories and such didn't suit many former soldiers. I gather there are many in similar situations. Lost, without direction or purpose in life. I am happy he had Carrie. I don't think I would have been able to shake him out of it on my own."

Sam stirred sugar into her tea, watching the liquid whirl around the spoon as if mesmerized. Her mind worked, forming a plan. Suddenly she jumped up and smiled at her new friend. "Thank you very much for talking to me about this, dear Mrs. Anderson."

The woman laughed. "If I am to call you Sam, you better call me Linda."

Sam nodded. "Thank you, Linda. I think you've just helped me solve a very difficult dilemma, or even two."

"I did? How?"

"I shall tell you everything if it works out." Sam walked to Carrie, still playing on the floor, and placed a kiss on her cheek. "I shall be coming out to visit you whenever I have free time if you don't mind. I truly miss female company. I've always had my sister to talk to or my best friend. Now they are both far away while I am here."

"I would be honored," Linda answered with a smile.

Sam waved to her new friend and hurried toward her waiting mount.

Chapter 19

The next day, Samantha walked toward the village with a basket covered by a thin blanket. The weather was beautiful, sunny, and occasionally breezy.

She found her husband in the fields this time. He was helping the farmers, shoveling dirt, and planting seeds. Sam smiled as she saw him. John wore fawn-colored riding breeches, black riding boots, and a wide-brimmed black hat. The sleeves of his white shirt were rolled on his forearms, the collar gaping open. Although calling his shirt white would be a stretch since it was mud-streaked and covered with flecks of dirt.

Standing there among the farmers, one hand on the shovel, muscles rippling under the sweat-soaked clothes that were clinging to his body like a second skin, he looked absolutely delicious. She wanted to run her hands along his body and bury her nose in the hollow beneath his throat. The thought brought on giggles, and she had to swallow a laugh before she approached him.

The minute she came up to him, the conversations around him ceased, as everybody started greeting her exuberantly. John turned around and regarded her with a frown. He waited until she finished with her greetings, then made their excuses, took her by the arm, and led her in the direction of the nearby woods. He didn't seem pleased to see her at all, and for a moment, she started having second thoughts about her plan.

"I thought I told you not to come here alone," he said when he stopped just by the line of the trees. He dropped her arm and watched her, still scowling.

"And good day to you too," she muttered and shifted the basket from one hand to another. She massaged her arm where he'd held her while dragging her toward the woods. He hadn't exactly hurt her, but he hadn't been gentle with her either.

John noticed her gesture, and his frown deepened. "Did I hurt you?" he asked gruffly.

"It's nothing," she said, lowering her arm and not looking at him.

"It is never nothing if I hurt you." He looked angry now. And then, noticing her basket, he took it from her hand. "This is too heavy for you. Why are you walking here alone with heavy loads? I thought I told you to always have someone with you?"

"Will you stop snapping at me? I brought you lunch!" she said, finally fed up with his attitude. "You don't have to be this surly with me. I wanted to spend some time alone with you, so I didn't bring a chaperone. Besides, I came right to you, so now you can act as the guard dog." She stubbornly tilted her chin and dug her heels into the ground. If he wanted her gone, he'd have to drag her out of there himself.

"You brought me lunch?" He sounded so surprised that she wanted to laugh.

"Yes, lunch. You have to eat, don't you?" She shrugged. "And I wanted to talk with you. So I decided we could combine these two activities and have a little picnic."

"You made me a picnic." He still looked dazed, staring at the basket in his hand.

"Well, the cook made the picnic. I just brought the basket here."

He finally looked at her. "I've got work." He gestured to the farmers.

"They can go on without you for half an hour, can't they?"

He looked as though he was about to protest, and Sam's heart sank. Then he nodded and turned to the farmers.

"I'm taking lunch," he called out. "You can relax for the next half hour if you like."

Sam smiled brightly at him. "Should we go to the stream?"

"Yes, I am filthy. I need to clean up." John looked at his clothes and hands and shook his head.

With that, they set out toward the stream through the woods. He held the basket in one hand and offered his other arm. They walked in complete silence until they reached the stream. Then he headed toward it to wash off the sweat and grime that had accumulated on his body since morning, and she set out to prepare their picnic area.

Sam spread out the blanket, set the basket in the middle of it, and settled on one side, taking out the bread, cold meats and cheeses, a couple of game pies, some fruit, and a bottle of wine. The cook had done excellent work assembling the basket. No wonder her arms ached from carrying it all the way to the field.

She turned and froze at the sight before her. John was standing in the water, knee-deep, in only his breeches. His bare torso gleamed in the sun, and his back muscles shifted with his every movement. He was extremely gorgeous, his body reminding her of a Greek statue. Her mouth went dry just looking at him. She had an inexplicable urge to lick the rivulets of water from his skin. She licked her lips. He turned then, his gaze heating with some unknown emotion. Sam swallowed but continued staring at him unashamedly. John gave her a salute and turned away to continue his ablutions.

After a few more moments, John joined her on the blanket opposite her. He'd dried himself near the stream and put his shirt back on, but his clothing still clung to his muscled back and Sam couldn't keep her gaze away. John took a bite of a game pie and regarded her curiously.

"I haven't had a picnic in... Well, let's just say a long time. Unless, of course, you count the cold, dried-up pieces of bread and spoiled cheese we ate during campaigns. We ate mostly outside too," he said between bites of food.

"The soldiers weren't fed very well, were you?" she asked, studying him. He rarely about his war experience with her. She didn't want to spook him. Usually, he avoided the subject like a plague.

He shook his head. "Sometimes we would go days without eating. It was worse if someone was injured. With no clean water or food, they were doomed to die." His face took on a faraway look as he talked, as if he'd quite forgotten she was even there. "We slept on the ground too. At first, it was uncomfortable..." He shook his head again and gave a tiny smirk but didn't continue his train of thought.

She was curious about what he was about to say but didn't

want to push him. Instead, she changed the subject. "How is Christopher working out?"

John took a sip of wine. When he set the glass back on the ground, he stretched out comfortably on the blanket. "He is a good worker. And works twice as hard as anybody." He popped a grape in his mouth.

"But you still have a lot of work on the estate, don't you?"

John nodded absently and popped another grape. "Adding one good worker isn't enough. I need dozens more if we are to farm in time, so we have a decent harvest in autumn. We also need to patch up old cottages for winter, clear the roads, not to mention our manor."

Sam nodded. She'd come up with an idea while in Linda's cottage the other day and had already put her plan into motion. If what John said was true, then her surprise would work out excellently for him. She smiled in anticipation of his reaction.

"What about you?" he asked and looked at her inquiringly.

Samantha wrinkled her nose. "The manor needs a lot of work. So I spend my days planning the grand renovation, buying the new furniture, and writing letters. All the pleasant things of being a mistress."

"You like it then?" He sounded surprised.

"I do. In all honesty, I thought I would be bad at this. Isabel always took care of everything. I barely helped with the chores. But our estates were well-established. I like that I get to build our manor from the ground up and set it up just the way I like it. I have my sketchbook filled with ideas for every room."

"I would love to see those," he said with a smile.

"You would?" Samantha's eyes grew wide. She'd never considered that he would have any interest in this. "I thought it didn't matter to you how I decorate the house."

"It doesn't." John shrugged. "I just want to see your sketches."

Sam's heart grew warm from his words.

"Come here." John beckoned her with his hand, and Sam shifted closer to him.

He tugged on her hand, and she collapsed on top of him with a yelp. He took her face between his hands and kissed her gently. His lips brushed hers, barely touching, like the wings of a butterfly, and she sagged against him in surrender. He continued feather-light kisses on her lips, then moved on to her eyes, her cheeks, and jaw.

Sam's hands drifted up his shoulders out of their own volition and entwined at the back of his neck. John turned her lightly until he was on top of her and moved his mouth to her throat. He kissed her more urgently now, licking at the place where her pulse thudded against her skin, and then even lower. She wished she could revel in his kisses and lose control of her mind, but she knew where this eventually led, and she stiffened under him. He raised his head and looked into her frightened, wide eyes.

She thought he would be angry with her or upset, but he just kissed her mouth as gently as he could and smiled at her.

"Do not fret," he said. "You don't have to be afraid of me."

"I am not," she said without conviction. He shifted his weight from her and rolled to the side without letting her go, holding her so they were still facing each other.

"Don't worry," he repeated, smoothing her hair. "I know I've hurt you, but I didn't mean to do it. It had been too long, and I lost control." He brushed his thumb over her cheek several times in a subtle caress. "But I shan't hurt you anymore."

"I don't want you to stop coming to my bed," she said, almost panicked.

His lips twitched as if he was holding back a smile.

"There must be something wrong with me," she said softly. "I've heard people saying that some women are just like that. They call them frigid, unable to relax and enjoy the act… I suppose I am like them."

She looked up into his eyes to see fury there. She was frightened of that exact reaction. If he knew there was something wrong with her, he would definitely stop coming to her. Why did she have to go and open her big mouth? But in the next second, his eyes gentled.

"Sweetheart," he said softly, "my lovely Angel." He kissed her on the mouth, teasing her with his tongue. "There's absolutely nothing wrong with you. I promise you."

"How can you say that when I know that it isn't like that for other women? I mean, I always hear about ladies flocking to St. Clare."

John's face contorted in a grimace, but Sam continued, unrelenting.

"Or, if you're right and it's not me then maybe your… your"—she waved her hand at his crotch—"your male organ is just too large for me."

John's lips twitched in laughter, but she continued, thoughtfully, "Perhaps it doesn't hurt with all men. Perhaps that's why women prefer St. Clare. His male organ must be too small to inflict pain—"

She was interrupted by a strangled sound from her husband, and she looked up at him. He made another choked sound before dissolving into fits of laughter. He dropped to the ground and wheezed with mirth. Sam had never seen John laughing like that. He looked so carefree and joyful that she couldn't help it; she laughed too.

Finally, he propped himself on an elbow and looked into her eyes. "Listen, I can't attest to St. Clare's *male organ*." He let out another chuckle before continuing. "I am certain it is a valid theory. However, I can tell you with complete certainty that there's absolutely nothing wrong with you. I... You just need to get used to this intimacy between us. We'll go slow. I shall not rush you, and I promise you, next time we make love, it won't hurt a bit."

Sam nodded, although she wasn't convinced.

John looked away for a moment and said through clenched teeth, "It's my fault. I pushed you when you weren't ready."

Sam reached up and kissed the side of his jaw. She then trailed her mouth to his ear and nipped at his earlobe. John chuckled softly, turned his head, and caught her mouth with his.

"That's enough," he said in a husky whisper after several minutes.

He was breathing heavily, and so was she. She was flushed, her breasts were aching, and she noticed that dampness had accumulated between her legs.

"I need to get back to work." He got to his knees and helped her up as well. "But I'll take you home first."

He started collecting the rest of the food back into the basket.

"Will you join me for supper tonight?" she asked, straightening her clothing and not looking up at him. She felt strangely embarrassed.

"I don't think so, Angel," he said huskily. "There's a lot of work to be done, and I've already lost a lot of time." He paused before continuing with a smile in his voice, "But I don't regret a moment of it."

Chapter 20

J ohn came home tired and aching from a long, hard day. He'd washed in the stream after work, so he sauntered into the manor with his clothing clinging to his body, his hair wet and still dripping slightly from the ends. He walked up the stairs and was about to go to his room and change for supper when he spotted the light coming from the library. John paused in indecision.

He knew that the library had become Sam's favorite room, and she was probably sitting there, reading a book or writing letters. The image appeared in his mind's eye, the dream he'd had since he received her letters during the war, of a blazing hearth and a loving wife reading to him. His heart constricted at the image.

Would Sam want him invading her privacy? Would she be glad for his company? He'd seen her just a few hours ago, and he'd missed her intensely, but he wasn't certain whether she felt the same.

Having lost the battle with himself, he ventured into the

room and peeked inside.

Sam was sitting curled up in a chair by the hearth, a book on her lap, her feet tucked under her skirts. John couldn't help but smile at the vision she presented. Her hair glowed from the firelight, and her eyes danced with humor. He wondered what she was reading. He stood there silently, watching her, drinking her in, feeding off of her innocence and the peace that surrounded her in this cozy room.

After a few moments, she must have noticed him, because she raised her head and smiled up at him. Her face lit up so brightly, and she looked so genuinely happy to see him, that a deep yearning appeared somewhere in the region of his heart.

"Have you had supper already?" she asked, closing the book and keeping one finger in place, so as not to lose her page.

"No, I'm not really that hungry," he lied. He was starving, but he didn't want to leave her to have his supper alone.

A little frown appeared between her brows. "But you've worked so hard. You have to eat."

"What are you reading?" he asked, hoping to distract her, and wandered farther into the room. She looked down at her lap as if checking the name of the book she'd been reading a moment ago.

"It's a collection of poetry, actually," she finally said. "I haven't read this one before. As vast as the library at Gage House is, I still find books here I've never heard of before. And there's still room on the shelves, so I can order more."

She was speaking enthusiastically about renovating the library, and he loved the sound of that. She was settling in and feeling comfortable at his estate.

"I'm certain you are tired but… Would you like me to read it to you?" She was chewing on her lower lip, and her eyes

196

still held that vulnerable light, as if she was afraid he'd refuse. *Not in a million years.* "I'll start from the beginning, for you. I haven't gone far yet," she continued in a rush.

"I'd love that," he said and settled comfortably on the floor next to her chair.

She got up, carefully stepped around him, and tugged on the bell. "First, I'll order us some sandwiches and warm milk. No matter what you say, you have to eat."

The warmth unruffled from his heart and traveled along his limbs. He felt a pleasant glow cover his body. Was this what it felt like to be cared for?

Sam settled back into the chair and started reading from the beginning. Her husky voice wafted around him, surrounding him with an atmosphere of peace. He sat, toasting by the hearth, his back propped against her chair, his head dangerously close to her skirts, her warmth and scent lulling him to sleep.

Shouts came from every corner. A man lunged at him, and John was able to duck and throw him over his shoulder. He took the knife and plunged it into the man's chest.

"Look out!" Ramsey yelled to him from the right. He was fighting two soldiers himself, laughing as he did so.

John turned, blocked the attack, and punched his attacker in the face. As soon as he hit the ground, John sank the knife into his heart. The blood rushed through the wound. John lifted his eyes from the knife and to the man's face. Only the next moment, the person in his arms turned into Sam. Her eyes, full of hurt and betrayal, regarded him in horror.

John's heart constricted in agony. He wanted to scream, but no sound would come out of his mouth. He clasped Sam's lifeless body close to his heart, clutching at her cold limbs.

He was jerked awake when the maid entered with the tray of food, and only then did he realize that he'd dozed off. His breathing was labored, and his eyes frantically searched the room for his wife. Sam stirred beside him and stood from her chair. John expelled a long breath of relief.

Sam took the tray and put it on the floor next to him. Then she collected her skirts and sat by his side, propping her back against the same chair she'd been occupying a moment earlier. John couldn't take his eyes off her. It was just a nightmare. His Angel was with him. Safe.

She sat so close to him that her shoulder brushed against his and her skirts were tucked against his knee. The small brushes and her warmth gave him comfort. He looked at her, mesmerized by her beauty, kindness, and spirit, wondering whether this was truly his life. How had he gotten so lucky?

She smiled at him and tilted her chin toward the plate. "Eat, I'll keep reading here."

He proceeded to do just that, nestled in the feeling of joy and peace. It was as if all his dreams about a peaceful life had finally materialized. And the nightmares? As long as he ignored them, they were bound to disappear.

* * *

The next few days proceeded in much the same way. John would come home to find his wife nestled in her chair, waiting for him with sandwiches, a glass of warm milk, and a book. She wasn't picky, so she read poetry, romance, Gothic books, and even scientific encyclopedias. He didn't care what she was reading as long as she was the one reading to him. He loved her voice. It was sweet and husky, full of wonder.

He loved looking at her too. Sometimes she curled up on her favorite chair, tucking her feet under her skirts, leaning against the back of the chair with a book in her lap. Other times she sat with him on the floor, leaning against him. He preferred the latter most of the time. But sometimes he enjoyed seeing her across from him, her hair glowing in the light of the fireplace. That way, he could see her entire face, the way her eyes glowed with humor when she read something funny, the way her throat rippled on a swallow, and her lips parted softly when she read something that disturbed her. He loved everything about those evenings, and he tried to spend as many with her as he could, even if he was too tired and lacked sleep.

She read to him, and later they discussed books, music, and art. Or rather, he listened to her talk as he made noncommittal grunts and occasional appreciative murmurs.

Being so close to her and yet parting at the end of the night sometimes felt like torture. It definitely made his days uncomfortable. But after using her for his own pleasure without giving anything back but pain, he decided to take it slow. He needed to let her relax around him more and make her feel comfortable without demanding anything in return. She was giving him too much as it was, and he didn't want to ruin it.

Besides, John loved her companionship more than anything. When he was with her, he forgot all the horrors of war, all the blood, mayhem, and ugliness that had been such a big part of his life for nearly a decade, and he found himself wishing he could spend more of his day with her. He had to restrain himself from taking a day off so that he could just spend the whole day frolicking in the woods with her, or spend it in the library, tucked against each other by the fire.

But he didn't trust himself to be around her for long periods. His mood swings still affected him. John still had the blasted headaches, especially when something inadvertently reminded him of the war. He'd wake up screaming and sweating, feeling suffocated if he rolled too far from the balcony doors. He needed to see the night sky instead of the ceiling, or he panicked until he got up and roamed around the estate at night. He wondered if Sam heard the noises he made at night. Although her room was several doors away from his, he was sure he was screaming loud enough to be heard down the hall, but she never said anything to him.

The nightmares and occasional fits aside, he still felt as if the world had finally righted itself. Until the day when everything went wrong.

John came to work early in the morning only to find several new workers. He frowned and wondered where they had come from. Still, more able-bodied workers could not possibly hurt. He approached the group of men.

"Where are you lads from?" he asked as soon as they were done with pleasantries.

"All over really," one of them answered. "We saw the advertisement in the morning paper yesterday and took the first hackney to Bedford. I assume more people will be arriving in the next few days too."

John's frown turned into a scowl. *What advertisement?*

"Good thinking, sir," Christopher remarked. "Hiring more soldiers, promising them the cottages once they're renovated. Should have done it sooner too, I reckon."

"Soldiers?" John looked at the group of new men more carefully. Their clothing was clean and pressed, but it was obvious it had seen better days. They looked ordered and tidy, but the weary lines on their foreheads and their haunted looks indicated that they'd gone through hell. The war.

A familiar noise buzzed in his head. He winced and took a step back. He didn't need more war chatter; he didn't need these painful reminders every day of the week. The men continued talking and getting acquainted, but John didn't hear them anymore.

"Christopher, you take the lead today, I need to go," he barked and left the field. His confused new tenants stared after him.

John didn't know how he reached home. His head ached, the buzz wouldn't subside, and his hands were shaking. Only years in the army and his trained body prevented him from falling off the horse in the middle of the road. He stalked into the manor, panting. His hands were clenched in tight fists and beads of sweat appeared on his forehead. He was angry with his wife because nobody else would be audacious enough to send the advertisement inviting the soldiers to his estate without even telling him. They'd spent every evening of the past week together and she couldn't have told him?

John rushed up the stairs. He needed to barricade himself in his room until he felt better; otherwise, there was no telling what he'd do in this state of mind. But as soon as he rounded the corner, he ran into Sam.

Her eyes lit up as she saw him and a smile broke out on her face. "You're home."

"Yes, thanks to you." He pushed past her and continued down the corridor.

"Are you angry with me?" she asked, following him. Her voice sounded confused and bewildered.

John whirled on her. "And why would I be angry? Because you went behind my back and invited all of England's soldiers to my estate?"

Her mouth opened in surprise. John fisted his hands tighter. He didn't mean to yell at her, but he couldn't hold back. He needed to hide out and wait for this mood to pass.

"I thought you'd be pleased," she said, a confused frown marring her beautiful face.

John took a deep breath so as not to implode. "You of all people know that I do my best to avoid soldiers, to avoid crowds of people and anything that would remind me of the war. You saw what it does to me! Why in the devil would you think I'd be pleased?"

She reared back as if he'd hit her. John closed his eyes, praying for patience. "I need to calm down. Please, do not follow me or God help me, I might hurt you." He turned on his heel and stalked farther down the corridor.

"But you were fine when Christopher joined you. You said he was your best worker!" His wife didn't heed his warning and stalked after him.

"Sam, leave me alone, I am warning you!"

"No, you don't get to shut me out just because we've had a hiccup in our relationship."

"A hiccup?" He opened the door to his chambers and stopped cold. The room was cleaned, the drapes missing, and his blankets by the balcony doors were gone too. He felt his wife hovering behind him in indecision.

"What in the hell happened to my room?" He turned on Sam slowly.

Her eyes were frantic, and she was twisting her hands in front of her. "I ordered it cleaned."

"I can see that. But where are my blankets?"

"I-I moved them to your room."

John took a step closer to her. "This is my room."

"Well, it is small and cramped. I thought you'd like to take your rightful place."

His eyes widened, nostrils flaring. "Where the hell is this rightful place of mine then?"

"D-do not curse at me," Sam stammered, her chest heaving.

"Sam, don't try my patience. Where did you put my things?"

"In the master's chambers," she said in a small voice.

"Ma—You mean the late baron's room?" He slammed the door with such force that it rattled on its hinges and stalked off in the direction of the master's chambers.

"Why are you so angry?"

"Why?" He halted and whirled to face her so suddenly that she ran into his chest. He took her by the arms, resisting the urge to shake her. "Didn't I explicitly tell you not to touch my room?"

"Don't yell at me," she whispered. He promptly let her go and ran his hand through his hair. "Your place is in the master's chambers," she continued quietly. "By my side. It is—"

John cut her off with a wave of his hand and stalked to the baron's rooms. He opened the door but didn't have enough strength to step inside the hated room. It was just the same as before. The drapes were different, the bedding was new too, and his things were occupying the drawers and over the hearth, but the room still felt the same. The same room his father had spent years in, hammering into his head that he was not worthy of it. The same room he'd hated with all the fibers of his being. He could just hear the baron's voice in his head: *"You're a worthless piece of garbage. Do not ever step inside of this room!"*

"John," his wife whispered from behind him.

"Get out," John pushed out between his teeth. This abominable place was not fit for her. He didn't want her essence mixed in with the ugly memories of the room. He didn't want to associate his failures with his angel of a wife. At the moment, however, she was the one raining misfortunes upon him.

"John, I think you—"

"I said, get out!" he growled and finally heard Sam's receding steps as she ran away from him. He closed his eyes and leaned his forehead against the doorframe. His breaths came in chaotic fits, his face was heated, and he couldn't control his shaking limbs. This had all been brought on by his wife's actions, yet none of it was her fault. He'd turned into something he'd never wanted Sam to see. He'd turned into the beast he'd been all through the years of war.

Chapter 21

S am galloped through the fields, enjoying the harsh whip of chilly wind in her face. Her face was feverish from embarrassment and anger, and the cool air seemed to have a calming effect on her. John didn't have the right to yell at her like that. True, she hadn't informed him of the decisions she was making, but she was just trying to surprise him. How was she supposed to know her tender and reserved husband would turn into a beast upon having his room moved to a bigger one?

Sam took a deep breath and slowed the horse into a trot. She wiped the tears from her face, not sure whether they were from crying or from the cold wind watering her eyes. She wasn't going to give up that easily on her marriage; it was only one tiny setback. Except that she'd wait for her brute of a husband to apologize to her first. The decision made, she continued trotting along, enjoying the cold weather and the dark clouds that befitted her mood.

She felt a few drops of rain hit her bonnet, and she raised her face to the sky. The clouds were dark and ominous, promising a summer storm. Sam urged her horse to a canter, but at that moment, the sky erupted and heavy rain fell from above. Sam saw a small shed in the distance and urged her mount in that direction. There was no way she was getting back home in this rain. At that moment, the sky was split in two and a magnetic, bright lightning hit the earth, followed by an angry clap of thunder. Sam's mount whinnied and reared in fright with such force that Sam had no hope of holding onto her saddle. She slid off her horse's back and rolled a couple of times as she hit the ground. Another clap of thunder frightened the horse even more, and it skittered away in the opposite direction of the shed.

Sam kneeled on the ground, watching her traitorous horse gallop away. She straightened her bonnet on top of her head, got up, shook out her skirts, and made a dash for the shed. A few moments later, she was safely enclosed in the dark, dank space. She looked around, still panting from her mad dash. The room was small and relatively clean. A tiny bed stood in the corner, a small table and a chair across from it with an oil lamp and a tinderbox on top. There was an empty hearth in the middle of the room.

Sam suspected the shepherd used this shed to rest in the evenings, so it held the bare necessities, but the empty hearth made her heart sink. She was cold and soaking wet. She'd need to warm up if she were to spend the night here, which she suspected she'd have to do since the rain showed no sign of slowing down. She shook out her skirts once more and tried to squeeze as much water from her clothing as she could. Sam took off her bonnet and untied her hair. It was tumbling out of her bun anyhow.

Sam took a deep breath. She should have stayed inside the manor. It was all her surly husband's fault. Now, she'd have to spend the night in this dingy old place, when she'd worked so hard on making him a warm and comfortable bed in his newly decorated, spacious room.

She wiped the errant raindrops from her face and settled on the bed by the table. *At least I know how to light the oil lamp.*

* * *

Sam was drifting off to sleep on the hard bed, lulled by the sound of rain beating an even staccato on the roof of the shed, when the door crashed open, bringing in a gust of freezing wind and raindrops with it. The dark figure entered the shed. Sam yelped and huddled farther into the corner.

"Oh, Sam, thank God!" came the achingly familiar voice. The shadow came closer, so she could finally see the outline of her husband's lovely face in the glow of the lamp. He stalked closer toward her, took off his hat, and threw it onto the table, then he settled in front of her, kneeling on his knees by the bed. "I've been looking all over for you. Are you hurt?"

Sam shook her head, studying her husband's troubled features. His gaze ran frantically over her body as he traced his hands over her limbs, feeling for injuries.

"Ow." Sam winced as he patted her thigh, and his head shot up.

"Does that hurt? I thought you said you weren't injured!"

"The horse threw me, but I am not hurt. Please stop shouting at me."

John wiped his face, looking anguished. "I am sorry, Angel, I didn't mean to shout at you. I've been worried sick. I've been out for hours, looking for you and—" He broke off and looked away.

He looked so forlorn and tired, as if he'd aged several years in one night. Sam reached out and stroked his face. John leaned into her touch and closed his eyes.

"I am unharmed," Sam crooned as her hand traveled up and weaved through his wet hair, her fingers stroking his scalp.

John stood suddenly, shook off his cape, and hung it on the back of the chair.

"Your hands are cold," he said angrily and stalked to the hearth. Realizing there was no wood, he cursed and looked around. Next, he took the lamp off the table and placed it near the hearth. Then he grabbed the table by the legs and hurled it onto the stone floor. Sam flinched and covered her face with her arm as the table fell apart with a loud thwack. A few more violent cracks and John had broken the table into a few pieces. He then placed the pieces into the hearth and dripped a few oil drops from the lamp onto the wood. He ignited the tinderbox and a few moments later, a tiny fire licked at the walls of the hearth.

John walked to the bed and ran his hand over her clothing again. "Your gown is wet," he said, his nostrils flaring in anger.

"John, would you cease growling at me?"

John closed his eyes and seemed to fight for composure. "I am not growling at you," he finally said. "Sam, can't you understand, this is all my fault?"

Sam raised her brow at him.

"Take off your clothes. I'll hang them near the hearth so they have a chance to dry while you warm up."

"You expect me to warm up naked?" Sam's eyes grew wide.

John's lips twitched in humor, and Sam was glad that he

hadn't lost all ability to smile.

"No, you won't be naked. Now come here."

Sam scooted from the bed and came closer to her husband. He started slowly but determinedly unbuttoning her gown, then untying her corset and layering her discarded clothing over the chair. His warm breath wafted over the nape of her neck, making goosebumps rise over her skin.

"Sam," he said hoarsely, then swallowed. "I hope you know that when I said to get out... I didn't mean from the estate. I was beyond angry, and I didn't want to physically hurt you. So I needed you out of my sight, a safe distance away from me."

Sam swallowed, thinking over his words. "You wouldn't have hurt me."

John laughed without humor, a hollow sound that made her stomach constrict unpleasantly. "You shouldn't say that, Sam. I could and I would hurt you. That's who I am."

Sam turned at that, the same moment her corset dropped to the floor. She stepped over it, standing in a single chemise and her underthings, shivering in the cold shed. But she had to make him understand. "You would never hurt me, John. No matter how angry you are. I am not afraid of you." She placed a hand against his cheek again, but he twisted away from her touch.

"I don't want you to have any illusions about me, Sam. Next time I'm in this mood, you run to your room and bolt the door. I can't control myself when I'm in a temper."

Sam shook her head, about to argue again, but he cut her off.

"You don't know me, Sam. Please, do not convince yourself otherwise. My painful past is what defines me. This anger

209

I have inside me has helped me survive, has helped me kill. God help me, I never want to hurt you when I'm in that state of mind."

"Very well." Sam took a step back and hugged herself, feeling colder than she had a moment ago. "Very well, I shall do as you ask if it makes you feel better, but I am not afraid of you. I know you would never hurt me."

John reached out and ran his hands over her arms. Then he took off his coat and placed it on the bed. "Sit," he said as he started unbuttoning his shirt.

Sam's mouth went dry as the shirt started gaping open, revealing his muscled neck and chest, heat rising from her throat to her face. If this was his idea of warming her up, it was working.

He took off his shirt and threw it over her shoulders, bringing his warmth and scent with it. Sam inhaled and huddled farther inside his shirt. John sat on the bed and collected her against his chest. Sam tucked her feet under her bottom and turned to settle comfortably in the circle of his arms, burrowing her head in the crook of his neck. She could smell his skin, the rain mixed in with his sweat, and had an uncontrollable urge to burrow her nose inside his warmth.

She pressed her lips against his neck instead and moaned lightly.

"Sam?"

"Hmm?"

"What are you doing?" he asked, laughter lining his voice.

"Inhaling your scent."

"I don't believe I smell that good," he said with a chuckle.

"For me, you smell like home."

John drew her deeper into his embrace and kissed her on

the top of her head. "I am sorry," he whispered.

Sam raised her head and looked up at him. His eyes were troubled again. She wanted to wipe that look from his face and never see it again.

"I am sorry I yelled at you and let the anger get the better of me. I shall try to rein in my temper." He shook his head. "I can give you millions of excuses for why I acted that way, but none of them will be enough."

"How about you give me one?" She kissed him lightly on his chin, his stubble tickling her lips. "Give me at least one excuse. I want to understand you better."

John heaved a troubled sigh. "My father wasn't very good to me. I do not have pleasant memories of this place, especially not the master's chambers. I am a third son and..." He grimaced, and Sam's heart ached for him. "I was never meant to inherit this place. That chamber was never meant for me, and I never wanted it either."

She licked her lips. "You can't live constantly in the past, afraid of your memories, unable to move on because of them. We can make new memories, lovely memories in that room."

He shook his head. "I don't know how."

"Then let me show you." She leaned in and pressed her lips against his.

It was a soft, comforting kiss. She didn't mean to arouse him. But John crushed her closer to him with a groan and took her mouth with his, licking against the seam of her lips, urging her to open for him. As soon as she did, he plunged his tongue inside her heat, devouring her. He tasted of ale and him, that taste of him that was extremely alluring. She shyly touched her tongue against his, and he groaned.

"Sam," he growled against her lips. "We shouldn't... I can't take you here."

"I want to." She plunged her fingers into his hair, drawing his head closer to hers, kissing him with all her ardor. She wanted to make him forget all his troubles, to distract him, to heal him. She knew she couldn't, it was a journey he had to make on his own, but she could at least comfort him in the cold of the night.

He softly laid her down with her back on the bed and kissed her chin, her throat, and ventured lower, licking and nibbling on her flesh. He reached her breast and took her nipple into his mouth through her shift. Sam moaned and arched against him, drawing her breast farther into his mouth, wanting to feel that contact again, that feeling that shot from her breast and settled between her legs. He swirled his tongue, and there it was again.

Sam put her hands on his head and held him tight. He kissed, licked, and nibbled on her nipple, driving her insane. She moaned, unable to form a coherent thought. He moved on to her other breast and the cold air wafted against the abandoned nipple. She covered it with her hand, and John immediately nudged it away, covering her with his palm. He played with her nipple, drawing circles with his fingers, pressing it, pinching it all the while his tongue did wicked things to her other breast.

Sam was writhing under him, her hair tangled on the bed, her legs shifting restlessly, needing something to fill the void at her center. As if sensing her turmoil, John spread her knees apart and settled in the cradle of her thighs. He covered both of her breasts with his hands and squeezed them as he ventured lower, nibbling on her skin through the shift. Sam wiggled under him, raising her shift higher along her thighs.

In one swift motion, John raised her shift to her waist. He then returned his hands to her breasts and started licking at her exposed skin. He licked his way down to her belly button, then dipped his tongue inside.

"John!" Sam wantonly raised her hips, searching for more contact, rubbing herself against his bare torso, needing him there at her center.

She felt him smile against her belly. Then he untied her drawers and took them off. He ran his hands against the insides of her thighs, above her stockings. His light caress sent tingles along her body, then he lowered his head and placed an open-mouthed kiss against her center.

Sam let out a gasp as a strange feeling shot through her. She didn't have time to contemplate the feeling, because the next moment, John was licking at her folds, drinking her in, thrusting his tongue inside her. All Sam could do was moan and twist under him, raising her hips at the same time, wanting more of the connection there, wanting to feel his stubble tickling her center, to feel his hot mouth devouring her, his agile tongue sending the feeling of pure bliss through her whole body.

She felt herself melting away and all she could do was feel. All the sensations gathered somewhere low in her belly, traveling lower and lower and then spreading along her nerve endings.

With a cry, Sam felt her body shooting off the bed. John held her fast and firm in his hands, while his mouth continued its sinful movements against her. She closed her eyes tight, bright light piercing through her subconscious. When she finally came to, John was lowering the hem of her shift and settling in bed with his back against the wall, gently placing her legs over his thighs. He picked up his cloak from the chair and covered her up to her waist with it. He then covered her upper body with his shirt.

Sam was breathing heavily, her eyes hooded, her mind jumbled. She still needed his touch, so she reached out her hand to him. He took it, slowly brought it to his lips, and placed a kiss on her fingers.

"Sleep, my Angel," he said, his voice hoarse.

Her eyes widened for a moment, surprised. Her gaze traveled down his body, where his erect length clearly protruded from his breeches. That couldn't be comfortable. "But... you..."

John shifted and winced, then readjusted himself in his breeches. "I'll be fine, love. Sleep." He raised her hand again and placed a light kiss on her knuckles, before lowering it and covering it with his clothes. "Rest, I'll wake you when it's morning."

Sam didn't have the strength or will to argue anymore. She huddled farther inside his clothes, surrounded by his comforting scent, and promptly fell asleep.

Chapter 22

John stirred the fire one last time. It didn't have much life left in it, and the shed had gotten colder. He needed to wake Sam, lest she freeze to death, but she was sleeping so peacefully that he didn't have the heart to rouse her. He covered her with their clothes and occasionally warmed the coat by the hearth before covering her with it again, but since the fire was dying out, he wouldn't be able to keep her warm much longer.

"Good morning," Sam said in a hoarse, sleepy voice from the bed. He looked up and smiled at the picture she presented. Her hair was tousled and tumbling over her face and shoulders, her eyes were still hooded with sleep, her cheek lined from sleeping heavily against one side.

"Good morning," he answered. He walked to the bed and sat on the edge. "Did you sleep well?"

"Mmm…" She stretched, pulling her arms from under the covers. She then sat up and enveloped him in a hug. "You're so warm," she croaked in her sleepy voice and placed her head on his shoulder.

John laughed and eased her away. "Get dressed, love. We need to get home. The fire is dying, and it will be freezing here soon."

Sam nodded and proceeded to get dressed. John tucked his shirt into the band of his breeches and threw his coat over his shoulders. Light shivers ran along his body at the warmth. He'd been cold most of the night, but he was used to being cold; he didn't mind that. Something else had bothered him though, much more than the freezing night air.

He'd spent most of the night with an erection and to say that he was uncomfortable would be an understatement. He'd spent the entire night in agony. He'd been certain he'd subside soon after pleasuring her, but she'd kept moving in her sleep and brushing against him, touching him and occasionally making delicious moaning sounds. He knew that he'd done the right thing. It's not as if he could have her on the cold and rough bed, without a mattress or even bed linens.

Serves me right. It was his fault they'd ended up spending the night in the shed after all.

"I am dressed." Sam's voice brought him out of his reverie. He looked at her. She was standing by the doorframe, bonnet on her head, a few strands of hair peeking out of it, a folded corset in her hands. She looked so beautiful, so innocent. Why had he married her? Nothing good could come out of their union. He'd ruin her before the year was out. He shook the grim thoughts out of his head.

"Let's go home. There must be a hot breakfast waiting for us."

* * *

Over the next week, John did his best to distance himself from his wife. He had lost his temper with her, and he didn't want that to ever happen again. He knew that the best way to ensure that was to keep away from her. He worked himself to distraction and stopped visiting her in the library.

John often ran up the stairs after work and stood by the door to the library, listening to the sounds inside, imagining her sitting in her chair, her feet tucked under her skirts, her lips in a thoughtful pout. He massaged the tense muscles of his neck and sauntered in the direction of his room.

He'd moved into the master's chambers after the night in the shed, as a reminder of who he was and what he was capable of turning into. She was too innocent to realize the danger she was in living by his side. He, the one person who was supposed to protect her, was the one person who could destroy her.

"John," his wife said softly from behind him, and he stopped in his tracks.

"Weren't you going to say hello?"

John grimaced and turned slowly to face his wife. "I'm sorry, Angel. I was hoping to retire immediately."

She nodded and fidgeted with her skirts before seemingly making her mind up about something and moving toward him. "Would you mind if I came into your room with you? I just wanted to talk to you about something. And seeing as how you are tired, perhaps I can do that while you change your clothes."

John wanted to refuse, he'd already opened his mouth to say no, but what came out was completely different. "Of course, Angel."

He cursed himself the moment he said it. Wasn't he trying to keep her away from him? *What about the dangers of you beasting out on her again,* his conscience screamed. But seeing her there, standing awkwardly, fiddling with her skirts, all he wanted was to scoop her up and kiss her senseless. He hated himself for being weak, but it was too late. A bright smile appeared on her face, and he fairly melted from the radiant glow in her eyes.

So he moved toward the room, Sam following in his tracks. The moment he entered, he started slowly stripping off his coat and waistcoat. Sam seated herself gingerly on the edge of the bed and watched him unashamedly.

John started on the buttons of his shirt and froze. Perhaps it wasn't the best idea to strip in front of her.

"What did you want to talk about?" he asked, peering at her from beneath his lashes.

"You've stopped coming to the library," she said with a slight frown. "Are you too tired for the readings?"

"I'm sorry, I've got a lot on my mind and this week has been really busy." He avoided a direct answer, and by the wistful expression on her face, she noticed it.

"It's been raining all week, so I wasn't able to see you at lunch either. I've really missed you."

John's heart leaped at her words. At the same time, he squirmed uncomfortably and moved to the window. He looked out into the foggy garden. *Why is it so bloody difficult for me to find peace?* He had everything he'd ever wanted, and yet he couldn't take full advantage of his life.

Sam heaved a sigh. "I was rereading the letters I wrote to Ben today," she said suddenly.

John was taken aback by the change in subject. He turned to her, propping one shoulder against the windowpane.

"He was the one who called me his Angel. He said I kept

him safe with my constant scribblings. That I saved him with my letters."

"He was right."

Sam shook her head. "I didn't save him in the end, did I?"

John chewed on his lip in thought before answering. "That's not how you saved him," he finally said.

She looked up at him in question.

"Sam, the war... you don't know what it's like. The death, the mayhem, the blood. Sometimes during a battle, you see so many of your friends die... It's impossible to describe with words. But having someone who cares for you, who worries over you and writes to you daily—it takes a lot of weight off your shoulders. When soldiers read the letters from their loved ones, they get transported back home for a short while. And that is how you saved him. That's how you saved me too."

Sam stood and walked toward him until she stood toe to toe with him. "Will you talk to me about the war?"

He shook his head. "No Angel, don't even ask. I shan't. It's too gruesome, too horrible for your innocent soul."

"How am I ever supposed to understand you?"

"You aren't. Sam... This marriage. It was a mistake."

Her eyes grew wide, and her mouth opened in astonishment.

"I shouldn't have condemned you to a life with me. I am a brute, a rude, rough soldier. There is not an ounce of gentleness in me, and you deserve so much better. I rationalized to myself that since I ruined you, it was the right thing to offer you my hand in marriage, but I've been selfish."

"No!" Sam exclaimed suddenly. "You weren't selfish then, but you are being selfish now. Will you ever try to listen to my side of things? To hear my opinions? Why do only your thoughts and feelings matter?"

"They don't. But you don't know the full truth—"

"Of course, I don't know the full truth!" Sam cried. "Because you won't tell me. I am tired of being the only one who works on this marriage. It seems like the only solution you ever come up with is to give up and run away!"

"I am thinking of you and only of you."

"Well, cease! Stop thinking and try listening. *I* miss you! I am *lonely* in this drafty old house. I am always alone, whether I wake up or fall asleep. I tried to fix it with our luncheons, and I loved our evenings together. But you..." She shook her head. "We live like strangers, and you seem to prefer it that way."

He ran his hand through his hair and spoke without looking at her. "We spend a lot more time together than most couples do. I know you probably think you want me around, but you don't. I have issues, Sam. Deep issues and I need to take care of them on my own."

"Why?" She looked up at him, her gaze full of hope and sorrow.

"Because I don't want to hurt you."

"John." Her voice was gentle as she looked straight into his eyes. "Do you remember that talk we had in the library, just after we got married? The time you said you didn't know how to be a husband?" She waited for an answer, so he nodded.

"Well, I don't know how to be a wife either," she said quietly then took his hands in hers. She brushed her thumbs over his knuckles and regarded him intently. "But I know how to be a good friend. You and me, we were friends first, remember?"

He nodded again under her inscrutable gaze.

"Why don't we start with that? Isabel told me once that

friendship is a partnership. It is not this one-sided thing, where a husband takes care of his wife and protects her from harsh reality. Friends share their worries and troubles with each other. Why don't you help me lift your burdens for you?"

"I don't know if I can do that, Sam." John shook his head. He untangled his hands from hers and turned away. "I have too many demons inside of me. I can't share all of them without dragging you down with me."

"How about you let me decide that for myself?" She came up behind him, and he turned to face her before his reflexes got the better of him. "Half-hour lunches and occasional one-hour reading sessions are not enough, John. I want to spend nights with you. Wake up next to you…" She looked at him, all wide-eyed innocence full of hope, and he didn't have the heart to deny her. He turned his face away before he gave in to an irrational impulse.

"You don't know what you are asking for," he said gruffly.

"Very well," she conceded quickly, too quickly. He didn't believe for a second that she'd back away that easily. "How about we spend more time during the day then? We can start with morning rides and breakfast."

She stood too close to him; he couldn't concentrate with her warm body almost pressed up against him. Her warm breath wafted around his neck; her scent muddled his senses. Suddenly, he wasn't interested in talking anymore.

"It's the middle of the night," he said softly. "How about we talk about it tomorrow?"

"At breakfast?" she asked hopefully.

"At breakfast," he repeated and tugged on her hand.

She braced herself not to fall, and her warm hands pressed against his chest. John bent down and took her into his arms.

He walked to the bed and gently deposited her in the middle of the mattress. He then took off his boots and climbed on top of her, covering her body with his. Sam smiled and pushed at his chest until he was lying on his back and she was straddling him. He raised his head and took her mouth in a warm, open-mouthed kiss.

She instantly sagged against him. He stroked her sides, her jaw, and cheek. He moved his hands on her with the greed of a hungry man. He licked at her lips until they parted and then plunged his tongue inside. He swept it inside her warmth, teasing her, daring her to follow his moves, and finally, she surrendered to him with a tentative stroke of her own tongue.

John groaned into her mouth and lost all control. His hold on her tightened, and he undid the sash of her dressing gown and pushed it down her shoulders. Then he turned her onto her back and nibbled on her neck. He stood from the bed, quickly shed his breeches and drawers, and climbed on top of her.

He kissed her as gently as he could, which was quite difficult with the need burning inside of him. But he would keep himself in check tonight. He wouldn't hurt her if it killed him. He lowered his head slowly and kissed her on her jaw, her collarbone, and lower. He licked his way down her chest toward her breasts, and when he reached his destination, he suckled on her nipple through the fabric of her shift. Sam moaned and arched into him.

He kept suckling and nibbling alternatively on both of her nipples, while his hands traveled up her legs and he hiked up the hem of her shift to her waist. He murmured endearments against her skin as his hand moved higher up the inside of her thigh. When he reached the patch of curls in the triangle between her legs, he was afraid she would stiffen again, but she just moaned, holding on to his shoulders as tightly as she could.

He started stroking her there, gently, lovingly playing with the petals of her femininity and finding moisture there. She started whimpering and making sweet sobbing sounds at the back of her throat.

"Shh," he crooned to her. "Relax, just lay back and let me do this."

"John, please..." she begged him. He settled heavier on top of her and sucked on her neck. At the same time, his finger that was making light feathery explorations of her soft folds plunged inside her center.

Sam arched up and gave a soft cry of pleasure. She clutched at him harder and dug her fingernails into his shirt. John found a little nub inside her folds and started circling it with his thumb, which seemed to drive her mad because she almost shot off the bed. He lowered her hips back to the bed with his other hand, while another finger joined the first one inside of her. He started rhythmic movements with his fingers, entering her and withdrawing, while at the same time his thumb kept circling the most sensitive part of her.

Finally, she started sobbing in time with his rhythm and pulsing around the fingers inside her. John grinned, continuing his careful movements with his fingers. John wasn't experienced in lovemaking, and before the night in the shed, he'd had no idea, that he would feel just as exhilarated by giving her pleasure as she did. The idea of making her senseless with pleasure was driving him to the edge. When he drew final shudders from her, he placed his cock against her hot, wet center and plunged into her in one swift thrust.

She stiffened instantly.

John went still and waited for her to adjust. She didn't move, just breathed quietly.

"Am I hurting you?" he asked in a husky whisper, praying she would say no, praying he could start moving again.

"No," she said just as quietly.

Then she took his neck in her hands, lowered it to her mouth, and sucked on it gently. He groaned and started moving frantically inside her. He drove into her hard and fast, not caring that it would end all too quickly. All he felt was her hot, pliant body under him, and around him. All he heard were her rhythmic cries urging him on. After several blissful moments, he shattered inside her, and it felt like he'd found catharsis.

* * *

Sam was lying in the crook of his arm, exploring his body with her fingertips. She looked so peaceful that he never wanted to leave the bed. He knew that he had to, however. He kissed her lightly on the forehead and moved to get up. She looked at him, her eyes wide, her gaze startled. He regretted taking her in his bed. It would have been easier if he were in her room.

"Come," he said. "I'll take you back to your room."

"What?" She drew the sheets higher over her body. She looked taken aback, as though not comprehending what was going on. "Why?" she finally asked on an exhale.

"Because you need to get some sleep. And me too." He moved to haul her into his arms, but she moved away from him.

"Why can't I sleep here?" She sounded like a little child denied her favorite candy. It made him want to smile.

"Because I am a restless sleeper, and you won't get much sleep with me. And neither will I." She opened her mouth to argue again, but he stopped her. "Please, Sam. We agreed to trust each other, didn't we? Just trust me on this. You don't want me sleeping beside you at night."

Sam swallowed, a tiny ripple appearing in her throat. She seemed so vulnerable; he wanted to take her in his arms and soothe her. But he couldn't give her an inch in this. If he did, he'd end up relenting and letting her stay the night. That wouldn't end well at all. She rose slowly to her feet, as regal as a queen, collected her dressing gown from the floor, and walked toward the door. John made a move to accompany her, but she smiled at him and said, "I can find my own way. Thank you." With a light kiss on his cheek, she left his room.

John stood looking at the closed door, then he looked down at himself. He was still wearing his shirt. He had been so eager that he'd forgotten to strip off his shirt and hadn't bothered taking off her shift. Oh, how he wanted to explore her entire body with his tongue, licking every nook and cranny, suckling on those rosy nipples, tasting her sweet essence. His cock grew hard again just thinking about it. He took himself in hand and groaned. The urge to go to her and have her again was almost unbearable.

He couldn't spend too much time in bed with her. He could have hurt her. Even if not with his ardor, he ran a risk of falling asleep with her in his bed. And with his nightmares being as violent as they were, he was afraid he'd hurt her in his sleep and not even realize it. With a sigh, he stripped off his shirt and settled down on his blanket by the French doors.

Am I ever going to be sleeping in a bed with a woman like a normal man? Or is normal not an option for me anymore?

Chapter 23

Sam didn't get a wink of sleep that night. She lay there turning the wedding band on her hand this way and that. *My Angel*, it read. How could John be so tender and gentle one moment and so callous the next? She put the ring back on her finger and puffed an indignant breath.

How could he have turned her away after the passionate night they spent together? Was he ever going to let her spend the night with him? She was hurt by his callousness, but at the same time, something in his deep hurt eyes told her that it was more complicated than she made it out to be.

She needed to talk with him about it. She had been sure they'd reached some sort of accord last night; she had been certain they could work out whatever the trouble was with him not wanting to spend the night with her. But she'd been wrong.

She was broken out of her reverie by a soft knock on the adjoining room door, and before she could answer, John stalked into the room. She looked at him, then at the window, and was surprised to see a faint light streaming through the curtains. It was already morning, and she hadn't even noticed.

"Good, you are awake," he said quickly, coming closer to the side of her bed. He was dressed in his riding clothes, holding a crop in one hand and a hat in another. "Do you need your maid to help you dress?"

Sam was looking at him like he was mad, trying to figure out what he was talking about. Apparently, he read her mind, because one side of his mouth kicked up in a smile.

"The morning ride. You asked if you could join me last night. Or have you forgotten?"

She was still angry with him for the way he'd kicked her out of his room, but she hadn't slept all night, and she didn't want to waste her energy arguing about it.

"I don't need Gina to dress, but I need a cup of chocolate before we go," she said and swung her legs out of the bed. He looked at her bare ankles, then slowly raised his gaze, looking his fill.

"Did I ever tell you that you have beautiful calves?" He raised an eyebrow.

Sam took a pillow and threw it at him. John chuckled, placed the pillow back on the bed, and kissed her on her cheek.

"I'll make you some chocolate and leave a cup in the kitchen. When you are done, come down to the stables. I'll ready the horses and wait for you there."

He folded his body and gave her a quick peck on the lips. Before she knew what was happening, he was already gone.

Sam dressed in record time that morning, performed her morning ablutions, and came downstairs. She wore her most comfortable pale green riding habit, brown jacket, and matching brown hat and gloves. She saw a steaming cup of chocolate on the table in the kitchen and smiled. She had prepared lunches for him, had made him tea and warm milk in the evenings while waiting for him to come home. Now, he was finally doing things for her.

Regardless of how their encounter last night had ended, he'd come to wake her in the morning to take her riding as she'd asked. He'd made her chocolate and was waiting for her in the stables. A warm, fuzzy feeling dissolved the bitterness that had nestled in her chest all through the night. Contrary to her thoughts on what had happened last night, he cared about her and wanted to please her.

After indulging in sips of warm chocolate, she went to the stables to join her husband on a morning ride.

They rode in silence for a while, enjoying the light breeze and the quietness of an early morning. They cantered, then galloped for about an hour, before John finally slowed his horse to a trot. They were riding through the woods, carefully ducking under branches and avoiding cobwebs. The birds were singing and chirping from tree to tree, the sun was streaming through the leaves. It felt like they were in an enchanted forest in one of the fairytales her mother used to read her when Sam was a little girl. She was so absorbed by this fairytale magic that she was startled when John finally spoke.

"I have nightmares," he said in an even tone.

She glanced at him, bewildered, but he was looking straight ahead.

"They are violent nightmares. I scream at night, toss and turn. Sometimes I wake up strangling a pillow in my hands." He paused for a beat before adding, "I cannot recall a single night since returning that I have not dreamed of war."

She still didn't speak. She was not sure what she was supposed to say to that, or if there even was something she could say. Fortunately, he continued his monologue.

"It's ugly, Sam. It's so horrible, you cannot even imagine, and I pray you will never have to. The blood, the destruction, the faces of people I killed cursing me into hell, faces of my dying comrades begging me for help. Little children…" He shook his head, unable to continue. "It is something I can never get rid of. I wish I could guard you from it. That's why you have to know. I can never sleep in the same bed with you. It is too dangerous for you. These dreams, they never go away."

She was silent for a moment. "It can't be forever, there must be some cure," she finally said.

"If there is, I don't know it." He took a breath and let it out before continuing. "It isn't just that. Even if I didn't have nightmares, I can't seem to sleep in a bed anymore. When I was at war, I would dream of a feather mattress and a pillow… But it's too soft and the walls suffocate me. I sleep on the floor next to the balcony doors, so I can wake up looking outside. Otherwise, I can't breathe, and this panic tries to strangle me as if I am trapped."

Sam was trying to digest everything she'd just heard. Falling asleep and waking up in John's arms was something she wished for with all her heart. And she didn't believe for a second that he would hurt her, asleep or otherwise. All she had to do was prove that to him. *How?* She didn't know just yet, but she was certain she would find the answer. She would make her marriage into a romantic fairytale yet, no matter what obstacles were thrown her way.

* * *

John wiped the sweat off his forehead and looked ahead. He saw Linda, Christopher's wife, walking toward them with her daughter. It must have been luncheon time. They had been working on the east side of the manor, and he was hoping to finish with it today, but they hadn't progressed a lot thus far. Christopher's little girl ran excitedly toward the working men, and John saw Chris's face light up with a smile the moment he noticed his family. He hopped off the ledge he'd been working on and hurried to meet them.

John studied the scene with a wistful expression on his face. Christopher grabbed his daughter, put her on his shoulders, then walked on and kissed his wife gently on the lips. All the workers erupted in cheers and low whistles. Christopher waved a silencing hand at them, and his wife turned beetroot red. Public displays of affection might be considered bourgeois from the standpoint of polite society, but common folk relished in emotional ties. These people were bourgeois, and they were proud of it.

"Do you think I'll ever find a girl like that?" a low voice said by his side. John turned to see a sandy-haired young man standing by his shoulder, still looking at Christopher and his family. John recognized one of the new tenants who had just arrived several days ago. Malcolm something. He and Christopher were close in age, and their cottages bordered, so they had become fast friends.

"Perhaps," John answered with a shrug.

"Definitely," Sam said sweetly.

John turned and caught his breath. He would never be used to the effect she had on him. She stood on the road, a basket

231

in her hands, strands of her hair playing in the wind. "I hear former soldiers make for the best husbands."

"Good day, my lady," Malcolm greeted her with a bow. The other men echoed the sentiment as they greeted the lady of the estate.

"Perhaps we can organize a celebration or a festival and invite young women from the neighboring estates," she continued, and John's mood darkened immediately. The talk of a celebration, hundreds of people on his estate, sent an unpleasant shiver down his spine.

"Perhaps we should discuss it privately before breaching the subject to the tenants," he said between his teeth.

"Come now, Master, you wouldn't deprive your loyal subjects of a celebration, now would you?" one of his comrades said light-heartedly.

"Yes, we need the distraction. The beginning of the summer is a perfect time for a festival!" another one chimed in.

"It is time this land saw a celebration," one of the older tenants echoed, and John got even surlier. Sam just had to go and make a suggestion in front of the workers, didn't she?

"A summer festival! Sounds lovely." Sam beamed at the workers.

"What are you doing here?" John finally asked, tired of hearing the exuberant glee about the blasted festival. "Are you walking alone again?" He looked around, searching for her escort.

"I am not alone. I am with you." Her smile hadn't faltered. She raised the basket a little. "Since you are working on the manor, I thought maybe we could eat in the garden. It's closer to here than walking down to the stream, or even back to the house."

"If you keep feeding me like that, I shan't be able to fit through doors soon," he said darkly.

John didn't know where that came from, but he was annoyed with her and was trying to pick a fight no matter what. He was already angry at her about the idea of a festival, and now, she further ignited his temper by endangering herself. He walked right up to her with angry, ground-eating strides.

Her gaze grew puzzled, and she started chewing on her lower lip. The action drew his gaze to her lips and sent jolts of awareness through his body. He wanted to draw her lip from under her teeth and suck on it. He was suddenly aroused, and that made him even angrier.

"I don't need you feeding me like a child," he grumbled. "I'd appreciate it if you didn't distract me during work."

"You didn't mind before."

"Well, that was before you started throwing ideas of celebrations in front of our tenants. So, we need to finish the manor in time for summer." He turned away, determined to walk away from her, angry.

"It was just an idea, John, no need to get surly again," she said, sounding confused. "If it's that unpleasant of an idea for you, we don't have to do it."

"Good. Then we won't do it."

"I just thought it would be good for the villagers. It's not like they have much to look forward to. And now that half of them are former soldiers... They deserve festivities. Would you be so selfish to deprive them of a celebration?"

John groaned inwardly. *She is right.* The people deserved a holiday, a celebration. Some time to relax. They'd gone through war, and many of them lost their loved ones, their lands, homes, and work. Now they were working harder than many of them ever had. The least they could do was throw a celebrative festival at the beginning of the summer. His foul mood didn't let him answer with grace, though.

"Very well," he said. "Do what you like. But I shan't be here to see it." He turned his back on her and left her standing there with a lunch basket and big round eyes, full of hurt. But he was determined not to think about that.

* * *

For the rest of the day, John took on the most exhausting physical labor. He hauled wood, moved stones, and ran back and forth between locations bringing necessary materials and throwing away heavy rubble. He was tired, filthy, and sweaty at the end of the day when the men went down to the stream to clean up. Christopher walked beside him on the way there, clearly wanting to say something, but not sure how to start.

"If you want to say something, just say it, Chris," John barked when they were nearly by the stream.

"Very well." Chris cleared his throat. "I think you are overreacting to the celebration. Lady Ashbury has her heart in the right place."

"She knows how I feel about big crowds, loud noises, and a crushing atmosphere. It was one thing to invite the soldiers over for work, but I can't deal with a party."

"None of us can, my lord." Chris threw him a sideways glance. "You need to remember that we've all been there. Some soldiers have it easy. They don't suffer as much, some of them get to move on. But not the men who are here. We all needed a fresh start, an escape from the nightmare that was war."

"For some of us, the nightmares haven't stopped." John halted in his tracks and leaned his back against the tree. "Nothing's changed for me."

"That's because you are still running." Christopher looked sheepish and apologetic. "I don't mean to presume to give you advice…"

"You've already started; you may as well speak freely till the end."

Christopher scratched his jaw and looked away. "I was worse than you when I came back. I drank. Heavily."

John gave a humorless laugh. "Haven't we all?"

"No, you don't understand. I would wake up and start drinking. And I kept drinking until I passed out just so I couldn't hear the screaming in my head. I couldn't even look at my own daughter. I ignored my wife, my mother. It took me a long time to get where I am, and I am still not as I was before the war."

"I don't think there's *as before* for men like us, Chris," John interjected during a pause.

"Maybe not," Chris agreed. "But there is *normal*. Whatever that normal is, and like it or not, you are not going to get there alone. I got this far only with the help of my family."

"You mean, I have to share the horrors of war with my innocent little wife? Is that what you did? Because I am not inflicting that ugliness on her, just to be rid of it myself."

"You won't be rid of it. But sharing the burden does make it easier." Chris paused and kicked at some pebbles with his foot. "No, I haven't told Linda about the horrors of war. The real horrors, I mean, the ones that keep me up at night. But she is not the only person I have in my life. Now, I have these men. They know what I went through. Believe it or not, most of them are going through exactly the same thing as us. But unlike you and me, they don't have loving wives willing to help them through it."

A loving wife. John's heart leaped at the thought. The guilt from the way he treated Sam earlier suddenly made itself known, eclipsing the heady feeling. He tried to shift his attention back to Christopher.

"Maybe this festival will help them find their families, too. But these men are the ones we can share our burdens with." Christopher paused again and looked at John.

John could feel his gaze on him, although he stood leaning against the tree, with his head lowered, his eyes closed. At the pause, John looked up at him. Christopher looked like he was going to divulge some secret or something he didn't want to say.

"I started talking with Malcolm one night," he finally said. "He had trouble sleeping in his cottage when he moved in. I had trouble sleeping in general. I would go out after Linda fell asleep, walk around the grounds."

John understood that all too well. He'd walked his estate grounds too many times at night, either because sleep evaded him, or because he was awakened by some especially nasty nightmare and he didn't want to go back to bed.

"I saw him outside, lying on his blanket, looking up at the stars." Christ huffed something between bitter laughter and disbelief. "Just like we used to do… sans the blanket."

He smiled then as if remembering the good old days. "We started talking. You can't imagine how good it was to talk through all the issues with someone who understands, who's been there. How liberating to finally talk about the war without censure, without people making you into a hero, or pitying you. It feels… good. Maybe you ought to try it."

They stood there in the woods, looking at the ground, listening to sounds of water splashing, and the workers' banter at the stream. John's mind went blank. He didn't know how to digest what Christopher had just said. He probably needed time to himself for that.

He pushed away from the tree and clapped Chris good-naturedly on the shoulder. "Let's clean up before the sun goes down."

Chris nodded and they both set off in the direction of the stream.

* * *

Sam sat at her vanity in her nightgown, brushing her hair, when she heard movement in her husband's room. She had planned a romantic late-night supper for him tonight, but after his cold reception at luncheon, she'd decided she wouldn't go through with it and dressed for bed. It was a little before midnight when she heard him come back, a lot later than he usually arrived. He was probably still angry about the festival, which she thought was absolute rot.

Sam was about to blow out the candles and crawl into bed when the adjoining room door opened, and John entered the room. He was wearing his dressing gown, with nothing underneath. The enticing V at his throat and chest revealed his naked, suntanned, and well-muscled body. Her mouth watered. His hair was still wet, probably from bathing in the stream, something he often did, rather than cleaning himself in the bath.

Sam swallowed and put her brush on her vanity table. "I was about to go to bed."

"I was looking for you in the library. Did you skip the reading today?" he asked as if nothing was wrong.

"No, I read after supper, but I got tired quickly," she said without looking up at him. She heard his soft tread on the carpet, coming closer to her.

"Not a problem, you'll have to read over the chapters I missed tomorrow."

She felt his hand playing lightly in her hair. He was so close she could smell him. Her favorite scent, soap and spice. So familiar, so lovely. She wanted to lean into his hand and brush her head against his palm like a cat. But she kept herself still.

"I am sorry about today," he finally said quietly. "I acted like a jackass. I am a jackass." She thought she heard a smile in his voice, so she looked up at him, a puzzled frown marring the skin between her brows.

"There you are," he said gently. "I've missed you. Will you forgive your brute of a husband?"

She stood up and walked toward the bed. "I don't know yet. Are we having a festival?"

"Whatever you want, Angel."

"And you'll be there?"

He let out a puff of laughter. "As if I'd leave you alone with an estate full of men." He smiled at her then, that crooked smile of his he used so rarely. The one she loved more than anything in the world, and she couldn't stay mad at him anymore.

"Come, Angel, come to bed with me. I need you."

She opened her arms, and he took full advantage of her generosity. He made love to her gently at first, and then fiercely, pumping into her with such ardor, as if trying to give all of his love to her in a single night. Sam fell asleep in the warm embrace of her husband for the first time since their marriage. Only to awaken alone again.

Chapter 24

S am sat on a log by the stream, sketching Carrie, as the child frolicked by the bank. Linda stood a couple of paces away from her child, ready to swoop in if she fell or wandered farther into the water. Sam sketched as the wind played with Carrie's hair, her slight frown as she studied a rock. It was the fifth, or perhaps sixth, sketch she'd made of the babe. She found it fascinating to catalog the ever-changing expressions on her face.

As the festival neared, Sam found herself seeking out Linda's company more often. They'd planned the celebration together, although neither of them had any experience in organizing an event as big as this, but that wasn't the main reason Sam enjoyed Linda's company. She was one of the rare souls who understood the burdens marriage to a former soldier could bring.

"Can you imagine the festival is just three weeks away?" Linda said as she collected a stone Carrie handed her and placed it in the pocket of her skirt.

"No." Sam smiled as she continued sketching. "Sometimes I think we will never be ready for it. But my sister, Isabel, is coming in a sennight, and she will be able to help."

"She is not married, right? Maybe we can find her a husband here?" Linda grinned at Sam.

Sam chuckled. "Perhaps."

"Unless, of course, she needs to marry a title."

Sam puffed a breath of laughter. "I don't think she cares one way or another. But she would be a perfect hostess. Besides, our brother, Gage, wouldn't let her settle for less."

"Well, we need as many women as possible present at the celebration or most of the village's current population will be sorely disappointed."

Sam chuckled as she studied her sketch. She'd sent out plenty of invitations to neighboring estates, inviting as many people as she could. She guessed women would flock to the Ashbury estate after the rumors surfaced that the estate had gathered over a dozen former soldiers.

Isabel was arriving soon too, with her brothers lagging a little behind. There was only one invitation that had gone unanswered, and it was the one she worried about most. *Evie.*

Sam hadn't heard from her since the day Evie left for the Somerset estate. The journey there had probably taken her about a fortnight and the mail would take longer still, but surely she would've sent a missive by now?

Sam felt bad that she hadn't tried to do more for her friend, even though Evie had urged her not to worry. As much as Sam believed Evie capable, she couldn't help but wonder if she was letting her friend come to harm.

Sam resolved to do something about Evie's situation as soon as the festival was over. For now, she had her tenants to worry about, but if she got no news of Evie by then, she would enlist John's help and they would bring Evie down to their estate no matter what. She was certain John would help her come up with a plan. After all, they were sharing their burdens now, and their marriage was shaping up to be similar to one she had always dreamed about. She rotated the pencil in her hand, studying her sketch.

"How is Christopher faring at work?" she asked Linda.

"Oh, he is quite happy. Proud even. I believe he is Lord Ashbury's right-hand man. He's quite boastful of that fact."

Sam smiled. "And how is he feeling overall?"

Linda looked up at her with a puzzled expression on her face, but understanding dawned and she gave Sam a reassuring smile. "It takes time. Little by little all the scars of war are disappearing."

"John says…" Sam placed a pencil inside her sketching notebook and closed it. "John has trouble sleeping on the bed. Does Christopher—"

Linda interrupted her, nodding vigorously. "He is better about it now, but sometimes I still find him outside, sleeping on the cold, wet ground."

"You do?" Sam's eyes widened.

"Yes." Linda nodded again with a wide smile. "I don't pretend to understand. And I don't need to. I don't need to make a fuss about it either. If he finds that's what he needs to do to feel better. I let him."

Linda turned then to Carrie, who extended another rock. She took it and placed it in her pocket and patted her babe on the head. Linda seemed so carefree and blithe. Sam almost couldn't believe that she'd gone through much worse times with Christopher than Sam herself was going through with

John.

Her words, however, gave Sam an idea.

* * *

Later that night, Sam entered John's chamber as soon as she heard him come in. John stood in the middle of the room, fastening a clean pair of breeches, and was otherwise naked. Sam paused in the doorway, watching the play of candlelight on her husband's muscled arms and back while he finished buttoning up. He turned to her then, a devilish gleam in his eyes.

"Couldn't wait for me to come to you, huh?" he said as he slowly advanced on her.

Sam almost forgot the reason she came to his room. She tried to collect her wits before he seduced her completely.

"No," she said, looking anywhere but at his gleaming chest. "I have a surprise for you."

"A surprise?" John's eyes widened a little. Then he winced and came even closer. He ran his hands up and down her arms and looked at her tenderly. "I love that you don't give up on the idea of surprising me. I was worried I frightened you out of that notion."

"I shall never stop trying to keep you guessing." Sam's smile was wobbly, but she couldn't help but remember her failed attempts at pleasing him with surprises. It was different now, wasn't it? He wouldn't react the same way, no matter his feelings.

"You always do," he said in a low voice, almost a whisper. Then he lowered his head and brushed his lips over hers. Sam stifled the urge to lean into him.

Instead, she jerked out of reach. "Yes, well… Don't distract me. Put your clothes on and follow me." She turned on her heel, ready to stalk out of the room, but he caught her arm and turned her back to face him.

"What, no kiss for your husband? Haven't you missed me?" he asked as he moved her closer to him until their mouths were a hair's breadth apart.

"You are diverting me from my goal," Sam breathed almost inaudibly, staring at his full lips so close to her own.

"Which is?" he asked just as quietly, tracing her jaw and cheek with his knuckles.

"You need to get dressed." Sam made a quick step back and ran out of the door before John pulled her into bed. His husky laugh followed her out of the room.

In several minutes, John entered her room dressed in a shirt he'd thrown over his head and hadn't bothered to tuck into his breeches, and a pair of old boots he used to roam around his estate.

"Well," he said, raising his arms and turning this way and that. "I am ready. Lead the way to the surprise."

Sam smiled at him, gave him a swift peck on the lips, and before he could put his hands around her, handed him the bundle of blankets to hold. He raised his brow in question, but she just smirked and beckoned him to follow her. She led him out of the manor by the side door and walked for several minutes in silence before reaching a naked lawn between the gardens and the woods. She turned to him and gestured to the bundle in his hands.

"You can put it here." She pointed to the ground.

"Here. On the ground."

Sam nodded in answer, looking smug.

"Very well, then."

John put the bundle on the lawn and knelt before it to untie the knot she'd used to keep the blankets together. When he was done, Sam helped him spread the blankets and left a couple of them as covers, although it was too hot to use them at the moment.

"Lie down," she said, her lips twitching at his bewildered expression.

"You want me to lie on the ground..." he intoned slowly.

"No, you daft man, that's what the blankets are for. I want you to lie on them." She laughed then and settled on one side of the blankets herself. She lay down on her back, facing the sky. Slowly, John took his boots off and joined her on the covers. They lay side by side for several moments, not talking, just gazing at the stars.

"When Ben was at war, he would write to me that he loved looking at the stars. It made him feel peaceful."

John made a grunting sound but didn't say anything more.

"It was the only thing we had in common. The sky." She smiled. "We would watch the stars and try to describe what we saw in them. I became obsessed with the stars, and I read legends about constellations, but I didn't like them. So I came up with my own."

"I remember," John said with a smile.

Sam peeked at him curiously, realizing what he meant. He'd received a good portion of those letters by mistake after Ben's passing.

"Did you know him?" Sam suddenly asked.

"Benedict? No. We probably crossed paths, but no, I don't remember him. I am sorry. I wish it could have been different."

"Do you? How?"

John heaved a sigh. "You know there's another legend about a constellation that I think fits our story."

"Which one is that?"

"About Hades and Persephone."

Sam laughed out loud. "You are not Hades."

"And you, I imagine, are more beautiful than her. And you brought prosperity and fertility to my estates. I just wish I could give you the kingdom you deserve. Not these ruins and a surly husband. A version of hell, wouldn't you say?"

Sam turned to her side and studied him with a frown. "I don't equate living with you to hell."

John grimaced, still watching the stars. "That's because we don't spend a lot of time together. I promise you, you would feel differently if I were around more. The war... it changes you. Not that I ever was particularly gentle."

"You are gentle," Sam protested. She laid her head on John's shoulder and hugged him.

John gave a huff of laughter. "You must be the only person in the world to ever think that."

"What about Lady Clydesdale? I thought that you were in love." She heard the bitter jealousy in her own voice.

John nodded. "We were... but it was a long time ago. I was but a child."

"What about your other relatives? Do you have anyone else?" Sam felt oddly disgruntled that John was all alone in this world, except for her and his estate. Certainly, there was someone else. Coming from a large family, she couldn't understand not having the full support of your relatives.

John heaved a sigh. "My brother, Josh, died young. But the eldest, Jeremy, had a family. He was a lot older than me, over a decade older. And he was married and moved to a different estate while I was still at school. I know he had plenty of daughters, but I never saw them."

"What became of them after he died?" Sam asked, stroking his arm.

"I don't know."

"You don't know?" Sam's hand froze mid-motion.

"By the time I became a baron, the property they lived on had been gambled away by my father. I don't know where they went after that."

"And you never tried to find them?" Sam sat up, looking at John with a frown between her brows.

"I never knew them."

Sam raised a brow.

"What would you have me do, find them and invite them to our estate?"

"Yes! They are your family. You don't know what conditions they are living in. If their property was gambled away, they probably had nowhere to go."

John grimaced uncomfortably. "I never thought of that."

"Well, obviously." She huffed.

"You're right. I shall ask my solicitor to find them first thing in the morning."

"Good." Sam nodded and lay back down on the blankets. "Are you certain there are no more of your wayward family members we need to hunt down?"

"I am certain," John said with a chuckle and lay down beside her. "I hadn't talked to Jeremy since I was about seven years old. I never saw his family. I never gave them a thought. They were never real for me."

"Weren't you ever lonely living like that?"

John chuckled again. "Not everybody's families are as tight-knit as yours. But yes, I suppose I was lonely. I never told you this, not entirely in any case. But when I received your letter, I gave up hope of ever returning home. To tell you the truth, I didn't have anything to come back to." He paused, and she felt cold even though she was wrapped snugly in her husband's arms. "My father never held any affection for me. My brothers followed suit. My mother was the only one who seemed to care about me, but she died when I was young. I told you about Julie and how heartbroken I was after my communication with her was cut..."

He kissed her lightly on the cheek. "I was angry, bitter at first. But after a while, all emotions were just jumbled inside to the point of numbness. I stopped caring about anything. I went out on campaigns like suicide missions. With nothing to dream about, nothing to lose. And then I received your letter." He smiled at the memory. Sam was watching him, transfixed.

"You signed your letter 'Your Angel.' But you have no idea how on point you were. You saved me. After that, you became my northern star. My constant. Every time I would grow desperate, I'd lose a friend, or get injured... Sometimes I'd be delirious with fever, lying in the hospital, and all I had to do was look at one of your letters, and I'd have this feeling of peace. Something to guide me home."

"I love you." Sam didn't know how the words escaped her lips. She didn't mean to say it; she wasn't even consciously thinking it. The words just slipped out from the bottom of her soul and landed on her lips.

John dipped his head and kissed her. Sam took his head in both her hands and answered his kisses, fervently, desperately. She felt extremely vulnerable after telling him she loved him.

And since he hadn't said it in return, she wanted to feel that love in his passion. As though John could feel her need, he clasped her closer to him, slanting his mouth over hers, drinking her in, licking at the corners of her mouth. His roaming hands were hot everywhere on her body. He turned slowly and gently laid her on her back and settled on top of her.

He hiked up her skirts and discarded her drawers. Sam felt cool air waft around her legs and her private place. She wanted to squirm, while John studied her form with passion-filled eyes.

"You are so beautiful," he said before covering her body with his once more. He kissed her again, while his hand played at her feminine folds, making her twist and writhe beneath him. She felt emptiness at her center, and she wanted to be filled by him everywhere in her body, her soul. Sam trailed her mouth down and sucked on his throat. John groaned and dipped one finger inside her.

Sam moaned and raised her hips, searching for more contact. The feeling was delicious but not nearly enough.

"John," she whispered, out of breath. "John, please, I want you inside me."

She blushed as she uttered the words, and John gave her a wolfish smile.

He lowered his mouth to hers and murmured against her lips, "Take me then. Guide me inside you."

Sam felt as he fiddled with his breeches, and a moment later, his hot shaft sprung from the confines of his breeches. Sam slowly reached out her hand and took him. John groaned and threw back his head. He was hot and thick. His skin was silky beneath her fingers. She tentatively stroked his length, watching every one of his facial expressions. She ran her hand over his length from the hilt to its head.

John seemed to hold his breath. Sam saw a tiny drop of moisture on the tip of his head. She ran her thumb over it, and John hissed.

"That's enough playing, love," he croaked. "Guide me inside you."

Hot waves ran through her body at the thought. Sam slowly brought his length to her center. John ran his length against her folds, and Sam dug her fingers into his shoulders and whimpered in frustration. She wanted more of him; she needed all of him.

"My dear Angel," John whispered and thrust inside her in one swift motion.

Sam gave a short cry as he filled her. She felt the glorious fullness, and she never wanted it to end. John rocked against her, and she moaned again. A slight tingle originated at the place where the hilt of his shaft rubbed against her. Sam moaned and rocked her hips, mimicking his earlier action. John grinned at her. He placed his hands on either side of her face and started rocking against her, sending delicious shivers up her body.

Small whimpers left Sam's throat with his every movement. She held on to him tightly, meeting his hips with hers with every thrust. The tingly feeling gathered low in her belly and spread all over her body with every rocking of their hips.

John was looking into her eyes intently, his face marred with a grimace of concentration.

"Just a little more, love," he said, speeding up his thrusts. "You're almost there."

Sam felt the sensation gather in her belly and burst inside

her. She closed her eyes and saw tiny stars surrounding her. It was as if she'd landed in the sky with those constellations, surrounded by the feeling of pure joy, love, and contentment.

She opened her eyes and saw John hovering above her. She could still feel him hard and full inside her. John took her by the waist and turned onto his back so that he was lying and she was straddling his hips. Sam felt the surge of power with the change of position. She was the one in control now. At the same time, she felt bereft of his comforting weight and the heat of his body.

"John," she moaned. "Touch me."

John smiled. He dipped his hands inside her shift and caressed her naked body. Sam rocked against him and moaned at the sensation. John took her hips and started guiding her carefully on top of him.

"Just like that, love," he moaned. "Move on me, just like that."

Sam repeated the movements with her hips, moving up and down his shaft, while his hands roamed her body, moving upward. Finally, his fingers brushed against her nipples. Just a little. Sam whimpered in frustration and pressed her breasts against his hands, searching for more contact.

John laughed but held his palms against her nipples in a way that brushed against her softly but didn't give her the full satisfaction. Sam rocked on his shaft, at the same time rubbing her nipples against his hands with every movement.

Moans were escaping her with every touch, every caress. She was whimpering loudly now, screaming in pleasure, not caring if anyone heard her.

Another wave of pleasure hit her. She saw bright stars again, the warmth unfurling low in her belly. Her body was covered in perspiration, and she felt pleasant exhaustion settle over her. Sam fell against John's chest, and he immediately put his arms around her. He rocked against her two more times, and she felt his hot liquid spill inside her. John froze, holding her tightly in his arms.

After a moment, he covered them both in blankets, with him still inside her, and kissed her gently on the lips.

"Sweet dreams, my love," he said into her hair.

My love. It wasn't exactly an admission of love, but after the glorious lovemaking, these words only proved to her what she already felt. He did love her too. She was certain of it.

* * *

John woke up when he felt a slight stirring at his side. He opened his eyes and saw his beautiful wife staring up at him. Her tousled hair was strewn partly over his shoulder and partly over the blanket next to her. Her sleepy eyes were heavy-lidded, her lips plump. She smiled up at him as she saw him open his eyes and stretched lazily. He couldn't remember the last time he'd felt this pleasure in waking up.

Her warm body was cuddled next to his, and he felt his arousal poking at her hip, ready for action. He got up, buttoned his breeches, and gently hauled her into his arms. Sam whimpered but settled comfortably in his arms. It was morning, and the servants would already be up and about, so he didn't want to embarrass his wife by making love to her on the lawn outside of the house. Instead, he carefully carried her into the house, up the stairs, and into his bedroom.

She rested her head on his shoulder and held on to him all the way until he carefully lowered her to his bed. When she saw where she was, she looked up at him, surprised.

He smiled at her. "I am not done with you yet."

John drew his shirt over his head and dropped his breeches. Sam's gaze lingered on his aroused flesh. He gave her a moment to have a look at him before climbing on top of her and making love to her all over again. Yes, he definitely enjoyed waking up with his wife.

Chapter 25

S am waved her handkerchief in the air like a white flag. She'd arrived home a few minutes before from a lunchtime rendezvous with John and had just enough time to straighten her clothing and coiffure when she saw the approaching carriage out her window. It bore the Gage family crest, so she knew it was Isabel.

"Goodness," Isabel breathed as she stepped out of the carriage and hugged her sister. "You look quite happy."

"I am!" Sam couldn't hold her radiant smile at bay. "I am most happy to see you. I've missed you!" She hugged Isabel again and, placing an arm at her waist, ushered her inside the house. They stepped inside the manor, and Isabel stopped to look at the place.

"It is very nice and bright in here." She looked around.

"Yes, well, we've painted everything in light colors. The late baron liked brown and gray, but we've stripped the walls from his dark influence. The renovations are not done yet, but most of the rooms are ready to receive their first guests since the remodeling. Yours," she said with a pointed smile, "is the nicest."

"Truly?" Isabel smiled in return. "Gage doesn't get the nicest room?"

"Do you see Richard helping me here? I sure don't." Sam chuckled and turned in the direction of the stairs. "We have seventeen guestrooms available, but I don't imagine we'll be using most of them for the celebration since a considerable number of guests will be using the cottages in the village."

Isabel shook her head in bemusement. "You look every bit like the mistress of this place. I am so proud of you, Sam."

Samantha looked at her sister and noted a glimmer in her eyes. "Oh, please, don't cry. Otherwise, I am going to cry too, and we shall turn into the two biggest watering pots in England."

Isabel laughed and wiped her eyes with the back of her hand. She then advanced on her sister and took her shoulders in her hands. "Mother would be so-so proud of you."

Sam swallowed audibly, a tear rushing down her cheek. She swatted at her sister's shoulder. "Now you've done it," she said with a nervous chuckle as she wiped the tear off her face and proceeded up the stairs.

"Have you heard anything from Evie?" Sam asked, a note of worry in her voice.

"Yes. As a matter of fact, I have a letter from her with me."

"You do?" Sam stopped in her tracks and turned to face her sister.

"Yes, it's in my valise. How about we get to my room, and I'll get it for you?"

"Oh, splendid! I hope it's positive news, I've been so worried about her."

They made it up the stairs and turned left into the family wing. Sam paused in front of the door before pushing it open.

"Here's your room." She smiled as she observed the wonder settle on her sister's face. The room was done in cheerful tones of yellow, orange, and pink. Something that would definitely put a smile on her serious sister's face. The walls were covered with paintings of beautiful landscapes, and small pillows were strewn about. It would have resembled the chambers of a Turkish sultan if the colors weren't so cheerfully feminine.

"This is lovely," Isabel finally breathed.

"Yes, I've had some time, and I decorated each guestroom in a different style. Now, hand over the letter, and I'll order a bath for you. Then we'll have some tea, catch up, and I'll show you the rest of the rooms. And the garden. The garden is just lovely!"

Isabel made a full revolution about the room and laughed at her sister. "I am so glad you are happy, Sam!" She then scrambled to her valise and rummaged through it. "Here it is!"

Sam took the letter and had an urge to rip it open right there and read its contents. "My quarters are just down the hall, but if you need anything, just ring this bell and Mrs. Lawson, the housekeeper, will take care of you."

She grinned and ran out of the room. Sam reached her quarters in a flash. She settled behind her writing table, opened the letter, and skimmed the contents.

Dear Sam,

I imagine you're extremely worried about me, although I've told you, there's no reason to be. We just arrived in Carlisle a few weeks ago, and I've been introduced to Montbrook's sons. They are both here, and they have been nothing if not polite and welcoming. I've had a frank conversation with Lady Montbrook, and she assured me that they wouldn't push me into a marriage until next season. And even then, I shall be free to choose my own groom.

As reassuring as this all sounds, I know you will still worry. So I urge you to not fret. I shall be married by the end of the summer yet. After all, I have a wager to uphold, or did you think I had forgotten?

I hope you are happy, Sam. I have received your letters, and I am so envious of you having a summer festival. I don't think I shall be able to attend. I am on the other side of England and am unlikely to make the trip in time. But please, give me more details. What is married life like? What is it like to have a love match?

Yours,

Evie

Sam stared at the letter, mixed feelings churning inside her. Evie was obviously trying to cheer her up. No matter what she said, Sam would travel to Carlisle to visit her after the festival. She wouldn't feel better until she saw her friend with her own eyes.

After Sam showed Isabel the rest of the house and the garden, they settled in the library, having tea and biscuits. Earlier that morning, Sam had told John that she wouldn't be visiting him with a luncheon for the next several days, since she would be busy with Isabel and Linda finalizing their plans for the festival. He put on a great show of being disgruntled, but in the end, kissed her long and thoroughly, said he'd miss her, told her to eat well, smiled at her, and walked away.

She'd secretly hoped he'd be more broken up about it since she was already missing him fiercely.

"And then, we can have a ritual bonfire. Each villager can bring some old thing and burn it in a gesture of ridding themselves of a bitter past and starting anew. What do you think?" Isabel looked up from her notes.

"How do you come up with ideas like that?" Sam regarded her sister curiously.

Isabel just shrugged. "I suppose I pay attention to what happens at every event. When you don't need to fend off the suitors, you can observe quite a lot."

"Do you ever wish that your life was different? That you were married?"

Isabel twirled a quill thoughtfully in her hand. "To whom?" she finally asked.

Sam shrugged. "I don't know, to anybody."

Isabel laughed at that. "No, I do not wish I was married to just anybody. Nobody who has ever proposed to me would make me as happy as Ashbury makes you." She put her quill down on the table. "Sometimes I wish I had an attentive, loving husband, yes. But this is just a useless dream. I haven't met any man who could be that husband for me. So why wish? I have a wonderful family. A viscount brother who needs me. I don't think I could be leading a more fulfilling life."

"Do you wish…" Sam paused, looking down at her lap. "Don't you ever want to have children?" she asked, wincing at the wistful tone of her voice.

"Well, I like children, but with siblings aplenty, I think I shall have enough nephews and nieces to…" She paused and studied her little sister's downturned face. "Are—?"

"I don't know," Sam answered quickly, her face turning crimson. "I have missed my monthly…" She turned away uncomfortably. "And I have been nauseous lately. But not terribly. You hear these stories." Sam shrugged.

"But that's wonderful!" Isabel leaped out of her chair.

"I am not certain yet." Sam let out a breath and leaned heavily on the back of her chair. "I am not sure if John will be happy about it."

"Why wouldn't he be?" Isabel walked toward her and settled on a settee next to Sam.

"It's something he said before we married. He said he wasn't interested in raising children. He said he would father them if I wanted them, but he wouldn't take an active part in rearing them."

Isabel tucked a wayward strand of Sam's hair behind her ear. "Why wouldn't he want to raise his children?"

Sam shrugged delicately. "He said…" She took a long breath. "He said he didn't know how. He didn't have the best examples."

"Well, that's just silly." Isabel smoothed Sam's hair with her palm. "He didn't have much reference on how to treat a wife either and look how happy he's made you."

Sam laughed, a merry sound. "Oh, how I've missed you, Isabel!" The sisters stood and flew into each other's arms, hugging, laughing, and crying all at the same time.

* * *

John entered his dining room to the murmur of voices and the buzz of genuine excitement. He'd missed several suppers since his sister-in-law had joined their household. One of the reasons for that was because he wanted to give his wife some time to catch up with her sister and give them privacy. But mostly he did it because they had so much more work to get done before the upcoming celebration in just a few nights he didn't have time for lengthy family suppers.

Today, however, all his in-laws had finally arrived. At least everyone who was still in England. The youngest of the brothers, Alan, was still somewhere on the Continent, but the rest were currently in his dining room.

As he entered the room, the warmth spilled inside him. His wife was sitting at one end of the table, wildly gesticulating in an animated discussion with her brothers. Her elder sister was pushing the plates closer to her brothers, urging them to eat and generally mothering them. John had told them to start the meal without him, since he wasn't sure he was going to finish the work on time. But for some reason, his heart wasn't in it, and he rushed home, leaving Christopher in command. Now, looking at the people gathered at his table, laughing and talking at the same time, he was glad he was there. This was something he'd wished for without even realizing it. A family. He finally had a family.

He smiled as he strode into the room. The men started to get up in order to greet him, but he gestured for them to stay in their seats. He walked toward his wife, placed a warm kiss on her forehead, received a bright smile in response, and took his seat at the head of the table. Just like he'd dreamed when he was young. A kiss, a smile, and a table full of family members. The only thing missing was a babe rocking on his knee. He shook the thought from his head. This part of his youthful dream did not have a place in his life. Too many changes were happening at once as it was. He didn't need a babe to turn everything on its head again. Although as he gazed at his wife across the table, he could imagine her belly swelling with his child, and an odd pride settled in his chest. She could be with child right at this moment. He frowned at the thought.

"So, how are the renovations proceeding?" Gage, the eldest sibling, crashed into his reverie.

"Almost done. Not all of it, of course, but everything necessary for the celebration should be finished by the end of the day tomorrow."

"That was fast. I don't think I've ever seen an estate taking shape in such a short period of time."

"When you have strong, willing workers, everything is possible. These are soldiers. They are used to working in horrid conditions, day and night. You give them food and lodgings, and they will work miracles."

His wife was gazing proudly at him from across the table. Her eyes gleamed with love. He was ready to drown in the depth of those eyes. How could everything be so wonderful in his life all of a sudden?

"I'll have to borrow your workers then." Adam chuckled from his left side. "Mine are getting too lazy, I'm afraid."

"Enough former soldiers are looking for work. I am sure with your background in the Secretary at War's office, you can get along with them quite well," John said around a bite of food.

"Yes, well, unfortunately, we don't have extra cottages lying around, and no land to build them on either. But I can trade you my villagers for yours once your renovations are finished." Adam flashed his white smile.

"No trade." John smiled in return. "They've put blood, sweat, and tears into this place, quite literally. Just like we did." He looked at Sam, and she smiled too.

"Indeed, who knew that I would be a better landowner than you, eh, Gage?" she teased her elder brother.

"That's a good point," Richard drawled thoughtfully. "We'll just hire Sammy here as the estate manager, and she will take care of it all. What do you say, Adam?"

Adam laughed good-naturedly. "You'll have to ask her husband, I'm afraid."

"If these are my only two options, then you take the soldiers. My wife stays," John said, looking his wife over intently, more of a lingering caress than a look. She flushed crimson and looked down at her plate.

They proceeded talking about other things, problems with crop yields, animal husbandry, new prices for building materials with the current state of the economy, and other things. John found it quite pleasant to share his worries and concerns with people who genuinely cared about his state of affairs and were eager to lend a hand or at least offer advice.

He wondered what it would have been like for him to grow up surrounded by such a family. If maybe he would have turned out differently, had fewer burdens, fewer troubles on his shoulders. By marrying Sam, he had gained strong allies in her siblings.

He wondered, once again, how his sister-in-law and his nieces were doing after the death of his brother. Had they received the letter John's solicitor had sent them? Sam was right. No matter the past, they were his family, and they were female. Which basically meant that they were helpless on their own. Unless, of course, his brother's widow had remarried.

In any case, the girls were his nieces, and he'd developed an urge to see them.

After supper, the men went to his study and went over some of the estate matters. Curiously, John couldn't wait to get done with work and see his wife. With the errands out of his way, he went up to his room, to find his wife snuggly nestled inside his bed. She looked up at him from under the covers as he entered the room.

"It is too cold on the floor without you," she said sheepishly. John smiled at her, stripped off his clothes, and joined her on the bed.

"You won't be cold for long," he said in between kisses. "I promise you." And with that, he proceeded to make long and leisurely love to her.

Chapter 26

As the celebration neared, more and more guests started arriving each day in the village. Most guests stayed in the village but Sam's relatives stayed with her and John at the manor. Sam's monthly courses didn't resume, but aside from that and light nausea, there were no signs of her being with child. She dreaded going to the doctor, but she dreaded talking to her husband even more.

Every night, she would fall asleep thinking she would tell him the next day, and every morning, she woke up coming up with more excuses to postpone the conversation. On the one hand, she wanted to be sure before she told him, which meant summoning a doctor. On the other hand, she wanted John present when the doctor confirmed or denied her suspicions.

I'll tell him after the festival, she decided on the morning of the celebration. She wouldn't risk ruining tonight by telling him her suspicions, just in case he didn't take well to the news. But why wouldn't he? It's not like she could get with child all by herself. It took two people, after all.

Another worry was the unaccounted-for guests: John's sister-in-law and her daughters. John had written to his solicitor several weeks ago and hadn't received any news yet. She hoped they were well. She also hoped they would be gracious enough to accept his invitation and act civil toward him, no matter what had happened in their family in the past.

Sometimes she thought that the worry over the festival and all the other issues were making her nauseous. Perhaps the stress was also delaying her courses. Worrying about possibly being with child didn't help matters either.

Breathe. Just breathe. She looked around the celebration spot.

The estate was decorated with leaves, flowers, and fruit, like a garden of prosperity. Isabel had worked really hard, turning the scenery into a tiny replica of the Garden of Eden. All they needed were the cherubs and the picture would be complete. The food was laid out on the wooden tables right there in the garden. Linda was helping the cook and other maids in setting the lavish feast. The punch was decorated with grapes and other fruit. Wine and ale were also set in abundance. The village had probably not seen such a banquet since its inception.

Sam looked up from setting the table and saw her husband striding toward her. He came up short just in front of her and gave her a swift kiss on her lips. She smiled to herself. He always did that now, showered her with small signs of affection. A kiss here, a touch there.

"Everything looks perfect, my Angel." He looked at her with such affection in his eyes she wanted to drown in it. "You are perfect."

"Not in this gown, I am not," Sam joked as she looked at her dirty day gown and the white apron tied around her waist.

"You are perfect in anything, love." He tucked a stray lock behind her ear. "Although you must know that I prefer you naked."

"John!" Sam turned crimson and looked around to make sure nobody had overheard his remark.

"What?" He laughed. "I can't tell the truth in front of other people?" He snaked one arm behind her back and held her close. "Go on then, you need to change. The celebration starts soon."

"We still have a few hours," Sam said, looking at the sun, still shining high in the sky. The festival would begin a few hours before dusk.

"Exactly. Just enough time for what I have in mind." He nipped on her earlobe and drew her toward the house, while she giggled all the way to the front door.

Just as they entered the hallway, John stopped dead. Sam looked up in the direction of his gaze and saw a middle-aged lady in the middle of the hall with six younger ladies around her. The youngest, still a child of about twelve or thirteen, was holding her hand. All of them were beautiful but with worry-strained features. Their clothing was clearly over-washed and oft-mended.

Sam looked from the group of women to her husband and then back again. He'd clearly lost the power of speech, and she decided not to fail him and act as the hostess she was. She smiled brightly at them and stepped closer, leaving her speechless husband frozen in the doorway.

"Welcome to Ashbury Manor. I'm Lady Ashbury and I am most delighted to make your acquaintance."

The women, as if shaken from their unmoving tableau,

finally looked at her and curtsied. The middle-aged lady moved closer to her and stopped only a few feet away.

"Pleased to meet you. Mrs. Amelia Godfrey." She sank into a curtsy, and Sam slid a discreet look at her husband.

He was studying the bedraggled girls with a look of horror in his eyes. *Godfrey.* It was John's last name, Sam's last name now too. These women were their family. John's sister-in-law and nieces.

"And these are my daughters," the woman continued. She proceeded to name all six girls, but to Sam's disgruntlement, she hadn't managed to remember even one. She still felt shaken by their unexpected arrival, although it wasn't exactly unexpected. They had been awaiting them for days. She just hadn't imagined their reunion happening like this. Her reaction was better than her husband's, however, and she thanked God she hadn't lost all her manners.

Thankfully, John eventually found his voice and regained the will over his leg muscles. He joined Sam in a few strides and stretched both hands toward Mrs. Godfrey in a gesture of extreme familiarity.

"We are delighted to have you here, Mrs. Godfrey," he said, clasping her hands in his. "You've arrived just in time for the festivities. They don't start for a few hours, so you have plenty of time to have a nap after your journey and relax. We shall have a proper family reunion and a conversation on the morrow."

"Let me show you to your rooms." Sam took her cue from her husband and led the group of women up the stairs and toward the family wing. Since most of the rooms were already occupied, Sam settled her nieces, some of whom were almost the same age as her, in twos, and gave their mother the nicest room still available in the house. She ordered them baths and told them to rest in the family parlor while awaiting the celebration.

They all looked exhausted. She did not know how long their journey had taken, so with a few words of hospitality, she decided to leave them to their own devices, leaving her personal maid Gina and a housekeeper in charge of getting them settled comfortably.

With that done, she went in search of her husband. He hadn't looked well when she led his relatives away, so she thought to give him some comfort before the celebration, but he was nowhere to be found. With too much to be done, after a while, she had to give up on tracking him down and went about her own preparations for the festival.

She wore her favorite lilac gown, the one she'd worn on her wedding day. The low neckline beautifully accented her bosom, and the color went well with her golden tresses. She knew for a fact that John also loved this dress. He hadn't been able to take his eyes off her the last time she had it on.

Sam wanted to look beautiful for him. She was eager to see him again and worried that something might have happened to him, or that he'd taken off after seeing the long-lost family of his eldest brother. He almost never spoke of his family with her, and she deduced from what he had said that it was a sore subject for him. Aside from the strained relationship he'd had with his father, she suspected what could have been nagging at him after seeing his brother's widow. She saw it in his face, just as he'd stopped short in the doorway. *Guilt.*

The family was obviously suffering, having no funds for food and clothing. John hadn't given them much thought since he came back from the army. He hadn't even spoken of them until she started poking and prodding. He cared for his villagers much more than for his own flesh and blood. In the meantime, they were probably counting pennies and stretching every piece of bread on their table so they could eat another day. Sam's stomach churned from the thought. She needed to give up thinking about things she couldn't change. They were here now. She and John would make certain they never suffered again. If she ever found him, that was. She was worried he'd lapsed back into one of his mood swings. She sighed a long weary sigh and headed out of her bedroom door.

Sam finally found John about an hour later. He was merrily drinking ale with the workers in the midst of the celebration. She squeezed her way until she stood right next to him.

"Wouldn't you rather accompany me to the dance floor?" she asked, gently taking a mug of ale from his hand.

He held the mug tighter, so she couldn't draw it away. "Sorry, Angel. I'm afraid I'd rather drink."

Sam drew a tight smile over her face. "And I'd rather dance."

She finally wrestled the mug from his hands and put it on the table. Then she took him by the hand and drew him away, accompanied by the low whistles and appreciative murmurs of the villagers, who'd witnessed their brief struggle.

Despite her claims of wanting to dance, she walked right through the dancefloor and stopped only as they reached the woods.

"What are you doing?" She whirled on him as soon as she stopped in a clearing far enough from anyone's hearing.

"I am celebrating." His speech was a bit slurred. *Is he foxed?* "Isn't that what you wanted me to do? Celebrate?"

"Since when does celebrating imply drinking? I thought

you gave up indulging in spirits!"

"Well, I decided it was time to give them another chance." He tried to turn away from her, but she put a staying hand on his arm.

"John," she said soothingly. "Look at me."

As he did, she almost gasped. She saw such pain in his eyes that she wanted to wrap him in a hug and never let him go.

"I failed them," he said hoarsely. "Just as I've failed everybody."

"Stop that!" she said harshly. "You didn't fail everybody!"

"I've failed my father, my fellow soldiers, my brother's family." He paused and ran a hand through his hair. "Isn't that enough?"

"You haven't failed me! I am here, and I am happy because of you. You haven't failed these villagers or the soldiers who moved here and found their home. Look at them! Happy, content. You"—she pointed a finger at his chest—"made it happen. And how can you say you've failed your father when you've restored the land he abandoned? And as for your brother's family—"

John interrupted her with a dismissive wave of his hand. "I failed my father by being born. By surviving the war, when none of his actual children survived in the peaceful country."

Sam stared at him, uncomprehending, as he went on.

"I am a bastard. You didn't know it, did you? Not legally, as my parents were married when I was born. But I am the child of an unknown lover my mother took in her husband's absence." He laughed bitterly. "Don't tell me I didn't fail you. I haven't told you the truth about me. Would you have married me if you knew?"

Sam just stood there in shocked silence, unsure of what she

was hearing until his last words finally registered in her mind. "Is that how low of an opinion you hold of me? Do you truly think the circumstances of your birth have ever mattered to me?" She narrowed her eyes when she'd rather punch him painfully in his gut, or his head. Any part of him, really. She wasn't that picky.

"It could have been a valet or a footman," he said with a grimace. "You thought you married a baron, but I might be a servant's son. Your children could have the blood of a serving-class fop," he sneered.

Suddenly, she felt like she was going to be sick. Nausea hit her hard, and she didn't feel like standing there and putting up with his drunken self-pity. She might be carrying his child at this moment, and he was standing there, feeling sorry for himself and taking it out on her. Insulting her and sneering at the mention of their unborn child.

"You know what?" she shouted at him. "I don't give a fig whose blood my child has in his veins. As long as he doesn't inherit this ridiculous habit of self-pity to the point of being pathetic. All I need from you is for you to be a decent-enough father, but to be honest, right now I don't think I want you around my child when he comes!"

Sam didn't realize she'd put a protective hand over her abdomen as she vented her frustration until she saw the direction of his gaze. His eyes were wide and filled with abject horror and disbelief. Was he that disgusted by the idea of having a child with her?

"You are increasing," he said quietly without taking his eyes off her abdomen. It was a statement of fact, not a question.

"No," Sam said and took a step back, without removing her hand from her abdomen.

"Yes, you are," he said, advancing on her. "Why didn't you tell me?"

He caught her by the arm as she retreated one more step.

"I'm not with child," she said with little conviction.

"I don't believe you," he hissed between his teeth. "Tell me the truth!"

"I don't know!" She shook her arm from his tight grip and stumbled back as he let go of her. "I haven't had my courses in a while, but I need to see a doctor to be certain."

"How long?" he whispered. All of his drunken stupor seemed to have left him.

"What?" she asked, confused.

"How long have you suspected you might be with child?"

"A few weeks," she answered weakly.

"You should have told me."

"I did just tell you! It might be nothing. I don't know yet." His attitude was starting to really frighten her now. *You should have told me.*

And what would you have done about it?

"I can't be here right now." He turned and walked away from her before she could utter a protest.

"Wait!" she called after him anyway, but he was already gone. Blended with the darkness, leaving her completely and utterly alone.

Chapter 27

J ohn walked around the grounds of his estate, listening to the joyful murmurs of the villagers and the guests. People were dancing and drinking merrily. In less than half an hour, the bonfire would start. He'd brought out his uniform to burn. No more past, he'd vowed. And just a few minutes ago, he'd thrown his vow out of the window.

When he was at war, he'd dreamed of nights like these. A celebration going on in his garden, families playing on the lawn, sweethearts stealing kisses behind the rose bushes. He'd wanted to have a home, a place that was his, a place full of happiness and laughter. Just like the one he had now. And most of all, he'd wished for a lady, his lady. A kind, beautiful soul, who would love him no matter what, greet him after hard days of work, read to him, smile at him, worry over him, and sleep beside him.

He had never wished for children. He didn't know how to cram them into his thoughts. He had never been around children, and his own childhood was not a very pleasant one.

But with a partner like Sam, he would figure it out. He knew it.

A partner. What a novel idea for a wife. Not someone to protect and look out for, but someone who shared his burdens equally and looked out for him in return. She was a revelation. And he did not deserve her.

But hadn't he come to the same conclusion when he decided to marry her? That she was entirely too good for him, and he took her anyway? Well, now was the time to pay up. She lived with his surly attitude, with his violent mood swings, his coldness and indifference, and she still hadn't complained. She plowed through, meeting his stubbornness with her softness, his rudeness with her kindness, and once again, he'd insulted her, offended her, and left her alone on the periphery of the festival during the celebration that she organized.

He turned and looked around, looking for her through the crowds of people. He'd finally found her standing beside her sister, a smile on her lips. But he knew better. Her eyes were sad and distracted. *My fault.*

He hurried toward her as her sister whispered something close to Sam and slowly walked away. Just at that moment, Sam looked up at him. Her face changed instantly into a guarded mask, her eyes inscrutable.

"I'm sorry," he said without preamble, as he drew close to her.

She didn't say anything. Just shook her head.

"I'm an arse."

She smirked.

"I love you."

She looked up at him then, her eyes wide. John smiled at her, a genuine smile that constantly tugged at his lips when she was near.

"I do," he said simply, putting his arm around her and drawing her close. "And if it turns out you are with child, I shall love him too."

"Or her." Her voice was muffled as she spoke, her face pressed against his shirt.

"Especially her." He nuzzled her hair and smiled against her temple. "Can you forgive me?" he asked, brushing a soft kiss on her hair.

She looked up at him and put her palm against his cheek. "I love you," she said with a transfixed smile on her lips and a lovely glow in her eyes. *My beautiful angel.*

"I'll never tire of hearing it," he whispered hoarsely.

Just then they heard the beat of the drums, the signal that the burning ceremony was about to begin. John took Sam's hand, and they both moved toward the fire. As the Lord and Lady of the estate, they were the ones to start the ceremony, by throwing their objects into the fire first. John raised his uniform and smiled at Sam.

"No more past," he vowed aloud.

"No more past." Sam smiled at him and raised her debutante gown. "We've suffered enough," she said to her gown and threw it into the fire, laughing. John's uniform followed, accompanied by the villagers' cheers. John put his arms around his wife, and they stood watching their villagers throwing their own past into the fire.

They went back home a short while after that. He made slow and deliberate love to her, making her moan and sigh and cry out his name. He needed to feel her in his arms, around him, hot and tight. He needed her to drown out the past, to clear up the way to the future.

The past, however, wouldn't be drowned out that easily.

* * *

John woke up in the middle of the night in a cold sweat. His wife was sleeping a few inches away from him, on her side, her back to him. She must have been so used to his nightmares by now that she didn't even rouse anymore. He was sleeping much better since they'd started sharing a bed, or more accurately, a floor. He wondered if the reason was the hard work that tired him out, the rigorous lovemaking they engaged in every night, or the reassuring warmth nestled beside him all night long. Or perhaps the magic combination of all of the above, maybe even something else added to the mix.

He hadn't been working the previous day, so that might have been the reason for his restlessness now. He looked out the window. The sky was light, perhaps minutes before dawn. Good thing the sun rose so early in the summer; he could do a lot of work in daylight. He gingerly edged away from the sheets, so as not to wake his sleeping wife. She looked so peaceful, with her golden hair strewn about the pillow, her naked limbs tangled in the sheets. How he loved just looking at her. He could spend eternity this way.

John washed, shaved, and dressed in about fifteen minutes, and then went out on a ride. He thought about his widowed sister-in-law and her six daughters, and what he could do for them. He could build a cottage on the estate. The Ashbury estate had never had a dowager house, but it certainly needed one. It would take a long time, though. In the meantime, they could all live in his manor, if Sam didn't mind. Of course,

Sam wouldn't mind. She'd insist upon it.

The alternative was to set them up in his London townhouse. Perhaps not a bad idea, considering the girls needed new wardrobes and a governess. He could provide it all for them. He could go to London with them for a while and take care of everything for them. After all, he wasn't needed as much at the estate anymore. All the necessary renovations were done, and the rest could be done without his supervision. He'd leave Christopher in charge, give him instructions, and start living as a baron should. The leisurely life of an aristocrat. He snorted at the idea.

After years of killing, fighting for his life, and trudging through enemy lines, was he finally about to have the peaceful life he had dreamed about? It felt unreal. John smiled and urged his horse to canter back to the house.

* * *

Sam sat on a log, sketching the scenery. She heard footsteps behind her and smiled.

"Beautiful," John said as he came to stand beside her.

"Yes, the view is truly splendid, isn't it?" she asked without lifting her eyes from her sketch.

"I didn't mean the view." He sat by her side and tucked a loose curl behind her ear. "I meant you," he whispered huskily.

She laughed and finally turned to look at him. "You look well."

"Why wouldn't I?" He raised one eyebrow.

"I don't know. I didn't hear you wake up today. Did you get up early?"

John let out a long breath. "Yes, I had a nightmare again." He rubbed his chin with the back of his hand. "They are getting farther apart though."

"That's wonderful." She smiled and got back to her sketch. "What did you do today?"

"I met with Mrs. Godfrey. Amelia."

"Oh? What did you talk about?"

John heaved a weary sigh. "Added to my troubles, I am afraid. Their life was not easy, Sam. The late baron apparently didn't care for the girls, so he never visited them. Jeremy was the heir, and he received a generous allowance, but that all ceased the moment he died. He didn't have his own savings, and since his death was unexpected, he didn't have time to make arrangements with his father about his family. Since then they've saved and scraped as they could."

Sam looked at him then. John's gaze grew troubled again. She placed a hand on his knee and squeezed. "No more past, remember?"

John gave her a wobbly smile. "I was thinking of taking them to London. I mean, they are welcome to stay at Ashbury Manor as long as they please, but the girls need new wardrobes. None of them have ever had a season, although some of them are of age."

"There is no rush, is there? This season is almost over. Perhaps we can all go together before the start of the next season?"

John smiled tenderly at her. "Anything you wish, Angel."

Sam returned to her sketch. "Since you dislike the crowds of the season, we could go a few months before, get the Godfrey girls settled into the townhouse, and leave before the *ton* arrives in full force."

"Excellent idea."

Sam picked up her sketch and placed it before John. "What do you think?"

He looked at the sketch for a long while, then raised his smiling face to her. "Beautiful."

"I love your smile," she said wistfully. "Here, go sit on that rock."

"Why?" He regarded her warily.

"Because I want to sketch you." She shifted to a more comfortable position. John shook his head with a smile and did as she asked. He sat on the rock looking to all the world like the formidable soldier that he was.

Sam laughed at him. "Are you getting ready for battle? I want to draw you smile."

"I can't just smile on command."

"Think happy thoughts," she said cheerfully.

"Hmm." He pretended to think it over, scratching his chin. "Like making love to you?" He raised an eyebrow.

"If it makes you smile," she said with a smug smile of her own.

"Oh, it does, absolutely." He gave her a predatory smile, and she laughed.

"Not that smile," she said with a chuckle. "That smile is dangerous."

"Truly? How so?"

"Oh." She waved her hand dismissively. "It makes me want to drop what I'm doing and hump you."

John choked with laughter. "Hump? Like a dog?"

Her smile turned into a grin. "Exactly," she said smugly. "And that"—she pointed her sketching pencil at his face—"is exactly the smile I was hoping for, my lord."

They laughed, and she sketched for what seemed like hours.

They got back home for supper and filed into the dining room with their large family. The room bristled with noise, banter, and laughter as everyone settled down around the table. John leaned closer to Sam as he helped her into her seat and whispered into her ear, "I want to fill this house with this many children."

Sam looked at over a dozen people at the table and blinked. John winked at her and went to occupy the head of the table.

Life was finally perfect.

* * *

Sam woke up that night to muffled noises and something that sounded like thrashing. She had to wait for her eyes to adjust to the dark before finally rousing from a dreamlike state. After a moment, she realized what was happening. John was having a nightmare. Again. He seemed like he was trying to shout, but his throat was constricted. His entire body was tense, and his hands were drawn into fists.

"Shh, John, you're home." She tried to soothe him and lull him back to sleep like she used to do when they'd just started sharing a bed, but he didn't seem to respond to her. She drew out her breath and put a soothing hand over his arm.

That's when everything changed. Suddenly he was upon her. His large body covered hers, and his hands were on her throat, throttling her. His eyes were wide open, but they seemed frantic in the dark as if he didn't know what was happening.

He was heavy and strong, and she couldn't struggle if she wanted to. His hands were clasped so tightly that she couldn't draw a breath, much less scream. She felt herself turning crimson. Not enough oxygen was traveling to her brain, and her mind grew foggy. She tried to take in a breath or get him off her. Her hands flailed by her side and then everything went black.

When Sam opened her eyes, it might have been an eternity or just a few seconds later. She felt strong arms surrounding her, and she was tucked against the hard wall of a chest. She was then placed on the soft bed. *What is going on?* Why was she being transported to a bed?

She heard muffled noises: footsteps, hushed whispers, some arguing. Her mind still felt groggy, so she groaned and turned on her side.

The next time Sam woke up, the light was bright in her eyes, and a strange buzzing sound invaded her ears. She moaned and tried to turn away from the offending light when she felt warm soothing hands down her sides.

"Do not fret, sweetheart," Isabel said softly.

Sam opened her eyes and studied her sister's worried face. She swallowed and noticed that her throat hurt. She cleared her throat and tried again.

"Isabel," she croaked. "Where's John?"

"Try not to speak, darling. The doctor said not to overtax your throat."

Sam frowned. *The doctor? What is going on?*

She reached her hand out and touched her throat. It was sore, and she felt a slight swelling. Then a memory flashed. John's hands on her throat, his body crushing hers. Was it a memory? Or was it a dream? John's nightmare!

The events of the night came crashing back to her and gave her a sharp headache. Sam winced in horror. She looked around the empty room. Where was John?

"The doctor said that the injury was not serious. You just need to drink warm tea with honey and take care to not talk a lot, and you should heal."

Sam laid a gentle hand on her sister's arm. "John," she croaked.

"He's..." Isabel looked away. "He's busy."

Busy? She didn't believe that for a moment. She knew John wouldn't leave her side, especially after what he did to her. He was probably guilt-riddled and ashamed. She wanted to go to him and soothe him, but she felt weary. John had probably spent all night with her anyway, and now he was resting.

But a strange feeling nagged at the back of her mind. She couldn't concentrate enough to decipher it, so she decided to let it rest for now. She filed away this feeling in some chamber of her brain. She'd think about it when she was well-rested.

Chapter 28

When Sam opened her eyes again, the room was dark. At first, she thought it was night, but when her eyes adjusted, she saw a crack of light behind the thick drapes. She got up and drew them apart, letting the sun in. It was probably midafternoon, judging by the position of the sun.

Sam was alone in her own room. She couldn't remember the last time she'd spent the night in her own room. Ever since they started sharing a bed, she'd spent all of her nights in John's bedroom. She looked down at herself and saw that she was wearing her chemise. She decided to get dressed before she ventured out of the confines of her room.

Sam went to the dressing room and selected one of her day gowns that she could put on without the help of the maid. Once she drew it on, she moved to the looking glass and froze. Her gaze immediately settled on her neck. It was swollen, and she could clearly see black and blue handprints on it. She shuffled closer to the looking glass and almost cried from the ugliness of it. She ran a hand over the bruises. They smarted, but it no longer hurt to swallow.

"One, two, three," she said. It didn't hurt to speak either, although her voice was still hoarse.

She went back to the dressing room and took out a long scarf. She draped it around her neck and set out of her room.

Samantha checked her husband's bedchamber first. The room was dark, the drapes shut. The bed was carefully made up, and his blanket was missing from the floor by the balcony doors. Samantha left the room and went down the stairs.

The house was quiet. When she'd gone to bed that fateful night, there were so many guests, everyone running around, chatting, laughing. Now, the place felt like a mausoleum. Although she loved this house, after all the energy she'd put into the renovations, it still didn't feel like home without the boisterous noise of people.

Carefully looking into every room she passed on her way, she finally found Isabel in the library.

"How are you feeling?" Isabel's brows drew closer over her eyes in worry.

"Well," Sam croaked. She put her hand on her throat. "It doesn't hurt as much."

"Good, good." Isabel indicated a chair next to hers. "Do sit down. Do you want some warm tea? With honey, perhaps?"

Sam nodded and sat in the chair. "Where's John?" Sam asked as she settled in the chair and straightened her skirts.

"He's…" Isabel paused a bit, on her way to the servants' bell, and looked over her shoulder. "He's not here."

She made the final two steps toward the bell and rang it. After asking the housemaid for tea, she settled back in her chair, making a great show of straightening her skirts.

"I've noticed," Sam said hoarsely. "Where is he?"

"In London," Isabel answered without looking at her.

"In *London?*" Sam shot from her chair so fast it nearly toppled back.

"Do be calm, Sam! Please, sit down." Isabel softly, albeit firmly, forced her sister back into the chair.

"What is he doing in London?" Sam's voice quivered as she asked. Why was he in London, how, and with whom? While she was suffering here all alone. Well, not exactly alone, but she wasn't with him either.

"He..." Isabel cleared her throat. "Richard made him leave." Sam's eyes widened in disbelief.

"Not that he put up much of a fight. I suppose John agreed with the decision. He hurt you, Sam."

"Not deliberately!" Her voice cracked, and she tried again, quieter. "He had a violent nightmare." Sam's eyes filled with tears, and she willed them back.

"Sammy, sweetheart, people don't just strangle their loved ones in their sleep."

"He didn't mean to," Sam said, tears gathering in the corners of her eyes. "He's had nightmares since the war, you wouldn't know that. But I did. I just didn't think..." Sam's voice faltered. Her lips began to tremble, and she had difficulty drawing a proper breath.

"Relax, sweetheart, please. Just breathe." Isabel's hand tightened around Sam's. She reassuringly squeezed her fingers, then let go. "I'm sure he wouldn't have left if he didn't hold himself solely responsible."

"Of course, he feels responsible," Sam spat back, irritated and angry. Tears freely rolled down her face now. "Wouldn't you? I am not harboring a wife beater, Isabel. He had never hurt me before, and he didn't mean to hurt me then either."

"Sammy, he could have killed you!"

"I can't have this conversation with you right now." Sam wiped her tears with the sleeve of her gown. "You can't possibly imagine what he must be feeling. If what you are saying is true, I have to go to him."

"Richard won't allow it," Isabel said softly.

"Richard is not the master of this house. And he is not the master of me."

At this moment, the maid entered bearing the tray of tea and honey.

"Forgive me, I've lost my appetite." With these parting words, Sam stalked out of the room.

Sam returned to her room and pulled out her valise. She started collecting her clothes and stuffing them inside. Unfortunately, after about three minutes of vigorous activity, she started feeling dizzy and had to sit down. She was so angry her hands shook. She couldn't get her nerves under control, and she could only think about what kind of destructive path her husband was on. He'd either locked himself inside his townhouse and was drowning in self-pity, or he was drowning his troubles in drink. She didn't want to think about that; she wanted to get to him as soon as possible. How could Richard do that? Why would he send him out of the house? Tears pricked at the back of her eyelids. She had to stop. She'd never get anything done if she were crying every five minutes.

There was a knock on the door. Sam didn't want to see anyone unless it was her husband, so she didn't answer.

"Sam," Richard called. "May we enter?"

We. A family council, probably. Sam smirked irritably. Her family had no right to intervene in her affairs. The door opened a crack, and Isabel's head peered inside.

"Good," she said, looking at Sam, then at her brothers. "She's decent."

Sam huffed. All three of her beloved family members entered the room. The same family members who'd thrown her husband, the rightful owner of this estate, out of the house.

"You are not going anywhere." Richard's voice was hard and brooked no argument.

Sam wasn't cowed by it, even for a moment. "Why would I listen to what you have to say?" she said, lifting her chin in defiance.

"First, because of the bruises on your neck." Richard indicated her scarf-wrapped area with his hand. "Second, if you won't do it for yourself, at least think about the babe."

"What?" Sam's eyebrows lowered in a frown. "What are you talking a—"

She froze mid-sentence. In her turmoil, she'd completely forgotten about the possibility she might be carrying a babe. "How do you know about that?"

"The doctor," he said simply.

The doctor. She remembered being inspected by a doctor. He must have confirmed she was increasing. She couldn't quite identify the jumble of emotions that hit her. Tenderness, happiness, protectiveness, horror, or some combination of all of those. Sam swallowed, not quite knowing what to say to that.

She was with child. And John was not with her.

"Does John—"

"He knows," Adam interrupted swiftly. "Sam, we want you to know that it was his decision to leave."

Sam huffed her disbelief. "Truly?" She sent a pointed glare

at Richard.

He raised his hands in mock self-defense. "Fine, I *suggested* he leave. But he did agree with me. Trust me, no power on Earth would make him leave you if he didn't want to."

"Why in the world do you still want to go back to him after what he did?" Adam looked genuinely angry and perplexed.

"Oh, for God's sake, he didn't mean to!" Sam yelled in a hoarse whisper. She cleared her throat and tried again. "He didn't mean to."

"So, when he kills you next time, is that supposed to be a comfort to us?" Adam fairly barked.

"He won't hurt me." Sam's chest heaved in indignation.

"Sammy." Isabel's soft voice interrupted her seething anger. "But he did."

Sam wanted to cry in frustration. Her family did not want to listen to her at all. They'd made John the villain, and they were not relenting.

"It's his child," she ventured her last protest before her strength gave out.

"And he'd be here to protect it if he weren't the danger," Richard said as softly as he could.

* * *

John sat quietly in his study, blankly staring at the wall. He had arrived in London a few days ago with Mrs. Godfrey and her daughters, helped them find a governess, paid for their new wardrobes, and kept himself as busy as he could. Now, the errands were done, and he felt lost, aching, frightened.

He couldn't find a hole to hide in anymore. He was worried about Sam, about his unborn child. What was Sam doing now? Was she eating well? Was she avoiding horse riding? Was she dressed warmly enough?

The questions and thoughts just would not go away. The nightmares had intensified. Now, when he saw the face of someone he'd killed, of someone bloodied and dying, he always saw her. His angel, dying by his own hands. He couldn't let it happen. If staying away from her meant he was keeping her safe, so be it. Nothing good had come from their marriage for her. He'd only brought her pain and misery.

He had taken her away from the bosom of her adoring family, brought her halfway across England to a crumbling estate, and then left her there alone to take care of home renovations. But ignoring her had turned out to be the best thing he had ever done, because after they started sharing their days and nights, when he finally felt happy and content, the worst had happened.

So, what now?

A knock sounded at the door like an answer to his question. Hope lit his eyes, and he whipped his head in the direction of the closed door. Was it her? Had she come for him?

Mrs. Godfrey's apologetic face appeared instead.

"Mrs. Godfrey. Do come in," he said dryly. "Do you need anything else?"

"No," she said with a smile. "I hoped we could have a conversation."

John nodded, although a conversation was the last thing he wanted.

Mrs. Godfrey settled slowly in the chair opposite his. "My lord," she started slowly. "My girls and I appreciate all that you've done for us very much. We never expected to be cared for by my husband's family. I know it should have been so, but your father… Well, you know he never regarded my girls as family."

"Can I be honest with you?" John tilted his head to the side.

"Of course."

"I hadn't even thought about contacting you. I know I should have, and I feel ashamed that I didn't do it earlier. But it was my wife. She was the one who insisted upon finding you."

To his surprise, Mrs. Godfrey just smiled in answer. "Lady Ashbury has a beautiful soul. It is on her behalf I came here right now."

"What do you mean?" John leaned forward. Had she contacted them?

Mrs. Godfrey cleared her throat uncomfortably. "I just mean that she needs you now. With her. You left her vulnerable and alone and it is not fair to her."

John shook his head. "You don't know what you're talking about."

"Perhaps not," she said thoughtfully. "But when things grew hard, when I had trouble with my girls, or when we were scraping pennies after Jeremy's passing… My first thought was always that I wished he was with us. I didn't need his money, nor his physical strength. I just needed to feel his presence. If Lady Ashbury is suffering as much as you, I dare say she is wishing for the same."

John stared ahead, his gaze glassy. Maybe Mrs. Godfrey was right, and Sam did need him. But he doubted he would be any kind of help to her. Not in the state he was in at the moment. Perhaps not ever. If he ever could be relied upon for his family, things needed to change. Within him.

Chapter 28

Carrie squealed in glee as Christopher tossed her lightly in the air and then caught her against his chest.

"Don't you worry you won't be able to catch her?" John asked as he neared the playing father and daughter.

"Mo'! Mo'!" Carrie chanted, bouncing in Chris's arm.

"I wouldn't do it if I weren't sure I could catch her," Chris replied evenly.

He took the babe by the armpits with his one arm and lightly threw her up in the air again. Carrie giggled as she landed against her father's chest, and he hugged her to him.

"Run along to Mama," Chris said to his daughter as he sat her down on the ground. Carrie happily scurried away. "What brings you back, sir? I heard you'd left for London," he addressed John as Carrie disappeared inside the house.

"I did. But now I am back." John shrugged. "I came back this morning and found the estate empty."

Christopher nodded. "Lady Ashbury left with her family, shortly after you left."

John heaved a sigh. "Did she happen to say if she…" John faltered. He couldn't say the words out loud. She couldn't have left him. Not for good.

Chris just shrugged. "She talked to Linda the day before they left and just said that she needed the support of her family at the moment. That's all."

John nodded.

"Are *you* back for good? Or will you run away again?"

John threw him a startled look. "I didn't run away."

Chris just raised a brow at him. "You don't have to lie to me. You know who you are talking to, don't you? I've done worse things than you."

John let out a bitter laugh. "I doubt it." He didn't think Christopher knew exactly what had transpired between Sam and him.

Christopher just regarded him thoughtfully. "So, will you tell me or do I have to ask?"

John walked to a tree nearby, leaned his back against it, and closed his eyes. It felt easier somehow to talk with his eyes closed. Blocking the world out, not seeing the expression on Chris's face.

"I've had this dream," he started. "It's happened over and over again since I married. It starts the same way every time. I am back at war. The battle is raging around me. Someone attacks me from behind. I turn and deal the fatal blow. I hold the cold body of a felled enemy in my arms, only it's not the face of another soldier that I see... It is Sam. Lying on the cold ground, dying because of me.

"It happened exactly the same way. Only that night, it wasn't just a dream. I woke up to the continuation of this nightmare. I don't remember how it happened, I don't remember when the dream blurred into reality, all I remember is my wife's delicate neck under my hands, her eyes, full of hurt and betrayal staring at me... In horror." He shook his head. "It's not something I want to ever see again."

A lone tear streaked down his cheek, but John didn't have the strength to wipe it away. "I can't live knowing that the biggest danger to my wife is me. I can't in good conscious be next to her, knowing that I might hurt her again."

Silence greeted his narrative. Chris hadn't said anything, had offered no platitudes or reassurances, and John was glad for it. He needed to have it off his chest, but now that it was said, he didn't know what to do next. He opened his eyes and looked at Christopher.

Chris stood nearby, his hand behind his back, a thoughtful expression on his face as he studied the ground under his feet.

"Do you think," he finally said as he raised his face to John, "that you are the only person who has ever hurt their loved ones by accident? This is not the same, but I've accidentally shoved my child away in anger. I was wilder than you when I came back. The guilt that eats at you is worse than anything you can experience. I don't have an answer for that, because I still haven't gotten over the guilt I feel after the things I've put my family through. There is one thing I can tell you, though. And that is however bad you feel, no matter how much you hurt and rage, your feelings are not the only ones that matter. How do you think your wife feels every time you run away from an argument? Every time you do something in a temper or on accident and run off, leaving her to pick up the pieces all by herself?"

John shook his head. "She is better off without me."

"Does she share this sentiment? Because to me, it sounds like a load of self-pity."

John stared at Chris in thought. "What do you propose I do?"

"I wish I had an easy answer, but I don't. Something has got to change, though. You can't go on as you have so far. I know I wouldn't be able to. And it's not like you can cut yourself off from the world completely either. What you should know is that your wife is not the only one who can share these burdens with you."

"I wish I didn't have to burden her at all."

"Then don't. Look around. You're in a village full of soldiers.

We can help each other." Christopher paused. "And while you heal, may I suggest adjusting your sleeping arrangements?"

John let out nervous laughter, tears streaming down his face. He wiped them away.

"If you want to be a man your wife can rely on, you better start taking responsibility for your actions. Trust me, it is going to be difficult. But every time you feel like running away, how about you amble to my cottage instead?"

John patted Christopher on his shoulder. "Thank you."

Christopher just shrugged it off. "What are you going to do now?"

"I am going to find my wife and bring her back."

Chapter 29

The sun shone brightly in the blue, cloudless sky. Sam was walking in a field of violets, just as she used to do every summer since she could remember. It had been a fortnight since she last saw John. She'd argued with her family about bullying him away, about minding their own business, and how she was an independent married woman, but deep down in her heart, she knew they were right. At least in part.

John had left her without so much as a goodbye, while she was lying sick in bed. He'd left, and he hadn't even inquired after her wellbeing once. She couldn't be the only one invested in this relationship, trying to bring him out of his misery and wasting all her energy. Not anymore. Not since she had her precious babe to worry about.

So she'd left for her ancestral hall. And she couldn't have been happier. She enjoyed sedate long rides in the mornings—not one person in the household allowed her to go past a trot anymore—and shared meals with her sister and brothers, talking about all kinds of nonsense. She read a lot in her old library. And in the evenings, she ventured out for walks in the flower fields. Yes, she was happy. If she said that often enough, she was bound to convince herself.

She found her favorite boulder, the one she'd spent endless days on, sketching to Ben and later to John, albeit without knowing, and settled comfortably on top. She looked at the sun, watching as it sank below the horizon.

"The first time we met, you leaned over me and the sun cast a glow around your head like a halo. For a moment, I thought I'd died and gone to heaven. I thought you were an angel." Sam remembered John's gentle words as he'd gifted her the angel pendant all those weeks ago. She dipped her hand into her bodice and withdrew the pendant, rubbing it between her fingers.

Tears rolled down her cheeks. Another memory sprung to mind of a beautiful day such as this when she was sitting on a log and sketching John. He was so happy then, so carefree. She took the pencil out and opened her sketchbook to a fresh page. Sam started sketching John from memory, remembering his smiling face, his eyes glinting with mischief, the scar she barely noticed anymore. He was beautiful to her, and she missed him so much.

She turned page after page, filling her sketchbook with John's likeness. When she sketched, the whole world disappeared. It was just her and the memory of John. Perhaps, if she sketched him long enough, she would forget all her troubles. Even her bruised heart. She turned the page to start another drawing, but when she looked up from her sketch, it was dark.

"I suppose it is time to go home," she said to herself with a shrug and put a hand to her abdomen. "How I managed to see what I was sketching for the past several minutes, I shall never know."

She collected her items and moved toward the house when she heard the sound of a galloping horse. The horse and its rider were headed her way. She squinted in the dark, trying to make out the form of the rider. It was probably Richard. Although they might have just sent James, the footman, to fetch her.

When the rider was a few feet away, he leaped off the horse before it could stop.

"Are you out of your mind?" The achingly familiar husky male voice shook with anger and agitation. "What are you doing here in the dark?"

Her husband's form started to reveal itself from the shadows. He reached her in swift, long strides and took her by the arms, concern shining in his eyes. "Are you well?"

Sam couldn't shake herself out of the shock.

"Am I well?" she asked, bewildered, finally getting her wits back. "Now, you are worried?"

Once she gained her voice, she was determined to tell him everything she thought of him. He had no right to act concerned after leaving her that way. "After two blasted weeks? Where have you been, John? Were you worried about me then? Because I've been out every evening in the past fortnight!" She threw the words at him and had the satisfaction of seeing his expression changing to chagrin.

He pushed his hand through his tousled hair. "I know, I have no right. I was just so frightened when I came here, and you weren't home." He scrubbed his hand over his face and pressed his fingertips to the corners of his eyes. "Let me take you home," he said, extending his hand to her. "We'll talk about it there."

"I don't want to talk with you, John," she said harshly, jerking away. "And I am not going anywhere with you."

She started heading down the path toward her home, without looking to see if he followed. After a while, she heard the horse's hooves and a man's footsteps closer to her side. John reached her and started walking beside her.

"I am sorry," he said quietly.

He had a look of such misery that she almost threw herself at him, kissed him, and forgave him all his sins. *Almost*. And she probably would have a few weeks ago. Now, thinking about the babe, it was different. She couldn't have him leaving as he pleased, then apologizing and expecting to be welcomed with open arms. If he was going to be in this child's life, she needed to be able to rely on him.

"Have you noticed that you say that a lot? You apologize, but then you turn around and act the same way all over again." She stared straight ahead as she spoke, not looking his way. "What are you sorry for this time? For yelling at me just now, when you had no right? For strangling me half to death in your sleep? Or for leaving me without a word while I lay unconscious, battered, and bruised?"

John visibly flinched from the accusations. "For everything," he said quietly. "And more. You deserve so much more, Sam, dear."

"I know I do, John. But that is not the biggest issue here." She stopped and rounded on him.

"It's not?" He looked genuinely confused.

"The child," she said simply.

"What about the child?" His expression grew tense and

worried.

"Exactly, John. What about the child?"

"What are you talking about?"

"I am talking about your apparent lack of concern for our future child. You weren't happy about it when I told you, you ran away the moment my suspicions were confirmed, and now you're here, and you haven't even mentioned him!"

John drew a breath to answer, but no words emerged from his mouth.

"I thought so," Sam muttered under her breath. She turned from him and started walking away.

"You know that's not true," he called after her. From the volume of his voice, she deduced that he'd ceased following her. *Good.* She didn't need him. She put a hand to her abdomen. They didn't need him.

As soon as Sam entered her home, she was ambushed by Isabel. Once she removed her outer clothing, Sam looked questioningly at her hovering sister.

"Did you see him?" Isabel asked with raised eyebrows.

"Yes." Sam moved farther into the house. "He should be here shortly. He trailed me all the way home."

"What did he say?" Isabel asked as Sam started up the stairs.

"That he was sorry." Sam hadn't turned to her sister, so she didn't see her reaction, and she was too weary to describe the full encounter. Let John tell everyone for a change. She needed a rest.

She ordered a bath as soon as she got into her room. Her heart was fluttering inside her chest. *He is here, he came for me,* it sang. But her brain told her to cease the girly dreams. He was not the man she'd thought he was. He wouldn't fight for her. He wasn't the reliable man she needed him to be.

* * *

John was greeted at the door by the menacing figure of Sam's eldest brother. When he'd arrived earlier, Gage was out of the house. Now, he would have to confront him in order to get to his wife.

John raised his hands in a gesture of surrender. "If you want to hit me again, Gage, feel free."

"Give me at least one reason why I shouldn't?"

John shrugged. "There isn't one." He widened his stance and beckoned Gage with both his hands.

Gage smirked and turned away before planting his fist into John's face. John stumbled and hit the door behind him. He wiped his face with his fist, watching the blood smear his gloves.

"That barely even hurt."

"Oh, for God's sake!" Isabel exclaimed from the top landing and hurried down the stairs. "Richard, you can't keep hitting people."

"Not people! Just him."

Isabel raised her brow at him.

"What do you want me to do? Stand by and watch as he hurts Sam?"

"No, but he is her husband. You can't keep him away from her."

"I am not letting him into this house."

"Where do you propose he sleep?"

"It is not my problem!" Gage crossed his arms over his chest and planted his legs apart in a stubborn stance.

John heaved a sigh. "I just want to speak to her."

"You are *not* taking her away from this house."

"Respectfully, it is not your decision to make. It is Sam's."

"Like hell it is!" Gage growled. "I am not letting her out and that's that."

John contemplated his next step for a moment, before turning lightly and punching Gage right in the face. The viscount staggered and fell on his arse. He blinked, looking surprised, before lunging at John and crashing him into the side table. John hit his lower back and felt a sharp pain, but adrenaline kicked in so he threw the viscount off him and dealt him another blow. A crash sounded, and both men turned, panting, at the sound. Isabel stood on the first step of the grand staircase, a broken vase at her feet.

"Would you stop acting like out-of-control adolescents?" she yelled.

"He—" Gage started but was swiftly interrupted as Isabel raised a finger in warning.

"Don't even start. You're supposed to be the head of this household."

"I am—"

"But Sam is not under your protection anymore. She is Ashbury's wife. So if he wants to speak to her, we are going to allow it."

"I will not give him a warm bed to sleep in after what he's done!" Gage said angrily.

"I don't need a bed," John said, already starting up the stairs. "A floor will do just fine."

* * *

Sam was lounging in her bath when a knock sounded at her door. She sat up, startled.

"I'm sleeping," she called out and heard a soft laugh.

"I doubt it," John said through the door. "Please, let me in."

Sam heaved a long sigh. She closed her eyes and shook her head mildly. "Why should I?"

"Because I've missed you."

The simple admission nearly tore her to pieces. She covered her face with her hands. "Please, leave," she said almost inaudibly. She doubted he even heard her.

"I just want to see you. I won't even speak if you don't want me to."

Sam took another breath. "Very well," she finally said. "Come in."

He entered and stopped at the doorway. Sam huddled farther into the bath so that only her head peeked out of the water, but the moment she saw John, she almost leaped out.

His clothing was in disarray, his nose bloody.

"What happened to you?" she asked in astonishment.

John waved a careless hand. "It's not important. Do you need help with the bath?"

"Your nose is bloody!"

John calmly took out his handkerchief, walked to the bath, and dipped it in, before wiping off his face.

"Don't tell me. It was Gage, wasn't it?" Sam seethed in anger.

"He had every right."

"No, he didn't!"

"Sam—"

"I am so tired of you men deciding everything for me. What is good for me, what is bad, fighting for me when I am the only one whose opinion matters in the end!"

John discarded the bloody handkerchief, then rolled up his sleeves and sat by the rim of the bath. "Gage is just trying to protect you."

"And you? What are you trying to do?"

John took the sponge, dipped it in the water, and lathered it with soap. "I'm just trying to help you bathe. Lean forward."

Sam blinked in confusion.

"Let me do this, Sam. It's the least I can do."

Sam leaned forward and hugged her knees with her arms as John started gently, tenderly washing her back. He moved her hair aside, and goosebumps covered her flesh from the contact. He proceeded to wash her neck, shoulders, and hands. Then he gently lay her down and continued to her feet and the rest of her body. His movements weren't seductive; he just carefully washed her as the maid would, slowly rubbing at her skin.

Sam was languid and relaxed, reveling in the tender ministrations of her husband.

"Sit up and throw your head back. I'll wash your hair."

"John, you don't have to—" Sam started to protest, but John looked at her pleadingly.

"Please."

Sam nodded and did as he asked. John took a pitcher of water and poured it on her hair. Then he lathered soap onto his hands and proceeded to carefully massage her scalp. The sensation was so pleasant Sam was tempted to moan.

John rinsed her hair and when he was finished, he took a towel and came to stand by the bath.

He extended his hand toward her. "Come, let me dry you now."

"Very well." Sam didn't argue anymore.

She got up with the help of her husband, then he wrapped her in a towel and swept her into his arms. He settled her on the blanket by the hearth and proceeded to dry her softly with towels. When the chore was done, he gently hugged her from behind and placed a tender kiss on her cheek.

"Good night." With that, John stood and walked toward the door.

"You're leaving?" Sam's eyes widened in astonishment.

"Don't worry, Angel, I will be right outside."

"What do you mean?"

"I am not leaving you. I promise." He winked with the last word and left the room.

Sam blinked at the closed door. What had just happened?

A few seconds later, she heard an audible thump.

"I'll be here," John called out. "I sleep on the floor anyway. What does it matter where?"

Sam couldn't shake the bewilderment out of her face. He was planning to sleep there. Outside of her door. The entire night.

Chapter 30

S am lay awake that night, staring at the ceiling. She hadn't quite recovered from the tender way John had given her a bath and then just left her. She knew he was doing what she'd asked, but she felt abandoned again. The next step had to be hers, but she still didn't feel confident enough to trust him. She was also afraid that if she let him stay, she'd cave under his pressure and relent under his kisses. At the same time, she was tired of living half a life, and without him, it was exactly that. And to be completely honest, she wanted to go home. To Ashbury Manor.

She hadn't realized how in two short months she'd started thinking of Ashbury Manor as her home. The thought took her aback. She had her friend Linda, her tiny, beautiful garden, and her precious, peaceful walking paths. Yes, she'd started thinking of Ashbury Manor as her own. She felt safe there, at home. Even more than she did here, in her childhood home, the one she'd grown up in.

Ashbury was different. It was hers. The home she'd

helped renovate from the ground up. The friendships she'd forged through hard work, dedication, and much effort. The bedroom she'd shared with her husband.

She sat up in bed. Would she ever learn how to fall asleep with a restless head? A glass of warm milk would help her feel better and fall right back to sleep, she was certain. She threw on a dressing gown and walked to the door.

She paused, wondering if she should get a candle, but decided against it. Sam opened the door, took a step, and nearly tumbled as she tripped over her husband. She shrieked but was able to right herself at the same time John caught her by her waist.

"Ugh, sorry. In hindsight, I should have moved out of the way and just slept by the wall." He rubbed his eyes and settled with his back propped against the wall.

"Or you could have slept in one of the guest rooms," she pointed out.

"Perhaps." He shrugged. "I didn't want to sleep away from you."

Warmth uncurled inside her chest. With a sigh, she seated herself on the floor next to John.

"The floor is cold, you shouldn't sit here," he said.

"Then you shouldn't be sleeping here."

"Sam…" Her name was more of a sigh. "I wish you would listen to me when I have concerns about your wellbeing. But I've learned the hard way that I can't make you do anything."

Sam nodded. "That's right, you can't."

"Then I'll have to alter my approach." With these words, John scooped her up and carried her back to her room.

"John!" Sam tried to wriggle out of his hold but he held her tight until he reached her bed and deposited her on top.

"This is how it is going to be, Wife. Take it or leave it. In the matter of your safety and wellbeing, I am not going to give you an inch."

Sam's mouth dropped open. "Is that supposed to be your apology?"

John settled on the bed next to her and took her hand in his, his expression pained. "It is, my dear, because if you won't heed me on this, I shall never let myself come close to you ever again."

"John—" Sam started slowly. John's eyes were hard but also filled with sorrow. At that moment, she wanted to drop everything, hug him, and never let him go.

"No, Sam. There is no way around this. I know you will forgive me. I can see it in your eyes. You are already contemplating going back home with me. You are so soft and kind, even when you shouldn't be. You will forgive me whether I ask for forgiveness or not, but that won't mean much, because I shan't ever forgive myself!"

Sam covered his hand with hers. "Hurting me in your sleep"—she swallowed—"it wasn't your fault."

John laughed bitterly. "Yes, it was, Sam. And you should expect better of me. You deserve better." He squeezed her thigh.

Sam closed her eyes, trying to keep her tumultuous emotions at bay.

"John," she finally said. "I am not upset with you for hurting me." John made a sound between laughter and a scoff. "I am upset because you left me there, sick and hurting. And that on top of just confirming that I am indeed with child. You didn't even say goodbye. Or leave a note. You just left!"

"And that's what I should have done from the start!" John

stood and started pacing the room.

"What?" Sam scrambled from the bed and stood there, hugging herself.

"Before we got married, I warned you about all this. That I have my mood swings, that I cannot sleep with anyone in my bed, that I am emotionally distant and will not be a good father—"

"Pardon me?" she interrupted in disbelief. "Are you saying—?"

John put out a staying hand. "Let me finish."

Sam looked at him begrudgingly but didn't argue.

"I told you all this, in hopes that you would stay away from me, and I would retain this wall I've built around myself. To protect everyone else from me." John raked his hand through his hair. "What I did not realize was how much I would start to crave your company. Your attention. Your smile. I started wanting to spend every available second with you. All my troubles disappeared when I was with you. I've finally started living again, and more importantly, enjoying life. I felt the peace and innocence of the world through you, and I didn't want to let it go. Even in my sleep."

He turned away from her, looking out the window. His gaze took on a faraway look. "I thought if I held on to you tightly in my sleep, you'd chase away the nightmares too." He looked at her then. "I was a fool."

Sam chewed on her lower lip, unable to utter a word. She swallowed a growing lump in her throat and chafed her hands against her upper arms. She was getting cold, but she suspected the cool room temperature was not the reason.

"I just put all the burdens on your shoulders and it's not fair," John continued. "I started disregarding the safety measures with you, sleeping with you through the night, being rough with you in bed, letting my moods affect you. I just did what I wanted, pretending that nothing would happen to you. I thought *nothing can happen to my Angel.* God, I was so selfish." He shook his head.

"You were *never* rough with me, John. And the... the incident wasn't just your fault. I made you stay with me at night." Sam finally found her voice.

"That's just it, Sam. You didn't make me do anything I didn't want to. You had no idea what you were dealing with, while I did. I thought to myself, if we both want it, then it's fine, consequences be damned. And then the consequences came." He smiled sadly. "And you paid the price."

"John, I understand—"

"No, Sam!" He turned away and started pacing the floor again. "You really don't understand. You don't know what it feels like to kill. To feel the light go out in the eyes of the person you've murdered. You don't know what it feels like to crush and ruin everything around you. But that is not even the most frightening part. The most frightening part is to realize you've hurt someone you love so much and it could have been worse. I can't sleep, Sam! I haven't slept ever since that night, because every time I close my eyes, I see your face... Your horror-filled eyes the moment you realized what was happening."

John closed his eyes and Sam saw a tear trickling down his cheek. "You don't understand the agony of waking up in a cold sweat because you're afraid you did it again. It feels like losing your mind. You don't understand, and it's probably for the best. But I can't—No, I shan't put you in danger like that again."

John's voice had grown hoarse by the time he finished his recitation, and he swallowed. Tears streamed down his face.

Sam slowly walked to her husband and put a hand against his cheek. John closed his eyes and covered her hand with his.

"I know you needed me when I left you, but I just fell apart. I couldn't be around you then, I would have made everything worse. So, no, Sam. This is not an apology. I shall not ask for your forgiveness. I've failed you too many times for that to be possible."

Sam withdrew her hand and nodded. "Where does that leave us then?"

John took a deep breath and wiped at his cheeks. "Right back where we started. Except with me trying as hard as I can to keep you happy."

"What about your moods and nightmares?"

John heaved a sigh. "I am not alone in this, you know. I have you and when it's something too gruesome for me to share with you, I have Christopher and the other soldiers to rely upon."

Sam cast him a curious glance. This was the first time he'd ever voluntarily admitted he needed help and he was willing to reach out to get it.

"I can't promise I'll be a good father. I don't know how to be that yet. I shan't promise you to be the perfect husband. But I shall try hard to be what you deserve. I can't promise you I shan't be violent in my sleep, so we'll have to go back to the previous arrangement where we sleep separately. But I promise I'll be the last thing you see before you fall asleep and the first thing you see when you wake up. And I can't promise you to be carefree and worry-free all the time. But with you,

I almost feel innocent again. It's not going to be easy, Angel. I can promise you that also."

"I don't want easy," she whispered, standing on her tiptoes and placing a kiss on his cheek. "I want real. I want you, and I want our messy little family."

John laughed and lowered his lips to hers. He kissed her softly, slowly, then he picked her up in his arms and lowered her to the bed. He then settled next to her.

"Will you take me home with you now?" Sam asked. "I love my family, I truly do, but they are suffocating me with their patronizing."

John laughed. "I will," he said and placed a soft kiss on top of her head. "And if it makes you feel any better, I did get to punch Gage in the face."

"You did?" Sam turned to look at John, her eyes wide. "How are you still alive?"

"I am a soldier." John looked offended. Then he hugged Sam closer and whispered into her hair, "Your sister might have saved me."

Sam laughed, settling comfortably against John's chest. John hugged her close to him, putting his hand against her abdomen. It felt warm and reassuring.

"Does the babe move yet?" he asked.

Sam let out a short laugh. "No, love. It's too early."

"Mm." John rubbed her abdomen in soothing circles, and Sam felt herself relaxing even more.

"John?"

"Yes, darling."

Sam smiled at the endearment. "Do you mind if we go visit Evie at her Somerset estate before we head home?"

John moved away and looked at her wearily. "Sam, my love,

didn't I just say I shan't do anything that would endanger you or the babe? The journey to Somerset is long and rough."

Sam lowered her eyes and made a pouting face.

"No, don't even try that look on me. I'll not budge on this. I can promise you this, however. I shall find a way to transport the duchess to our estate."

"You will?" Sam's mood brightened instantaneously.

"Yes, I promise. You will see your friend before the summer is out."

Sam hugged him tightly and kissed him soundly on his lips. She then moved to kiss his jaw, then his neck. She started unbuttoning his shirt and kissing every piece of flesh revealed.

"Sam?" John's hands tightened in her hair. "What are you doing?"

She untucked his shirt from his breeches. "I haven't been made love to in over a fortnight."

"Good to know." John chuckled, helping her draw his shirt over his head. He took her in his arms and placed her in the middle of the bed, hovering over her.

"And I want that remedied." She smiled at him suggestively and bit down on her lower lip, drawing his gaze to her mouth.

"Happy to oblige."

John kissed her lips, her neck, and all the way down to the bodice of her shift. Then he took the bodice between his hands and ripped it. She gave a soft yelp.

He smiled against her chest. "Sorry," he said, clearly not meaning it. "Too impatient."

He took her pendant in his hand and placed a kiss on it. Sam hitched her breath. John then proceeded kissing, licking, and softly biting his way down. He suckled her nipples, then moved lower. He paused, hovering over her abdomen, then kissed it gently, tenderly. He then opened his mouth and licked her belly, making Sam giggle.

"It tickles."

A low grunt was his answer. He moved even lower then, nudged her knees apart, and settled in the cradle of her hips, holding her thighs tightly with his hands. When he kissed her in her most intimate place, she almost flew off the bed. He proceeded licking and suckling on her there until she couldn't think, understand, or remember anything. She could only feel. Sam moaned and sighed, bunching the sheets by her sides. His agile tongue was doing wicked things, drawing circles upon circles among her folds, tickling and driving her insane. Sam cried out as she reached the blinding apex, the feeling of floating among the stars. Then she slowly came down to earth, completely spent and blissfully tired.

John settled beside her on the bed, placing her head on his shoulder. He wrapped her in his arms, kissing her forehead.

"Sleep," he said, his voice hoarse from passion.

"But we didn't…" She looked up at him in confusion. "You didn't."

"Tomorrow." He kissed her forehead and smiled. "You need your sleep. I'll wake you tomorrow."

Sam smiled and settled comfortably in his arms. If that was the way he was going to apologize every time, she was not about to protest.

* * *

Sam and John set off for the Ashbury estate the next day. Gage was not happy about it, but no force on Earth could hold Sam away from her husband. Because of Sam's nausea,

313

they traveled at a slow pace and decided to stay in inns as much as they could. On the second day of the journey, it was pouring rain, so they could barely see anything outside the window. Sam was resting her head against John's shoulder, her eyes closed, his arm curled around her protectively.

"How much longer before we arrive?" Sam asked without opening her eyes.

She felt John peer outside the window. "I don't think it's much farther. Although I don't see anything other than the heavy rain beating against our windows. Aren't you glad I insisted we didn't go to the Somerset estate now?"

"Ugh," Sam groaned and tried to find a more comfortable position. "This feels like torture."

John shifted in his seat to make sure she had more room. "I am certain we are coming upon our London townhouse. We can spend the night there if you wish. Or even wait several days before we set out to Bedford. I am sure Mrs. Godfrey and the girls would be glad for the company."

"I've missed Ashbury Manor," she pouted.

John grinned at her. "Did I tell you that you became a lot more demanding and a bit whinier since you started increasing?"

"Don't say that word," Sam pleaded. "It is making me nauseous again."

"Poor darling." John collected her against his chest again and drew soothing circles down her back.

After a short while, their carriage drew to a halt and John exited the vehicle. The wind blew the rainwater inside the carriage and all over him as he opened the door. John carefully handed Sam down, and they sprinted up the steps.

The moment they entered the house, they were greeted by

shouting and angry epithets being thrown around. A soaked but richly dressed lady was arguing with their butler and Mrs. Godfrey. A portly middle-aged man uncomfortably stood by her side.

"What the devil is going on?" John barked, and everyone suddenly grew quiet.

The visitors turned and John beheld Lady Montbrook's angry face and Lord Montbrook's uncomfortable gaze. Lady Montbrook's face turned red and furious the moment she saw Sam, and she stalked toward her.

"You!" She pointed her finger at Sam. "It's your doing!"

John took a step forward, placing himself between the irate lady and his wife.

"I'd choose your words if I were you," he warned.

Lady Montbrook didn't seem to hear him. "What did you do with her?" she yelled, peering behind John.

"What did I do with whom?" Sam peeked behind John's back.

John tucked her behind him with one hand. "What in the devil are you talking about? And choose your words carefully as you answer. You might be a lady, but I won't hesitate to throw you out of my house."

Lady Montbrook bristled at the threat, and her husband just shifted uncomfortably from one foot to another.

"Barbarian!" the lady spat at him and then peeked at Sam again. "Our niece, Eabha! The Duchess of Somerset is gone! And I know it's your doing. Where did you take her?"

John slowly turned to his wife, placing his hands on her arms. Her eyes grew wide with terror. "She's not in Somerset?" she whispered.

"Steady, Angel. Breathe," he said just as quietly. "What do

you mean she's gone?" He turned back to the Montbrooks, wearing his most intimidating sneer. "When did she disappear?"

"She ran away from the bloody Somerset estate, not so much as a note was left behind. This was soon after she received a letter from you, so it must be your doing!" Lady Montbrook huffed.

"Cease sneering at my wife!" John barked. "What else happened before she disappeared?"

"Nothing! We took care of her as best we could. That ungrateful brat!"

"That's enough!" John barked. "It is time you left." He pointed at the door.

"Won't you do something?" Lady Montbrook finally addressed her silent husband, and he just shrugged. The lady huffed in frustration, puffed out her chest, and thundered out of the townhouse, her husband following in her wake.

Sam rounded on John as soon as the door closed after him. "Evie is gone! Where could she be?"

"No reason to get so upset, Angel. You need to calm down," John tried to soothe her.

"Calm down?" She started crying and couldn't collect her breath. "How can I calm down? If only I'd done something sooner..." A sob escaped her, and she covered her mouth with her hand.

At that moment, Mrs. Godfrey came rushing down the stairs.

"Oh, how glad I am to see you two together!" she almost sang. "And just in time, too. That toad was getting on my last nerve."

Sam chuckled through her tears at the epithet.

Chapter 30

After the greetings were over, Mrs. Godfrey handed Sam an envelope. "This came for you about an hour ago."

Sam looked at the letter and closed her eyes in relief. "It's from Evie, excuse me." She rushed up the stairs and into her bedchamber with John on her heels. She unsealed the envelope with the letter opener and unfolded the missive.

My dear friend,

By the time you read this, you will probably know that I have disappeared. Perhaps not. Either way, I urge you not to worry. I am safe and I am happy. The truth is, Lady Montbrook wanted to marry me off to one of her sons. I overheard the conversation, and it wasn't very pleasant. I felt this was her plan all along, ever since I arrived at the Somerset estate, or perhaps even when she arrived in London. Forgive me for not writing to you sooner, but I did not want you fretting over me.

I shan't bore you with details, I shall tell you all when I see you. For now, I need you to know two things:

I am away from the Montbrooks, and I am safe.

When we do see each other again, I shall be a married lady. I've eloped.

Much Love,
Evie.

Epilogue

One year later

Sam woke up in the middle of the night at the sound of the door closing. She opened her eyes and looked around. The place by the balcony where John usually slept was empty. So he was out again.

She stood, put on her slippers and dressing gown, and ventured out of the room. The stairs creaked under her footsteps as she made her way upstairs. She turned left when she reached the corridor and heard a low humming sound. Sam smiled to herself.

She walked to the door of the nursery and beheld her husband softly rocking the babe in his arms.

"Don't we have a nursemaid for that?" she whispered and ventured into the room.

John looked at her without stopping the rocking motions and smiled. "I didn't want to wake her."

Sam glanced at the peacefully slumbering maid and shook her head. She came closer and stopped to stare at the infant in John's arms. Their little angel. The babe wasn't sleeping. She was making soft cooing sounds and waving her arms in the air.

"Unlike her nursemaid, our little one doesn't seem to want to sleep," John whispered.

Sam stretched out her arms toward John. "She must be hungry. Do you mind if I take her?"

John looked at the babe in his arms for a moment before nodding and handing her over. Sam slipped her breast out of her chemise and started nursing her daughter.

John raised a brow. "You know the nurse would be scandalized if she saw you feeding her. She'd start insisting again that we need a wet nurse."

Sam laughed. "It's good that she's sleeping then."

In a few moments, the child was contentedly sleeping in Sam's arms. Sam slowly walked to the crib and deposited the babe inside. John came up behind her and put his arms around her waist, gently stroking her abdomen.

"When do you think our angel will get a brother or a sister?"

"I can't predict those things," she said with a chuckle. "But as soon as we go back to our bedroom, we can definitely start working on it again."

John kissed her on the temple, then turned and looked at their daughter. "Good night, Angela, darling," he said.

Sam reached for the pendant hanging around her neck and stroked it gently. "Angels are watching over you."

THE END

Loved the book? Sign-up for my newsletter to get a bonus novelette about Chris and Linda:

https://sendfox.com/sadiebosque

By signing up, you'll also get new release alerts and bonus content such as extra epilogues, deleted scenes, and more.

Curious if Evie gets his Happily Ever After? What about Isabel? Read more from *Necessary Arrangements* series on Amazon.

Keep reading for a steamy deleted scene.

Fun Facts about this novel

Even though this is installment #2 in the Necessary Arrangements series, this is the first book of the series I actually wrote. I started writing it on June 27, 2020. The first draft was completed thirty-three days later. After that, it went through at least seven drafts and iterations, until it was finally published.

In the first draft of the novel, the prologue was over 4000 words and outlined the lives of the Lewis siblings prior to and shortly after Ben's death.

I listened to the album *One More Light* by Linkin Park while drafting the book. The songs "Nobody Can Save Me" and "Battle Symphony" were constantly on repeat.

You can find more fun facts and deleted scenes from the book on my website:
www.sadiebosque.com

Deleted Scene

Between chapters 24 and 25

The moment John saw Sam, he disengaged from the group of working men and ran toward her. He grinned as soon as he stopped in front of her and stood, waiting for his customary kiss on the cheek. Sam obliged him, and he took the basket from her hands.

"Do you want to go to the stream to enjoy our lunch?" he asked, leading her away.

"Mhm." Sam made a noise of acquiescence, tilted her head back, and closed her eyes against the sun as she walked. It was a beautiful, sunny day. A rare sunny day and she wanted to enjoy it. It had been a week since the night they spent under the stars, the most precious week of her life. She and John had finally started sharing a bed together. Well, not a bed exactly but rather a bunch of blankets by the side of the French doors in his room. First, he worried that the floor would be too hard for her, but she convinced him that she didn't mind.

He finally agreed to spend their nights there on the condition that if she were uncomfortable, she would scramble back into his bed and sleep there. So far, she had never used that option. She would sleep on the cold, wet grass if it meant being with him. The only feeling better than falling asleep in his arms was waking up next to him.

His nightmares came less frequently, and when they did, she managed to soothe him by gently whispering in his ear while petting his arm.

He told her not to wake him from nightmares, otherwise, his reaction could be violent, but so far he settled down every time she soothed him. She was sure all his worries were for naught. But he was still unconvinced.

They spent most of the day together too. Their luncheon hour spread, with them eating, talking, and kissing under the sun.

This was the day Isabel was supposed to arrive, and Sam was over the moon about that. She couldn't wait to share her life with her sister. This was the happiest she ever remembered herself being, and she was ready to shout it to the entire world.

John brought her to their usual picnicking sight and spread the blanket. They followed the same ritual every day. She would set the picnicking area while he washed, then they ate and enjoyed each other's company. Sam settled comfortably on the blanket, watching her husband's bare back as he performed his ablutions. He was splashing in the sun, and Sam had a sudden urge to join him. So she took off her bonnet, kicked off her slippers, rolled down her stockings, and set them all aside. She tiptoed carefully to the bank of the stream and stepped into the water.

"Oh! It's so cold!" she yelled, frozen on the bank with just her feet in the water. She was holding her skirts over her ankles, her shoulders hunched, a grimace of pain on her face.

John turned to her and laughed. "Why did you think it was a good idea to step into a freezing stream?"

"You are knee-deep and you don't look at all cold!" She felt a cramp starting up in her toes and hastily scrambled back up the bank. John's rumbling laugh followed her out of the water. In her haste, she stepped on the pebbles or what might have been bare branches that poked at the sole of her foot. "Ow!" she yelled and raised her foot, which only worsened the pressure on the other one.

Suddenly she was scooped up into the arms of her husband. She started with a yelp, but as soon as she realized what was happening, she locked her arms around his neck. She pressed herself closer to his chest, not caring that he was dripping water and making her gown wet as well.

John made a couple of steps and sat on a thick log, placing her carefully on his lap.

"Show it to me," he said. "Does it still hurt?"

Sam twisted her leg and surveyed her foot. There was no bleeding, just red marks from the pebbles. "I shall live," she said brightly.

"Good." John lowered his head and took her mouth in a scorching kiss.

Sam laughed into his mouth before his tongue swooped inside and she forgot how to think. His hands were roaming her body as he kissed her fiercely. Sam pressed herself closer to his naked torso, running her hands over his arms. She loved the play of muscles as he tensed. She loved the feel of his silky skin beneath her fingers. She wanted to trace every inch of his body.

Sam felt his hand traveling up her skirt and squirmed. A

tingle appeared between her legs, and she wanted to feel him there. She shifted until she was straddling him and pressed herself against his hard, erect length. John groaned and shut his eyes tight. Sam smiled at his expression of pure bliss mixed with agony. She lowered her hands and quickly started unbuttoning his falls, while his hand traveled farther up her skirt. He found the slit in her drawers, and his fingers ventured to her private place. Sam moaned and pressed herself firmer into his hand. John chuckled, then took her earlobe into his mouth and sucked on it.

Sam squirmed as he just played with her folds, not delving further, not satisfying her hunger.

Finally, she was able to undo the buttons on his breeches and took his erect length into her hands. It was thick and hard and incredibly hot. She moaned as her hands played with its length, traveling up and down, squeezing him.

With a growl, John lifted her up until she hovered above him. The head of his cock was lightly pressed against her center.

"John," she whispered, easing herself down his length, taking him in, marveling at the feeling of being filled by him. John squeezed her buttocks and looked into her eyes. She could feel his heartbeat accelerating, and his breathing came out in fitful gulps. Sam carefully placed her hands on his shoulders and sat down, hard.

John groaned and threw back his head. Sam traced her mouth over his exposed throat, licking at his Adam's apple, venturing lower.

"Sam," he croaked. "I can't..." He moved her on top of him in time with his rhythmic thrusts. Uncontrollable whimpers left Sam's throat with his every move. And she started moving her hips in time with his thrusts. John was watching every minute change in her facial features and somehow this intense perusal fed into her excitement. He placed his thumb over the pearl above her center, and she lost control. She saw a blinding light erupt under her eyelids and cried out as she spent several long moments lost in bliss.

When she came to, John was holding her close to his body in the protective circle of his arms. His hand was drawing soothing circles on her back, and his head was nestled on her shoulder. She was surrounded by his heat, and she never wanted to leave. Finally, the surrounding sounds penetrated her hearing, and she heard workers' banter and laughter, and the sounds of shovels hitting the ground.

Sam felt embarrassment heat her neck. They were out in the open; somebody could have ventured further and discovered them. They probably had heard her cries of pleasure too.

John placed a warm kiss on her shoulder and eased her away. "We need to get back," he whispered to her. Sam could only nod. She stood carefully, with John's help, and adjusted her clothing.

"What about luncheon?" She looked at their picnic spot, feeling forlorn.

John was putting on his boots as he spoke, "Do you mind if we distribute the food among the workers? I'll have a bite, but I feel like I've spent enough time away from work as it is. Besides, I've already had the tastiest treat." He grinned at her, and she blushed.

"Come." He swept her into his arms again. "I'll deliver my bride to her slippers. Don't want you to hurt yourself again."

Sign-up for my newsletter to get a bonus novelette:

Deleted Scene

https://sendfox.com/sadiebosque
By signing up, you'll also get new release alerts, and bonus content such as extra epilogues, deleted scenes, and more.

Also by Sadie Bosque

Necessary Arrangements Series

Prequel Novella
To Fall for a Duke by Christmas
Main Series
A Deal with the Earl
An Agreement with the Soldier
A Bargain with the Rake
An Offer from the Marquess
An Affair with the Viscount
A Wager with the Gentleman

The Shadows Series
Return of the Wicked Earl
Secrets of the Wicked Viscount
Curse of the Wicked Scoundrel
Ravishing His Wicked Lady
Taming His Wicked Duchess
More coming soon…